Kate N Nkanza is an MA Creative Writing student at Birkbeck University.

She works for Transport for London and volunteers as the Education Director for DfAD, where she runs short story competitions at Chitokoloki Primary School in Zambia.

Her poems have been published in anthologies and the Zambia Post. Her short story Broken Promises has been published on The Mechanics' Institute Review (MIR) website.

She lives in Kent and has two god-children, and two dogs.

UNTOLD TRUTHS

Kate N Nkanza

Published by Kate N Nkanza

Copyright © 2016 by Kate N Nkanza

www.katenkanza.com

ISBN 978-0-993586316

A CIP catalogue record for this book is available from the Britain Library

For Mum, Dad and Aunty Kamona

Acknowledgements

Thanks go to my Dad, who turned me into a bookworm. My Grandfather, William Nkanza whose story challenged me to become a better person and My Grandma Mwangala who was the greatest story teller, and my teacher, Sister Brendan and Mr Sandu who were such inspirational teachers.

Thank you to my mentor Clio Gray, for her time, knowledge and patience.

Matt Maguire at Candescent Press, for his guidance and brilliant final product.

To the Nkanza clan, thank you for all your support, I'm blessed to have such a family.

For encouragement and support, thank you Daniela Calogero Smith, Nina Collins and Portia who read every word, for your great faith in me. I'm blessed to have such friends.

To my oldest dearest friends Rose Gould (R.I.P) and Ling Mann, who never fail to amaze me, they always believed I had a book in me. Thank you for the marketing.

Special thanks to Nforngwen Manfred, thank you for putting up with me even when I was moody, miserable and couldn't write for days. For always being there, your patience, inspiration and wonderful memories.

For RK, thank you for the support, for being you.

Many thanks to, Evelyn KM, Annie Menyonga, June Lanasna, Nicki Keating, Dillip Shah, Maurizio, Emmanuel, Afua, Prisca and Siim Sinihelm. Thank you for all you have been and what you mean to me.

To all my friends, too many to put down, but you know yourselves. I love you.

To Mark Roberts for all your support with my journey into this mysterious wonderful world of writing.

Chapter One

Catherine stood by the window of her Royal Oak flat staring at the lake. It was still dark, and she felt a cold chill run through her body, but it was nothing compared to the pain she felt deep inside her soul.

No! I can't be, she told herself, *I can't.*

Shaking her head in denial of the evidence right before her eyes, she tossed the second pack of Clear Blue aside, out of sight. Cupping her face in her hands, she wondered, not for the first time, why this was happening to her. For a few seconds, everything seemed strange, a mysterious breath of air wafted through her room; it felt dark and eerie. She reached for the nightgown which hung loosely by the bathroom door and wrapped it around her.

Despite the soothing soft music from her radio, or the inviting bed she found herself flattened against the wall. A great heat rushed through her body, and she shut her eyes 'Oh God,' she sighed. Her heart sank. She thought she had buried him in the past, along with all the pain he had caused her, yet not a day went by didn't she think about that dreadful day.

She woke up covered in sweat most nights tormented by the horrors of what had happened. Memories flashed before her eyes, and she fought hard to erase them from her mind. For a while time stood still, and the only sound she could hear was her breathing.

Her whole body felt weak, and she held on to the dressing-table. Hours later, she opened her eyes to find the bright light of morning sunshine reflected from her window. She drew the curtains right back and opened the window. Her neighbours' children were playing outside.

She swiftly moved away before they could see her.

Her mind drifted back to when she had come to view the flat. Four years I've been living here, she thought still finding it hard to believe that the flat belonged to her. The estate agent had told her right from the beginning that he had a long waiting list. It was a beautiful place, overlooking the canal; it had all the facilities expected in a modern apartment plus the swimming pool, twenty-four-hour security guards and a perfect location. These days she didn't have to wake up at 4.00 a.m. to start her journey to work.

Just when I thought I had everything, a lovely home, and a good man to love me, a good job and peace of mind, and now everything is falling apart, she thought. For four weeks, she had been dreading this moment, and now that it was real, she felt nothing but numbness. She blamed herself too for not taking the morning-after pill, for not dealing with it at that moment when it happened, when her world had come crashing down. She had been too frozen, too traumatized to think practically. Getting pregnant had been the last thing on her mind. Protecting her family and her friends had taken precedence over everything else she felt.

Those things don't happen to someone like you. A small inner voice whispered to her whenever she recalled that moment. As much as she tried to convince herself she was a strong woman, something inside her had changed. She tried to do things differently, little things like choosing assignments no one else wanted to take at work and avoiding group outings, or the defense lessons she was taking and kept a secret from everyone.

She took out another test kit and went to the bathroom, convincing herself she hadn't read it correctly; yet deep down in her heart, she knew that the sooner she accepted the truth, the better chance she had of dealing with it. The results had not changed. She stared at the test kid for a long time before going back to bed. She curled her body into a ball and wept. A blind rage like a fire swept over her, she wiped away the tears and closed her eyes.

At twenty-eight, she felt she had accomplished what some women her age couldn't even dream of doing. Of course, it had not always been easy. She missed spending time with her family and friends. Her mind drifted to David, the man she was madly in love with; the man she was so afraid of losing. Closing her eyes, for a moment, she wondered how to tell him and when to tell him. Unable to come up with answers, she eased her body out of bed and went to the living- room. She shook her head looking at the mess on the table. Sally – her putative flat-mate never cleaned up after herself and Catherine was tired of telling her. Her gaze suddenly rested on a picture on the wall. It was a picture of her brother. Tears clouded her eyes and for a moment, she tried to remember him just as he was when the picture was taken, on his twenty-fifth birthday.

I wish you were here now, she thought sadly. It was almost five years since Michael died; yet it felt like just yesterday. Not a day went by when she did not think of him. She tried now, just as she had so many times, to block out the memories but they came floating back. She could still see him in the coffin, his face looking so peaceful, yet not quite the same. Everyone told her it got easier as time went by, but not for her. Each year was worse than the last. She missed him terribly and wished she could find the strength to let him go. She tried to talk of him, not of his death, but of the life, they had shared together. Those thoughts somehow helped her to look at life the way she knew her brother would have wanted her to. Unable to control the dark thoughts, she fled back to her bedroom.

Warm tears slid down her cheeks, her throat tightened and she sat on the bed. Unable to sleep, she pulled the chair from her drawer towards the bed switched on her laptop and busied herself with emails. Her friends wanted to know why she was hiding; there were a few dinner and lunch invitations and a long email from Kim giving a full description of her honeymoon resort. Just then, her mobile phone rang, she picked it up while continuing to read her mail.

It was Kim.

'Kim?' How amazing! What are you doing writing me long emails when you should be out in the sun enjoying yourself?'

'Most people would be grateful to get a phone call,' Kim said laughing. Is Lover boy back yet? What would you say to the four of us going away when Jason and I get back? We have hardly spent time together the last two months.'

'David should be back next week. I will ask him,' Catherine answered nervously pressing her hands into her face. 'How is Jason?' she asked changing the subject.

'He's fine and trying to have a siesta. I don't think he's coping well with the heat.

I didn't realize Fiji would be this hot at this time of the year. The island is fabulous. Did you see the pictures I emailed you?'

'Not yet, but I promise I will have a look later, I just woke up.'

'Have you finished working on the feature for the Times?'

'I need to interview Nancy from the refugee organization. It has been difficult trying to arrange a meeting with her; she's always out of the office. Nevertheless, I am working on it. I should be done before the end of the month. Which gives me exactly two weeks, I hope I don't miss the deadline.'

'Are you OK?' Kim asked alarmed. Catherine never missed deadlines; she was always on top of her game.

'Fine babes,' Catherine said with a faint sniff. 'I was up quite late last night. I did wake up to clean the house though and couldn't resist taking a nap after.'

'OK, speak to you later,' Kim said ringing off.

Catherine switched off her phone and tried to do some paperwork. As much as she tried to focus her mind on things other than the child growing inside her, it did not work. All she could see was his face hovering over her.

'No!' she gasped as the horror of it swept over her. 'Please, God, this cannot be happening.'

Somehow, she would fight back and not let him take control of her mind and body. For weeks, she had been terrified of him and anything that reminded her of him. She refused to let him take over her mind. Sitting up, she pulled out her S.T. Dupont pen and started working on her freelancing projects. She was so immersed in her work; she didn't hear Sally come into her bedroom.

'Catherine, are you awake?' Sally said moving fully into the room.

For a moment, Catherine froze. With her back to the door, she didn't turn round to face Sally.

'Are you okay?' Sally spoke from beside her.

'Don't you know how to knock?' Catherine snapped facing her. She wasn't normally so brusque with Sally; strangely enough, she was starting to enjoy having her around. Kim, on the other hand, said that living with Sally was a time bomb waiting to go off.

Ignoring the tone of Catherine's voice, Sally looked at her quizzingly.

'What's up? It's a lovely day outside, and here staring at that computer.'

'I'm fine,' Catherine said pulling a silk dressing-gown around her. She stretched out her hand for the newspaper while Sally stood awkwardly by the dressing-table.

'I know I'm not Kim, but I am still your friend, and I'm a good listener, so don't shut me out,' She murmured. 'Please tell me

5

what's going on with you. You haven't been yourself for days. Don't think I haven't noticed. You're not sick are you?'

Catherine swallowed, unable to speak. Her instincts told her not to trust Sally. Even though Sally lived with her, they had become strangers. The closeness they once shared as children was no longer there. A lot had happened. Flashes of all Sally's disasters sparked in her mind. She quickly blanked them away. Catherine had stopped trusting her even though in the last six months she had forgiven her.

She swung round and faced her. 'I'm pregnant,' she whispered.

'Are you serious!?' Sally said closing the gap between them. 'I'm so happy for you,' she added hugging Catherine tightly.

'Hey, don't crush me,' Catherine said, putting some space between them.

'Sorry,' Sally said, laughing. 'I just can't believe it. I mean, I didn't realize you were trying for a baby. Oh, I'm saying all the wrong things. What I want to say is I'm so happy for you and David.' She stopped talking as she watched the color drain from Catherine's face. 'Are you OK?' she asked alarmed.

'Yes, sorry, I am a bit tired today,' that's all. Can you keep the news to yourself for now? I need to tell David before he hears it from someone else.'

'Please don't tell me David doesn't know? You should ring him right away. I am sure he will be on the next flight here. That man is madly in love with you. He's going to be a great father,' she added.

'I will call him tonight.' As much as Catherine wanted to talk to someone about her fears, she knew Sally wouldn't understand.

For a whole month, she had gone over and over in her mind what to say to her friends, how to put into words how she felt, the feelings of guilt and hopelessness. Her mind had drifted from one scenario to the next, wondering if she had done anything to encourage him. Her body didn't feel as though it belonged to her.

All the long soaks in the bath or the showers never washed way the feeling of being unclean.

Kim's wedding had been heavenly sent. She hardly had to think about him. Everyone had been too busy with the wedding to notice her disenchantment, only Kim noticed. Catherine had watched her staring at her; sometimes their eyes met across the room, and she couldn't help noticing the anxious look in Kim's eyes. She hated lying to Kim every time she asked if she was okay, but she loved her friend too much to tell her the truth.

The whole episode still didn't make sense to her and, no matter how hard she tried; she couldn't find a way of telling those closest to her.

'You're happy, aren't you?' Sally asked bringing her to the present.

Catherine's face was taut and pale as she walked to the window and pulled the curtains. It was bright and beautiful, but she could not enjoy the scenery. Her mind was focused on the child growing inside her.

'Yes, of course,' Catherine said, hesitating. 'And remember what I said, don't say a word to anyone. Besides, I still need to confirm it with the doctor tomorrow.'

'Do you want me to come with you to the clinic?' Sally asked. The question brought Catherine back to the realities of what lay ahead.

'You can come if you like,' she said, her eyes fixed on the window.

'Of course, I want to come,' Sally told her. 'Anyway, I was going to fix myself some lunch. Would you like something to eat?'

'No, thank you. I think I will just stay under the duvet for another hour.'

As she lay there, she made up her mind to go and see her parents the following weekend. Her phone was ringing before she could focus and make plans. Easing herself into a sitting position, she wished she had switched the phone off. She stared at it for a long time, eventually, the ringing stopped.

She listened to the message, and it was David. She was relieved that she had not answered his call, she needed more time before telling him. She made up her mind to call Kim before Sally could beat her to it. She knew Kim wouldn't take it kindly if she heard the news from Sally. She couldn't help feeling Sally might just enjoy delivering the news to Kim before she had the chance to do it herself.

'What? 'Kim yelled. 'Are you sure?''

'Yes,' Catherine said, not wanting to believe her words.

'Have you told him?' Kim asked.

'No, I haven't had the chance.' She knew Kim was referring to David, and she didn't want to start explaining on the phone. 'There is something I've not said, but we'll talk when you get back.' She ended the call before Kim could ask her any more questions. She called her parents and her mother's first question was, 'Are you okay?' Making Catherine feel guilty for cancelling their lunch plans.

Her parents lived in Guilford, and she went to see them whenever she could find time, but for the past weeks, she had avoided meeting them and now that the wedding was over, she couldn't come up with any more excuses.

'Are you still there?' her mother asked, bringing her back to the present.

'Yes, Mum, sorry. I'm just not myself today.'

'I've been trying to get hold of you since yesterday. Your dad left for Japan this morning, and he wanted to say goodbye.'

'How long is he away for?' Catherine asked.

'He's back Friday. He's worried about you, too. Is there something we can do to help? You seem to be working all hours. Your dad said he saw you on CNN. I thought you gave that up.'

'It was just a one-off,' Catherine assured her. 'Everything is fine. I'm just trying to keep busy. Are you around this weekend?' she asked. 'I'm hoping to come and see you.'

'That will be great,' her mum said. It will be good to catch up. How is David?'

'He's okay,' Catherine answered her voice tight. She did not want to think about David, but that was going to be hard when everyone and everything reminded her of him. It was much later in the afternoon when she heard Sally call out to her. Quickly, she swung her legs off the bed and rubbed her eyes.

'Catherine, are you still giving me a lift?' Sally asked, her face peeking through the doorway.

'You might as well come in,' Catherine said, pushing her hair from her face. 'What time do you have to be there?'

'Four o'clock,' Sally answered. 'You don't have to take me if you've got stuff to do. I can always catch the bus.'

'OK, that's a great idea, it will give me a chance to catch up on some paperwork,' Catherine said getting up.

'Do you want me to fix you a drink? Tea?' Sally asked, looking her over.

'Stop fussing over me!' Catherine snapped.

She watched as Sally retreated from the room, without a word. Half an hour later, she heard her hovering by the door.

'Come in!' she shouted.

'What do you think?' Sally asked, doing a twirl. She was wearing a red Calvin Klein dress and Jimmy Choo shoes.

'You look great. Who's the lucky guy?' Catherine asked, dragging herself out of her bad mood.

'No one just thought I could dress up. I haven't worn this dress since I bought it.'

'Pull the other one, Sal. You don't dress up like that for the hairdresser.'

'I could never fool you, could I?' Sally said, smiling. 'Well, Jay said he might come and pick me up from the hairdressers.'

'You're serious about this one, aren't you?' Catherine said, looking at her.

'He's okay, easy on the eyes I guess,' Sally said giggling. She wasn't thinking about marrying the guy, but he made her laugh, and she enjoyed his company and, of course, he was always willing to buy stuff for her.

'Well, I hope things work out for both of you. We need another wedding before the mood wears off,' Catherine said jokingly. Catherine remembered Sally's last boyfriend. He was a married man who had made promises he couldn't keep, and she couldn't understand why it took three years for Sally to realize he was never going to leave his family for her.

Sally nodded her head as if in agreement, but she knew she was just buying time. She was not interested in a future with Jay. She didn't feel anything for him anymore but she couldn't bring herself to let him ago. Her heart belonged to someone else. She hated lying to Catherine, but she hoped one day she could open up and tell her everything, maybe then they could rebuild their friendship.

'If I'm not home by midnight, then I shall be in first thing tomorrow morning. You will be okay, won't you?' She hesitated, then forced herself to say it. 'I'm here if you need me. All you have to do is ask.'

'I'm not ill, Sal, I'm pregnant,' Catherine answered.

Soon after Sally left, Catherine took a quick shower and shook her head, thinking of Sally. The girl only had a part-time job and yet she wore the most expensive clothes and shoes. Catherine had concluded a long time ago that Sally was a girl who could get any man to buy her anything she wanted. She only hoped that things would not blow up in Sally's face one day.

Catherine had tried talking to her when she first moved into Kim's old room, but Sally was adamant she wasn't doing anything wrong.

'Listen, Catherine,' she had said to her. 'I don't have a well-paid job like you, so if the fine brothers want to buy me presents, who am I to say no?'

Catherine never brought up the subject again. The only thing she said to Sally was to keep those fine brothers away from the flat. She couldn't understand what had happened to the independent girl she had befriended on holiday. She had first met Sally when she was ten years old. She had never met a girl her age who talked so much or acted so grown up. Catherine had admired her for her sense of humour and courage. They had spent that summer together, and when she left Zambia, she had promised to invite Sally to England. It was ten years before they met again and they were now both grown-up women with a different perspective on life.

Catherine barely recognised her old friend. Gone was the fighting spirit and independence she had seen in her as a child. She still talked louder than anyone else, but she liked to be given everything on a silver plate. She lived with her cousin for a few years, and when Kim moved out, she begged Catherine to let her have the spare room. Catherine did not have the heart to say no and, despite Kim's objection to the idea, she decided to give Sally a chance. Sally and Kim never got on well; they just learned to tolerate each other for Catherine's sake.

With no one else at home, she felt tired and restless. She paced up and down the carpeted floor in her study, and when she couldn't think of anything else to do, she changed into her silk pyjamas and sat down in front of the television to watch Grey's Anatomy. She did not know how long she sat staring at the screen when her doorbell rang.

She ignored it, at first, hoping that whoever it was would go away. The person did not go away, and the sound got louder.

'Go away,' she mumbled, covering her face with a cushion.

The ringing persisted.

Tired of the noise, Catherine walked to the door, thinking it was Sally. She pressed hard on the intercom, ready to tell Sally off for forgetting her keys again. Shock waves ran through her body. Time stopped. She rubbed her eyes and closed them for a few seconds. Her heart was beating fast; too fast she was afraid it was going to pop out of her top. Standing there, flowers in his hand was David.

Chapter Two

Catherine felt the floor sway beneath her, and her pulse pounded in her ears. It can't be him! But it was, and she couldn't keep him standing outside any longer. She pressed the button on the inter-com and a few minutes later listened to his quick footsteps walking upstairs. She flicked her eyes at him, and they stared at each other nervously. She suddenly felt weird things going through her body.

'What are you doing here?' she asked. She wasn't expecting him for another week.

'Catherine?' he said slowly closing the gap between them. 'Don't I get a hug?' she heard him say, her mind still confused. She couldn't quite believe he was there in her living room.

'You look surprised, almost shocked. You do want me here don't you? I mean I can always go back,' he said, his grin widen-ing, to show his dimples and she felt her heart catch at how devastatingly handsome he was.

'Don't be silly,' she said, moving into his open arms.

He gave her a box of Godiva chocolate truffles and a bunch of roses.

Taking the roses, she placed them in a vase. 'You really know how to spoil a girl, don't you?' she told him brightly. 'You should have told me you were coming back today; I would have come to pick you up from the airport.'

'And spoil the surprise? No way. You should have seen the look on your face...priceless.' David said laughing.

She threw a cushion at him, making him even laugh louder.

She joined in and for a few seconds, she forgot that she was carrying another man's child. They sat together on the big leather sofa, hands intertwined as they listened to soft music. Time stood still as they faced each other. Catherine felt a great urge to pour out her heart to him and tell him about the baby, but, words failed her, she didn't know where to start and end. It was the first time since meeting him that she felt uncomfortable around him, and she didn't know how to handle it.

'I don't know what I would do if I lost you,' Catherine said an hour later as she lay her head on his chest, their legs intertwined. Their bodies were so close and their breathing soft and steady.

He felt her tense; something was bothering her. He could see it in her eyes, her body language. David propped himself up on his elbows and looked at her so adoringly that she felt butterflies in her belly.

'Look at me, I'm not going anywhere. I'll always be here, for as long as you want me. And even when you don't want me,' he added teasingly. His mouth moved over hers until her stomach knotted up, and she held on to him tightly.

'I know,' Catherine whispered, and looked lovingly at him. 'I suppose sometimes I'm just afraid to be this happy. I can't picture my life without you in it,' she added softly. She was about to ask him if he wanted dinner but he grabbed her to him.

'God, I've missed you,' he whispered hotly kissing her neck, her lips, and her cheeks.

'I missed you too,' she moaned as he kissed her again, pulling her on top of him, their hips pushing against each other. For a while, they slept on the sofa, their bodies entwined.

Two hours later, David opened his eyes. She lay on top of him. Her head was resting on his chest, her beautiful body warm and soft.

'I love you, Catherine, and don't you ever forget it,' David said, kissing her gently. 'I think we should go to bed before Sally walks in.'

'Good idea,' Catherine smiled up at him.

Once in bed they made love again, then she fell to sleep in his arms, David watched her sleeping. To him, she was the most beautiful girl in the world, and he loved everything about her. He wondered why she looked so sad. Something was wrong, and he wished she would open up and tell him about it. No one had ever made him feel so good before, and he was damned if he was going to let anything spoil what they shared.

Catherine's mind was in turmoil. She turned and tossed through the night thinking about David and the child growing inside her. She loved David with all her heart. He was to her, what a man should be – loving, caring and whole. He was such a good-looking man, kind and adventurous. She wanted to touch him, to feel his soft skin next to hers, but a part of her was afraid. She had tried several times to tell him, but each time she tried, all her courage and determination disappeared. She was confused and hurting. She knew he loved her and would most likely under-stand, but she was not ready to take that risk. She had never known such love or felt such strong feelings for any man before.

The following morning at breakfast, David dropped his bomb-shell. 'I know I said I would be back a while, but I have to be in Germany tonight. My secretary finally managed to arrange a meeting for me with a CEO of a company I have wanted to do business with for a long time.'

'But leaving today, when you just got home,' Catherine felt panic rising in her throat.

'You could ......come with me,' he hesitated not wanting to push her, noticing that sadness again, that something was trou-bling her. He remembered the first time his eyes fell on her, just as he was coming out of the Commonwealth House in Central

London. His chest felt as tight now as it did then, still the most beautiful girl he'd ever seen. Nothing would ever change that.

That evening, after dropping off David at Heathrow airport, she made her way to Guildford. The sky was cloudy and grey as Catherine's BMW sports car pulled into her parents' driveway. She parked next to her mother's car in the garage. She didn't know how her parents managed to live in the place, just the two of them. It was gigantic. Actually three now that Cora, their housekeeper, had moved in with them after losing her husband.

She let herself in; the Television was on mute. Music played in the background. She stopped to admire the new furniture. The house was still the same, and she could smell Cora's freshly baked scones as soon as she walked towards the kitchen. Smiling, she walked right through and within minutes, she felt Cora's strong arms around her. The elderly woman feasted her eyes on her. For a petite person, she was so strong, and her voice was sharp enough to make Catherine listen, with that Filipino accent that had never gone.

'Look at you; you look theen Aren't you eating? This is not good, not good at all,' she said, shaking her head. 'Are you sick? You don't want to be walking around all skin and bones; people think you no family that care. I will ask your mum if I come and visit next week. You need some meat on you,' she carried on while filling the kettle and shaking her head wildly.

'Don't make a fuss,' Catherine said, laughing. 'I'm no thinner than the last time you saw me. I saw Mum's car in the garage. Is she upstairs?'

'Yes, and she didn't say you was coming. I could have cooked your dish. Anyway, don't change the subject. Why you look so theen?'

'I'm okay, Cora, and I haven't been starving myself. I still eat, but I suppose I'm just lucky not to pile on the weight.'

'If you're sure,' Cora said, still unconvinced. 'Your mum said she was going to have a bath, but I'm sure she wouldn't mind if you went up before she goes into the bathroom.'

'I'll give her twenty minutes,' Catherine said, pulling up a chair to sit down, keeping her thoughts away from the baby, she chatted happily with Cora. As usual, Cora asked when she was going to marry David.

'You can't let this one go, he too handsome. When I was your age, I was married, and I had my two daughters.'

'Well, things have changed since then. It's hard for David and me we're both very busy, and the man is living in the air at the moment.'

'Air!?' Cora asked, looking strangely at her.

'Yes, he's always travelling somewhere. I've hardly seen him the last couple of months.' She suddenly felt sad thinking perhaps it was too late to be entertaining the idea of life with David.

'I think I'll just go and have a look around the house,' she said, feeling the need to avoid any more difficult questions. First, she went to her old room. Even though she had not lived at home since her university days, no one ever slept in there except her. In it were some of her old clothes and the cuddly bears she'd had as a child; she felt too attached to them to give them away. A picture of her and three of her four grandparents still hung on the wall. She smiled, remembering the day it had been taken. There were also pictures of herself and Kim when they were in pre-school.

It was such a long time ago, but it all seemed like yesterday. Nothing had changed between Kim and herself, apart from the fact that her friend was now a married woman. They had spent many happy times in her room. It was where they'd discussed their first kiss and the cute boys in school, where they had talked about their dreams for the future. Looking at the photograph, she could not help but smile. She and Kim had stood out; they were the only black children in their class. While her mother was of African origin and her father, half-American and Scottish, Kim's mum was Chinese and her father, black American. It was no surprise that the two of them had become the best of friends. She was shuffling through old magazines when there was a knock on the door.

'Hello, darling.' Her mum said coming into the room carrying a tray with a teapot and two cups. 'Imagine my surprise when Cora told me you were here.' She gave her daughter a hug and sat on the edge of the bed watching her.

'Are you all right?' she asked, looking at her closely.

'Yes, I'm fine. I don't need a reason to come and see you, do I?'

'Oh no, but you normally call, and you didn't sound well the last time we spoke. Anyway, let's have something to eat and then you can tell me all about what's been happening in your life. It's been a while since we had a chat.'

They took their tea with them to the living- room and her mother chatted on about work.

'Your dad is back on Friday; then we're off to Spain. You should come with us; it will be lovely to spend time together.'

'I wish I could, but I have a lot of work on at the moment. You should take Cora; she doesn't seem her usual self.'

'I did ask her, but she's not interested. Nothing much interests her since Lito died.'

'I will try and convince her to join you unless her children have invited her. She can't be here by herself for two weeks.'

'Good luck trying.'

Elizabeth could tell Catherine wasn't listening to her; something was bothering her. She sometimes wondered if her daughter truly knew how much they loved her. She seemed so grown-up and independent. She hardly slept a wink when Catherine had been in Rwanda reporting on the war, or the time she went to Israel. She hated to think what she would do if anything ever happened to her; she had already lost a son, and Catherine was the most important thing to her. Her husband, John, of course, told her she worried too much.

'I'm OK,' Catherine said reassuring her.

Elizabeth looked at her daughter unconvinced. 'Has something happened that you're not telling me? I can always tell when you're not honest with me. So let's hear it.'

Catherine did not answer straight away. Instead, her mind drifted back to her childhood. Her parents had always been there for her, never judged her for the decisions she made, but told her mistakes made people grow wiser. 'Just look at them as a blessing, because next time you won't do the same thing,' her dad always reminded her.

Looking at her mother, she knew deep in her heart that she could never tell them about the rape. They must never find out. 'I'm pregnant.' She said the words very slowly and softly. Her eyes fixed on her mother's face to see her response.

'Wow, I'm going to be a grandmother!' Her mum's face beamed with happiness.

'Wait till I tell your dad. This is the best news ever!' She put her arms around Catherine and hugged her tightly to her, but seeing the confusion on Catherine's face, she took both her hands. Fear gripped at her heart. 'There's nothing wrong with the baby, is there? I know I have always said I wanted to see you married before you start a family, but David is totally committed to you. Anyone can see that.'

'That's the problem, I don't know,' Catherine answered.

'Oh, my poor baby!' said Elizabeth. She could not believe her little girl was going to be a mum. 'You will be fine; it takes time to adjust.' The look on Catherine's face told her that something was not right, and her heart went out to her.

She couldn't help noticing the dark cloud, which fell over Catherine's face when she mentioned David's name. 'You and David are alright?' she asked.

Unable to give an answer, Catherine laid her head on her mum's shoulder and closed her eyes for a moment. She just couldn't find a way of telling her without taking away the ecstatic look she had seen in her eyes.

'Do you think I'll make a good mother?' she asked with sudden humour in her voice.

'Not only do I think so; I believe you will. I remember watching you, years ago when you were babysitting Anna. You were ever so gentle with her.'

'Wow, how years fly. I must remind her to pay me for babysitting duties. I wonder if she's OK. I haven't heard from her since her parents divorced. Is her father still living next door?'

'Yes and the new wife is causing him a few sleepless nights. He was complaining to your dad about her spending habits. Anyway enough about other people's lives. What about David? How is he taking it?'

Catherine stayed quiet, contemplating whether this was the right time to tell her mum the whole truth.

'He's fine,' she lied. 'We haven't sat down to discuss it yet.'

'It's always harder for men,' her mum said. 'But I can tell you once the baby is born; you'll be the one left feeling like the stranger because he will spend all the time staring at the poor baby. I remember when you were born, your dad used to drive me nuts. He would call almost every twenty minutes just to make sure you were okay, and when he got home in the evening, he would make such a big fuss over you.'

'What was I like as a baby?' Catherine asked.

'You were a good baby until you started crawling,' her mum said, laughing. 'Then we had to put everything away; nothing was safe. And Michael, well, he just thought you were another toy he could play with. He wanted to bathe you and feed you.'

She stopped as memories of the past overcame her. Catherine put her arm around her shoulder and changed the subject. She described her recent trip to Angola and the children she had met.

Five hours later, driving back to London, Catherine made up her mind to tell David the truth and be done with it.

Chapter Three

The next morning, Catherine woke up determined to make a decision about her future. For the first time in twelve months, she called in sick at work. Sally had made her practise her voice for hours before she had the courage to pick up the phone. She had heard Sally call in sick so many times; she could have become an expert had she hated her job.

'The thing about lying about illness is that you have to memorise it and stick with it. Otherwise, you'll get found out. Your voice needs to be right too, not too low and not too high. Just enough to make the other person on the other end believe you couldn't even get to the bathroom by yourself,' Sally said before leaving for college. Despite not being actually sick, Catherine did think about going to see her GP about her pregnancy. But after breakfast, she decided to do some work, her trip to the clinic was put on hold. Picking at her food, Catherine closed her mind to any thoughts of the baby and decided to do some work on the child trafficking project in Africa she was working on. She and Kim had spent three months the previous year zipping between Angola and Zambia, searching for fifteen young girls between the ages of eight and twelve who had vanished from several local villages. It had all come about following a frantic phone call from her grandmother in the middle of the night begging her to come out to use her journalistic contacts to help search for one of her worker's children who had vanished. The girl's father believed she'd been trafficked into Tanzania by his former boss, who was a well-known politician with a tarnished past. It didn't take Catherine long to learn some key information. Most of the people she and Kim had spoken to said the missing children's parents must have sold them to the traffickers for food and money.

With all its beautiful landscapes, lovely sunset and wild animals, Catherine realised there was a lot more going on behind closed doors in most of towns and villages in Africa. It was then that she met Melissa, the seven-year-old girl who had touched her heart. After months of searching for her relatives, Catherine had put Melissa in boarding school and paid for her education. During the holidays, Melissa stayed with Catherine's grandmother at the farm.

Thinking of Melissa brought back thoughts of her own baby, and she shoved her breakfast plate into the dishwater and went to the spare room, which she had turned, into her study room. She got her briefcase and pulled out letters and school reports from Melissa. Her eyes glanced over them, but somehow the words didn't make sense. She felt tears streaming down her face and she pushed herself into the couch. Between the sobs, she tried to weigh her options. She figured she had several options, none very appealing: She could have a termination and put a stop to the whole thing; She could lie to David, tell him the child was his and hope he would never find out the truth. She could tell David the truth and hope he would understand and support her; or she could walk away from David, have the child and try to build a life just for the two of them.

In the end she couldn't decide, so instead picked up Melissa's latest letter and wrote out a reply. She had also begun a tentative letter to David, telling him the truth, when the doorbell rang, followed by more knocks. Startled, she stood up, momentarily alarmed as she heard the scrape of the key in the lock. Richard's face appeared in the doorway and she gave a sigh of relief.

'I hope you don't mind, I got tired of knocking so I used the spare key.'

'Don't be silly, that's why I gave it to you...to be used and not admired.'

'I spoke to Sally this morning; she said you're not well. Are you feeling any better?'

Catherine sighed, not sure whether to carry on the lie. 'I'm feeling better, I hope you didn't leave work early just to come and see me,' she added suddenly feeling guilty.

'That, and the fact that I needed to get out. The old man is driving me crazy. He's convinced himself he's still young at seventy-nine and wants to go skiing.'

Catherine suppressed a giggle. She loved how he always worried about his father even though the old man was more than capable of looking after himself. 'I wish you'd called earlier. We could have gone to see that new play from South Africa.'

'I would have done if your phone had any more space to take messages, and your mobile phone was switched off.'

'I'm sorry,' Catherine apologized again. The truth was she had not wanted to answer the phone in case it was David and she wasn't in the mood to chat to any of her friends. She just didn't know what to say to them. 'Tell you what, why don't I make us dinner and you can tell me all about this new girl you've been seeing.'

'What new girl?' he asked looking at her curiously.

'Exactly, don't you think it's time you started dating again?'

He ignored her question. 'There's a new Thai restaurant in Putney. I thought we could check it out.'

Catherine laughed. She was not given up on him yet. She also knew why he was inviting her to dinner. It wasn't too hard to see through him. He was the kindest man, and it was a shame he had not found anyone yet to share his life with. He had so much love inside him, but then there was the dark side, which only she knew about and maybe that was the reason they were so close. He could talk to her without feeling vulnerable. She valued what they shared, and she understood why he was so protective towards her. He had been Michael's best friend and the best substitute brother anyone could ever wish for.

'I really don't mind,' Catherine argued. 'Besides, I need to try out this new recipe before David gets back.'

'I see,' Richard said jokingly, 'and for a moment there I thought it was all about me.'

It took a tortured twenty minutes to realise she was never going to master the recipe. It was just too complicated. Then she remembered that Cora had cooked some lamb and potatoes for her, so all she had to do was heat it up and make a salad. Catherine's mother and Kim had given up trying to teach her to cook, and her grandmother said she had better not marry a man who loved food. Unfortunately for her, David did.

After putting the lamb and potatoes into the oven, she took a shower then walked restlessly about the dining-room and waited for Richard. Of all her male friends, Richard was the one she trusted the most, but he was so protective towards her there was no guessing what he might do once he knew the truth.

She laughed recalling her brother telling that Richard had a crush on her. It seemed such a long time ago, and she was happy nothing had happened between them. He was to her the brother she had lost, loving and caring for her unconditionally. She ran to open the door as soon as the doorbell rang. He stood there with a bottle of wine and flowers.

'You didn't have to do this,' she said, putting the wine in the fridge.

'Well, after the trouble you have gone to with the cooking, it's the least I can do. Dinner smells good,' he said, and she laughed, wondering if he had thought they were going to eat takeaway.

'I can cook, you know,' she said, still laughing. It was a long time since they had last shared a meal. It felt great and for a moment, she forgot her problems and relaxed.

Richard noticed how she avoided the wine. 'Catherine,' he said, putting his plate aside, 'is everything okay?'

'Yes,' she lied. 'Why do you ask?'

'I haven't seen you for almost four weeks; you hardly pick up your calls and today you're home instead of going to work. Do I need to go on?'

Catherine stood up from the table without answering his question and asked him if he wanted tea.

'We can have it in the living room. It's cooler in there.'

'Are you going to tell me what's been bothering you?' he repeated.

Knowing she wasn't going to get away with distracting him, Catherine sat down and took a deep breath.

'I'm pregnant,' she told him, her eyes cast to the floor. 'And before you say anything, it's a bit complicated. That's why I didn't tell you earlier.' She knew she was not making much sense to him. 'I was raped,' Catherine whispered, and watched as the blood drained away from Richard's face.

'Oh my god! I cannot believe this, and you never said anything to me. Have you spoken to the cops?'

Catherine shook her head, cheeks burning with shame.

'I can't go to the police,' she said. 'They'd never believe me.'

'But of course, they will …' Richard began to say, but Catherine put a finger out to stop him.

'They won't believe me because the person who raped me was Brooke.'

Chapter Four

The smell of freshly brewed coffee wafted through to her room, and she knew Sally was back.

'Morning, Catherine.' Sally appeared dressed up in a pair of Levi jeans and a Mickey Mouse top.

'Well, good morning to you, too. What time did you get in?' Catherine asked reaching for her dressing gown.

'An hour ago, you look awful, should I get you anything before I go?'

'I feel awful; I should never let you talk me into making that call. Now I feel sick for real.'

'Sorry, maybe it's your body telling you, you need to slow down.' Sally said putting the banana she was holding into her handbag. She wished Catherine could open up and tell her what was bothering her. For a woman who was carrying a child for the man she loved. She seemed too sad and withdrawn. She had known Catherine for many years not to realise she was hurting. They hadn't grown up together but from age ten, she had always considered her, her best friend ... until now. Kim seemed to be the best friend she was never going to be. 'I'll see you later,' she said reaching for her handbag.

Left alone, Catherine did a few yoga stretches. She recalled the first time she met Brooke; she thought he was the rudest man she'd ever come across. She had met him through his elder brother, who was a doctor and a friend of Richard's. Brooke had made it very clear to her he disapproved of her relationship with his brother and for a while, she had not bothered to tell him there was nothing between her and his brother. When Brooke finally realised they were just friends, he went out of his way to pursue her.

He showered her with flowers and phone calls until she finally agreed to go out with him. She related to him in a way she had not been able to with her other boyfriends. He understood the pain of growing up different from other kids. She could tell him how she felt without feeling she was hurting him. For eighteen months they had the perfect relationship; she, like most of her friends thought they would one day get married.

It had come as a surprise to everyone when they broke up. Thinking about it now, she knew she had made the right decision. He wasn't the same man she had fallen in love with. Brooke could not cope with the pressure of her job. She was away most of the time on assignments, and it was during one of those periods that he cheated on her. Catherine kicked him out of her flat, but three months later he was begging her to forgive him and, much as she didn't trust him, she decided to give him another chance. But when he did it the second time, there was no going back for her; she simply told him it was over, and all his efforts to get her back had gone unnoticed. He had tried to use his charm on her friends and family, but none of them succumbed, and she had avoided him until the day of Stacy's party. She had met David by then, and they had been seeing each other for over six months. David was on one of his trips, that why he wasn't at the party.

She heard the front door slam and sounds of feet moving towards her. Instinctively she pushed her hands through the long hair and tied it into a ponytail. Richard walked in carrying his jacket over his shoulder. It was then she remembered they had made plans to have lunch together. An hour later, they left for his place. He was adamant he wanted to cook for her.

'Does David know?' Richard asked after they had their lunch. They were sitting outside his house in Chelsea overlooking the Thames. There was a lot of activities going on at Battersea Park. She watched as the cars lined up on the bridge stuck in traffic.

'We can go and check out the band later if you like?' Richard said softly.

Catherine shook her head. The beautiful sunny day was lost on her; her mind was filled with horrible thoughts of Brooke. For the first time since meeting him, she wondered why she had allowed him in her life in the first place. It was hard for her to think of him without hurting, she wanted more than anything to forget about him but she couldn't. A baby was growing inside her, a reminder of what Brooke had done to her, and he had made her forget about the beginning when everything had been good.

Her mind turned to David, his brilliant smile, his beautiful face flashed before her eyes. She felt hot tears starting, and she closed her eyes, suddenly feeling very tired.

'What am I going to do?' she said softly. 'He would never forgive me for this, for not telling him about Brooke. I wanted to tell him, I needed so much for him to hold me and tell me we were going to be fine. I love him so much. I cannot think of tomorrow without him in my life, and I just don't know what to do.'

Richard held her to him. He hated what this was doing to her. When she finally stopped, he tilted her head to face him.

He wiped away her tears. 'Why didn't you tell me?' he asked.

It was all beginning to make sense to him now: all those cancelled dinner dates, all the time she spent buried in her work. He had tried to catch up with her so many times, but she always had an excuse, and now he knew why she had been avoiding him.

'You should have told me,' he said.

'I'm sorry, I wanted to, but I never found the right time or the right words, I guess a part of me couldn't believe he did it, and I felt so ashamed and embarrassed. I went with him to his house, thinking that he only wanted to talk and I told him repeatedly that it was over between us, that I didn't want him in my life anymore, but it was like something had come over him. He was not the same man I used to know. I said no, but he wouldn't listen, and I could not fight him. He was too strong for me.' She stopped talking. Overcome by emotions.

'You should have reported him to the police,' Richard said. 'How can you be so certain it's not David's child? He asked. Still hopeful.

'It's not. He was in Asia for almost three weeks. When it happened, I wanted to report him, but I couldn't put my family through all that and his family, too. Can you imagine what would have happened if word ever got out? I have someone else to think about now and, no matter what I have to go through, I cannot put this child through it as well. I cannot believe I was with the man for almost three years, and there was a part of him I did not know existed.'

'You cannot blame yourself for this,' he told her. 'You trusted him, and he abused that trust. You did nothing wrong and don't you forget it. I just can't believe Brooke could do that to you. That man deserves to be locked up; you don't owe him anything, and I doubt his family would look kindly on him if they knew the truth. Maybe I should tell his brother.'

'You will do no such thing,' Catherine said, looking at him. 'I don't want anyone knowing about this. Please, promise me you won't breathe a word to anyone.'

'You can't let him get away with this,' Richard said, running his hand through his hair. 'What if he does this to someone else, how are you going to feel then?'

'It's all I think about. How can I forget, especially now that I have a reminder? And can you imagine what kind of life the child is going to have if word ever got out? I cannot do that to him or her. I think Brooke is clever enough to know better.'

'I'm sorry; I know it's a no-win situation with your job and everything else. I still think you should tell David. You can't walk away from that kind of love without a fight. You need to tell him. Let him know before he hears it from someone else; otherwise, you're going to regret it for the rest of your life.'

Catherine was silent for a while. She still felt dirty and humiliated. She had loved Brooke he had been a big part of her life, and now she realised that she didn't know him at all. He had wiped away all those happy memories she had of him, and now she couldn't think of him without getting upset. It was a relief to talk to someone about it; it felt as if a huge weight had been lifted off her shoulders, even though she was still afraid to tell David.

'I love him,' Catherine stated. 'I love him so much, but I can't expect him to understand what I'm going through.'

'Have you thought of other ways of getting out of this? I mean, you could always—' He turned away, ashamed of himself. He was a doctor and now he was giving her ideas about having a termination. He didn't know how else to help her. No one would blame her if she decided she couldn't go through with it. He had seen many women traumatized by rape. Most of them were not as strong as Catherine. It was not an easy decision for any woman to make.

'You mean have an abortion? It's not as if I haven't considered it. But I don't think I can go through with it. I will never be able to forgive myself. I went to Surrey to see Mum, and you know what? I almost didn't tell her. I was afraid she might be disappointed in me, but she was just so happy. She told me David and I would make good parents. I sat there and watched her face; I couldn't take away that happiness from her. I left her still thinking I was glad to be having this baby and for a moment I tried to convince myself I could make David believe I was carrying his child, but as soon as I got home I knew I was lying to myself. There is no way I could live with myself with such a big lie hanging over my head. I don't know what I'm going to do about my parents. I guess with time I will find the courage to tell them the truth.'

'Well, if you need to get away, let me know, I can book leave.'

She laughed. 'Great idea, I will think about it, would be nice to have a doctor on call 24/7.'

'I'm a pathologist,' he reminded her. I can do most things but not look after a pregnant woman,' he replied jokingly. He took their dirty plates and put them in the dishwasher. 'Would you like some tea?' he asked coming back to the balcony.

'Yes please,' Catherine said pulling herself into a sitting position. She shuffled through her bag, looking for the pictures from Melissa to show him, anything to distract her from talking about the pregnancy.

Watching her from the door, Richard felt an inner surge of anger towards Brooke. He wondered what would happen if he came face to face with him.

He crossed over, and sat down opposite her, resting his elbows on the table. A traffic jam stretched along the road to the park. Drivers hooted at each other.

'So glad I'm not caught up in that,' He said shaking his head.

Catherine grinned. 'The traffic on this road seems to get worse every year. Sometimes I just feel like selling my car and getting a decent bicycle.'

Richard laughed. 'Didn't you do that two years ago, and I remember it lasted for three months.'

'Oh yeah, thanks for reminding me, I must admit I did enjoy it, though. I could have done without a car for much longer had it not been for Grandma visiting.'

Much later, Richard watched her as she rested in the rocking chair. Her eyes were fixed on the activities going on in the park. He wished he could take away the pain. He could make Brooke pay for what he had done to her.

His mind drifted to Brooke; he never understood why Brooke had felt threatened by the bond he shared with Catherine. He went to the extent of accusing him of trying to break them up. It had been hard for him to separate himself from her but in the end, he had decided to stay away for her sake. He did not want to be the reason to break up their relationship. He cared for her too much. When she asked him if he was avoiding her, he simply told her he was busy with work. He had not wanted to make her feel the need to choose between him and Brooke, but now he wished he had been there to protect her from Brooke. He had promised her brother he would look after her, and he was failing miserably.

He deeply regretted introducing her to Brooke. A part of him never actually trusted Brooke and secretly he believed Catherine deserved someone better, but he had been quite happy for Brooke to prove otherwise. He had not been too upset when Catherine had phoned him in the middle of the night to tell him she had finally broken up with Brooke.

Brooke had become a frequent visitor to his tennis club, trying to make friends with him and begging him to speak to Catherine on his behalf. He did not seem to care that she was with someone else and, no matter what he said, Brooke seemed to have convinced himself that he would win her back.

Richard kicked himself now for not warning her about Brooke's obsession with her. Looking at her, he knew he had to do something to make sure she and David stayed together. The only person he could think of helping him was Kim, but she was away on her honeymoon.

Chapter Five

Kim stared at the phone for a long time. Her hand gripped the chair, and she took a deep breath. She wiped the tears with the back of her hand and left the apartment. She walked around in confusion for almost an hour before making her way to the local pub where Jason was having lunch with two guys he had befriended the previous day.

She saw him sitting, with his back to her. He looked happy and relaxed; she almost turned back, but her feet and heart weren't cooperating. Watching him, she was reminded why she loved him. It had been love at first sight for her, and she just knew the first time she met him that this was the man she was going to spend the rest of her life with.

He was tall, much taller than her, with piercing blue eyes and a smile to die for. He was a very confident person and at thirty-five, he had already made a name for himself as one of the best surgeons in the country. Like her, he was a workaholic; as busy people, they appreciated every second they spent together.

It was no surprise to her that her family had welcomed him with open arms. Her father had been one of his lecturers at Harvard, but he had not realised this until the day she took him home to meet her parents. She couldn't believe it was almost two years to the day, and now they were on their honeymoon.

Being the only child, hers was a very close family, and she did not want history repeating itself. Her mother told her she had eloped with her father because her parents did not approve of her marrying someone of a different race, but she loved Kim's father very much and, in the end, she had chosen to stay with him without their blessing and for ten years her grandparents had not spoken to her mother. They were slowly trying to rebuild their relationship, but Kim did not know much about them as they had not been in her life growing up. Caught in the past, she didn't see Jason until he circled her in his arms.

'What's wrong?' he asked looking cautiously at her.

'It's Catherine,' Kim said softly. 'She's in trouble; she needs me.'

'Right then, Mrs Carrington, what time do you want to leave?'

'Oh, Jason, I love you. Are you sure? I'm really sorry. I promise I will make it up to you.'

'We have a lifetime to have holidays. Right now Catherine needs you, and I know you won't have much fun till you see her, so if you start packing, I'll pay the bill and change our flights.'

'Thanks,' Kim said softly and hugged him tightly.

Whatever did I do to deserve someone like him? Kim thought as she packed their clothes. She didn't phone Catherine; she didn't want her to talk them out of going home.

Catherine couldn't stop crying. She had spent half the night turning and tossing. When the phone rang, she lay still, wondering whether to pick it up. The only person who would call her that late was David and he was the last person she wanted to speak to; her guilt was eating at her like a deadly poison.

'It's about time you called. I was beginning to think someone had kidnapped you or worse,' she said trying hard to sound cheerful.

'I was just about to hang up,' he said. 'Did I wake you up?'

'No I was reading, must have dozed off.'

'Would you like me to call you in the morning?' He asked, concerned that he had woken her up.

34

'No, it's okay. How's Germany?' She asked sitting up.

'The clients were really happy with my presentation so I think we may get the contract. I'm actually going out to dinner with the CEO tomorrow night.'

'Great, I'm so proud of you,' Catherine told him. She knew how hard he had worked on the project.

David owned an advertising agency, which he was now expanding into Europe. Most of his clients were among the movers and shakers of the corporate world. Catherine knew from the way he talked about his company that he was very happy. Like herself, he travelled a lot. She could count the number of nights he slept in his London apartment. They had talked about living together, but after what had happened with Brooke, she wasn't ready to live with him. She had almost changed her mind until the dreadful day when her life changed.

'I should be back over the weekend; I'll tell you all about it. Have you given any thought to going to the States with me for a couple of days? There is something I need to show you.'

'Can I get back to you later?' said Catherine. 'I do have some projects to complete, so I can't make any promises. 'I'll call you tomorrow night and confirm if I can come,' she said before hanging up the phone. Unable to fall asleep, she went to the kitchen to make herself a cup of tea.

Catherine knew whatever he had to tell her, or show her. It was about moving back to the States. It was all he'd talked about over the last six months. Not that she blamed him; his whole family lived there apart from his younger brother who worked in Japan. The only reason he was still living in London was because of her. As much as she loved him, she wasn't ready to move back to the States. She wanted to be closer to her parents. Life had changed for all of them after Michael's death. A dark shadow fell over her face. She stood still like a statue. It always happened when she thought about her brother.

The last thing she wanted was to hurt David. She needed more time to prepare herself. She had written to him, emailed him but always deleted the messages and the letters ended up in the bin.

The flat felt very quiet. Sally had left a message saying she was staying with her boyfriend for a week. Catherine was happy to be alone; she loved the quietness and peacefulness. She buried herself deeper beneath her silk beddings and slept.

She was woken next morning by a loud banging on her door. She tried to ignore it, hoping whoever was there would go away, but they didn't give up. She looked at her bedside clock; it was seven o'clock.

'Oh, my God!' Catherine said. Kim was the last person she had expected to see on her doorstep.

'What are you doing here? I thought you weren't due back till Friday.'

'Are you going to let me in or just stand there staring at me?' Kim said, laughing. 'We missed home, and you, of course.'

'Come here,' Catherine said, hugging Kim. 'I missed you. It's really good to have you back. What about your hubby? Don't tell me you've abandoned him already!'

'He's fine. We got back about three hours ago. I couldn't sleep, so I took a ride. How are you?' She asked looking Catherine up and down.

'I'm good,' Catherine answered avoiding eye contact.

'Then why aren't you dressed yet. Are you working from home today?' Kim looked straight at her. She wasn't going to let Catherine shut her out.

'Yes, and I'm fine.' Catherine gave her another hug. 'You want some tea before you give me all the glorious details of your honeymoon?'

They went to the kitchen together.

Watching her, Kim couldn't pretend anymore. 'Why didn't you tell me?' she demanded, as Catherine poured water into the kettle. 'No point in hiding, babes,' Kim went on without remorse. Richard told me everything. What are we going to do about that bastard Brooke?'

'I'm sorry,' Catherine purred… she blurted out everything she had been holding inside. Tears poured down her face, and she couldn't stop. She cried uncontrollably, and Kim held her in her arms. She soothed her back when she finally sobered; she wiped her face and took deep breaths.

'You poor, poor thing,' Kim said over and over. 'You should've told me. Don't tell me you have been going through all this on your own? You should have told me,' she said again. 'I wish you had reported him. He doesn't deserve your loyalty.' she said, but she knew the answer even before her friend could reply. She could feel Catherine shaking uncontrollably.

'I'm so sorry. I should've known something was up. You haven't been your usual self for a while, and I just assumed it was because of work.' Kim hardly knew what to say. She would never have expected this, not from Brooke of all people. 'I'm sorry, Catherine. I feel that I've let you down.'

'You have nothing to be sorry for. I should never have trusted him,' Catherine replied. 'I have been going through it over and over, wondering whether I did anything to encourage him. He has really changed. He isn't the man I once loved. It makes me wonder how much I knew him, or if I knew him at all.'

'Don't you dare blame yourself for what happened? No means no, Brooke is crazy; he needs to be locked up. Have you seen him since then?' Kim asked.

'No, but he sent me flowers at work. My whole body just clenched when I got them. I chucked them into the bin. He wrote me a note, well many notes actually, telling me he doesn't know what came over him. Can you believe he still thinks we can be together after what happened? And what annoys me most is the fact that he just dismisses my relationship with David. A part of me wants to see him punished for what he did, but I can't help feeling I'll be the one who's going to pay the price in the end. I just wish he would leave me alone and get on with his life. I got a call from his mother the other day asking me to lunch. I know that she and I used to be close once, but I can't face any of them right now, and you know how she loves her boys. She probably thinks butter wouldn't melt in their mouths, and I don't want to be the one to wake her up and make her realise that Brooke, for one, isn't a boy anymore. He's a grown man who needs help.'

'Have you told David yet?' Kim asked.

Catherine shook her head. 'I don't know where to start. I have tried again and again, and my courage weakens each time I try. I have talked to him in my mind so many times. How do I tell the man I love that I'm carrying my ex-boyfriend's child?' She dabbed at her face with a tissue. 'It's all a mess, and I don't know how to fix it. He wants me to go with him to the States next week, but I don't know if I'm ready to tell him just yet.'

'I think you should tell him,' Kim said. 'He's one of the good ones, and he won't walk away because of something you had no control over. At least, give him the chance to decide. You don't want to spend the rest of your life wondering if you could have worked things out. David loves you; he will understand. You can't let Brooke wreck everything for you. If you can't talk to David, then go and see a counsellor. What else do you have to give up before you start taking responsibility? I love you, and I want you to be happy, but you need to do this for yourself.' Kim understood why Catherine didn't want to tell the cops.

Her father was one of the country's top judges and her mother owned a publishing company. It was the kind of story the tabloid newspapers loved to tell, and people loved to gossip. She was doing this to protect not only herself but the people she loved, including Brooke's family. She realised most people might not believe her, considering the history she shared with Brooke and his family background. Not that she was one to be interested in what people said. Her family was more important to her, and she would do anything to protect them.

After sitting in the kitchen for so long, they went to the bedroom, and Catherine showed her the letters and pictures from Melissa.

'Oh my goodness, is this really her?' Kim said staring at the pictures. She could not believe it was the same girl they had met almost two years ago.

'You must be so proud of her,' Kim said, handing back the photographs to Catherine.

'I know; she has come a long way; grandma cannot believe the change either.'

'I think you should consider David's plan to move to the states,' Kim said changing the subject. I know you have a lot to think about, but don't be in a rush to give up on him. Just remember he's tall and handsome…. tall and handsome, got that, she repeated laughingly.

Despite the pain in her heart, Catherine smiled. 'I haven't stopped, and, to be honest, I'm tempted, but there is so much to think about. The baby for one thing and the fact that I don't know how he's going to react to the situation…'

'Well, you can start looking before you move; besides you can put this place on rent for income. I would hate to see you go of course, but this might be good for you. You don't need Brooke breathing down your neck.'

'I'll think about it,' Catherine said. 'I have been thinking about adopting Melissa,' she said changing the subject.

'That is such a big move especially now, have you given it some serious thought?' While we are on the subject of major projects, I think you should seriously consider the CNN job. You will be based in the States, and it will give you a chance to spend more time with David. I wouldn't worry about you two breaking up,' she added seeing the look on Catherine's face. 'He loves you too much, and he's quite a catch. You don't want him having too much time alone. He spends half his time the States already. Your aunt Miriam is over there, you can always pop round to hers if you get homesick.'

'I will, I promise. I still need to work out details about adopting Melissa before decided what's best for her. David and I had talked about it too before I found out I was pregnant. She will have a little brother or sister soon,' she said, touching her stomach. She stopped talking.

Kim watched her. For the first time in her life, she didn't have a clue what to do to help her best friend. At the same time, she realised Catherine was the only one who knew what was best for her. No one else could claim to know what she was going through unless they had been in the similar position. She reached out to her and hugged her tightly.

Sally came in two hours later, having had a fight with Jay. She went to check on Catherine and found her fast asleep, with Kim beside her. She was envious of their closeness and wished she could share the same bond with Catherine. She resented Kim for taking Catherine away from her. She had hoped, that now Kim was married, that things might change, but looking at them now she knew they were even closer than before.

She closed the door and left, wondering what Kim was doing there. *I hope that nice-looking man has seen sense and dumped her.* She thought, smiling to herself.

Chapter Six

As the summer breeze touched her skin, Catherine was glad she had agreed to come. It was nothing like she had expected. Surrounded by trees, roses and lilies, she wished she could stay forever. The house was isolated; it was in the middle of nowhere, an oasis of peace and tranquillity. The lake was ten feet away. She sat down next to David on the porch and let herself enjoy the beauty around her. He had said he had a surprise, but she would never have guessed it was a house. He had blindfolded her as they reached the gates, all she knew was that they were in Sagaponack, N.Y and when she finally opened her eyes, she was standing by the lake, facing the house.

'Do you like it?' David asked her.

Catherine was still, almost too shocked to speak. She looked at him as if to confirm what he was saying. 'It's beautiful. It is simply breath-taking. How did you come by such a beautiful place?'

'My lawyer saw it advertised, and he came to view it. I just knew when he told me about it that I had to come and see it for myself and two weeks later, I had the keys in my hands.'

'You mean you bought this house? It's yours?' She could hardly take it in.

'No, it isn't mine. It's ours,' David said, kissing her.

'Oh, my God!' she said, looking around. Brooke's face flashed in her mind. She clasped her hands together.

The house was built on a hill, with large glass windows overlooking the resplendent gardens and the lake; just the kind of house one would love to get lost in.

'All it needs now is a woman's touch,' he said, stroking her hair.

'I see, I do all the work while you sit back,' she teased.

'No babes, we work at it together, I love you, and I want us to spend the rest of our life together in this house if you will have me?'

'David Alexander! Are you proposing?' She asked in amazement.

'Maybe,' he said mischievously. He kissed her passionately and changed the topic. He had plans to ask her tomorrow night. The table was booked, and he couldn't wait to see her face when he proposed.

Catherine was too overwhelmed to speak. It wasn't the surprise she had expected. She had come prepared to tell him about the baby and, standing so close to him, with his arms around her, this didn't seem to be the right time. She trembled with fear. Hot tears filled her eyes, and she struggled not to cry.

Both Kim and Richard had begged her to tell David the truth, but she didn't know where to start. David was so happy; she didn't want to spoil it. Maybe this is the last time I will have him holding me so close. She thought sadly.

'Why the sad face? We should be celebrating,' David said.

He took her hand and walked towards the house. He showed her the bedrooms upstairs, the in -house swimming pool, sauna and the tennis court on the other side.

'Oh, David, it's beautiful,' she said, looking at the massive kitchen.

'Is that why you're crying?' he asked.

'Yes,' she said and impetuously moved into his arms, throwing her long legs around him and hugging him tightly.

Forgotten for the moment were her worries about the baby as

his arms closed around her and their bodies locked in a long embrace.

Her mouth did not leave his as he continued to kiss her, throwing away any doubts or worries she had. *This is where I belong*, Catherine told herself, kissing him back.

He pulled her closer into the circle of his strong arms. 'God, you're so beautiful,' he said, looking straight into her eyes.

Catherine could feel herself floating away as he touched her, his hands telling her what words couldn't say.

The next morning, after breakfast they went to see his elder sister and her family.

'Good to see you,' Natalie said, giving her a hug.

Catherine couldn't help but feel terrible at all the love and affection David's family showed her. They had welcomed her into their family and, strangely enough, she was beginning to understand what it felt like to have an elder sister. Natalie shared her most intimate details with her about her ex-husband, and they talked about clothes and men.

'Well, I'll leave you two to chat,' David said an hour later. 'I promised the girls I would take them shopping.'

'Don't let them trick you into spending too much,' Natalie said. The twins both burst out laughing and rushed to the car.

Natalie stood in the doorway, watching her brother with Catherine. They make a perfect couple, she thought, looking at Catherine, with her perfect light complexion and hazel green eyes. She was almost as tall as her brother was and possessed a smile to die for. He had always made bad choices when it came to women, but Catherine was different. People warmed up to her big bright smile. She was also an intelligent, independent, woman, so unlike those girls who had only wanted her brother for his money and status. With all of her beauty, though, Natalie couldn't help feeling that Catherine was afraid of letting anyone get too close, and it was only when David had told her about Michael and how close they had been that Natalie had begun to understand. She was reminded of her own pain when their parents had both died within the same year, and she had only managed to cope because of her children, her sister Gabrielle, and her brothers. They had been there for each other, more especially David. He had taken over the role of a dad for Gabby. It's a shame Mum, and Dad never got the chance to meet her, she thought sadly.

Catherine gave Natalie a mischievous grin. 'I detect good news, what's happened?

Natalie smiled. 'My divorce papers came through yesterday, I'm officially a single woman.'

'Wow, I'm so happy for you,' Catherine said brightly hugging her.

'Thank you,' Natalie said smiling. 'Come, let's cook.'

Natalie's kitchen was very big. Catherine could smell the chicken and lamb. There was also a big plate of fish on the table.

'How are you feeling?' Catherine asked.

'I don't know,' Natalie answered. 'For a long time, I was so bitter and angry. I wanted to hurt him just as much as he had hurt me. I didn't allow the girls to see him. Not that they needed much encouragement, watching their father making a fool of himself with a girl half his age, but after a while I guess I got tired of being angry, and I felt so much better. I shared twenty years of my life with him, and I realised that I was the one suffering by spending so much time thinking of ways of getting back at him. I am starting to enjoy being single again and I guess with time we might become friends.'

Listening to her, Catherine knew Natalie would be fine. She was less angry, and the bitterness had completely vanished from her voice. Not that anyone could blame her for being angry. The whole neighbourhood knew her husband had left her for a younger woman. His girlfriend lived only five houses away, and he had moved in with her.

'Have you seen him lately?'

'No. The girls spent last weekend with him. He told them he's moving to Los Angeles, so I guess I don't have to worry about bumping into him and his girlfriend. Anyway, enough of me – how are you and David doing?'

'Good,' Catherine said, suddenly remembering their time together that afternoon; their lovemaking had been so intense and sweet.

'I can tell, you both look so happy and relaxed,' Natalie said happily.

'Unfortunately, I still can't cook,' Catherine joked.

'Well, I wouldn't worry about that if I was you. David can cook and don't let him make you think otherwise. Besides, there are so many cookery books and TV shows these days. My ex couldn't even boil an egg and I blame his mother for making him think it's a woman's job.'

Catherine helped cut the vegetables and made the table while Natalie did the cooking.

When David and the girls finally came back two hours later carrying designer carrier bags full of clothes, the food was ready, and they helped take it to the table while their mother mixed the salads. Catherine sat opposite David, and she could feel her heart beating rapidly. He was so devastatingly handsome.

Candles flickered from the table's centre, making the atmosphere relaxed and romantic.

'This is really good,' Virginia said, putting some food on her plate.

'I agree. You should come more often.' Vanessa looked at her uncle and Catherine.

'Is that for my cooking or your shopping?' Natalie asked.

The twins laughed. 'We did have fun, though, didn't we Uncle David?' Virginia said.

'And we all know at whose expense,' said Natalie, picking up her glass of Cos D'Estournel. 'It's not often I get a chance to cook. The girls would rather eat burgers than a proper meal. Well, let's make a toast, shall we?' she added, raising her glass. 'I drink to your happiness.' She glanced towards Catherine and then David.

'Are you spending this Christmas with us, Aunty Catherine?' Vanessa asked.

'I'm not sure yet,' said Catherine. 'I'll certainly let you know once your uncle, and I decide. What about you two, any plans for your holidays?'

'We are going away skiing with friends for two weeks, and Dad wants us to visit him in LA, but we haven't decided yet if we're going to go,' Vanessa said, suddenly remembering their father wasn't the favourite subject at the moment.

'What do you think of the house?' Natalie asked, changing the subject. It was all her brother had talked about since viewing it.

'It's beautiful,' Catherine said. 'It's overlooking the lake and far away from the main road and other houses. It's so gigantic – I can't believe anyone would want to sell a house like that. You should come and see it for yourself. I'm sure you will love it.' She launched into a description of the house. Nothing more was mentioned of holidays or Natalie's ex-husband.

Later, much later, after having dessert and tea, Natalie turned to Catherine when everyone was busy watching television.

'Are you all right? You seem a bit distant tonight.'

'Yes, I'm okay. I guess I'm still suffering from jet lag.'

'You know you're welcome to spend the night here. We can catch up and wake up to a heavy breakfast.'

'I wish I could,' said Catherine, 'but we can't, David has a meeting first thing, and we have to do food shopping. I will come soon, though, I promise.'

They stayed on for another hour before saying their goodbyes.

'You have been rather quiet,' David said parking the car. He thought she had fallen asleep, yet her eyes were wide open. He couldn't help wondering if he had seen that same expression before he left for Germany.

'I'm OK,' she said, trying to smile. 'Just a bit tired.'

'Catherine, talk to me,' he said turning his body to face her. 'Something is bothering you; you hardly said a word on the way here.'

'There is something I need to tell you,' she began, 'but let's go inside.'

They went into the house and sat by the fire. She could not look at him, and she felt her throat dry. The words would not come out.

David waited, his heart pounding. He loved her and knew deep down something was wrong; he had never seen her look so confused before.

'You don't have to tell me if you're not ready,' he said, coming to sit next to her. He held her in his arms and whispered gently in her ear, 'I love you; you do know that, don't you? Whatever it is, I'm sure it can't be that bad.' Turning her to face him, he lifted her chin and cupped her face. 'What's wrong?' he whispered against her cheek.

He had told her over and over how much he loved her, and she knew he meant every word. It was hard for her to think of the impact the pregnancy might have on their relationship.

David was everything she had ever wanted in a man, he was not like anyone else she had ever dated and even her father, who was always critical of her past relationships, told her mum that he was a good man. She hated herself for the situation she found herself in; as for Brooke, he was the last person she wanted to think about and yet her mind couldn't help wandering back to that day.

'Catherine,' she heard him say, 'I can't help you if you don't tell me what's bothering you.'

'I don't know how to say this,' she began, suddenly wanting

some space between them. 'I'm pregnant, David,' she said slowly.

'What! You are?' he said excitedly, closing the gap between them. 'How could you think I would be upset? This is the best news ever. Is that what's been worrying you?' he asked. Suddenly he felt her trying to pull away from him and he stood still, confused.

David kept his eyes on her, not saying anything.

'You're not the father,' Catherine said, tears filling her eyes.

She had almost lied to him, told him it was his baby, but she couldn't. She didn't want any future they had together to be based on lies.

She watched as the blood drained from his face; silence filled the room.

Fear grew in her heart. She had not meant to hurt him, and now she couldn't take away the words. She felt him drawing away from her, sensed his bitter struggle for understanding of the ramifications of what she had just said.

'David, I'm sorry,' she said, wiping away her tears.

David was very quiet for a while, his face motionless.

He felt as though someone had taken a knife and stabbed him straight through the heart. This can't be happening, he thought. He loved her, and she had betrayed him. He wondered how long the affair had gone on. He struggled to stay calm as images of her naked with another man flashed through his mind. He could not understand what had happened to the love they shared. Less than two hours ago, she had said she loved him.

'David,' he heard her say from a distance. 'I'm sorry.'

'Is that all you can say?' he said turning to face her.

Catherine wanted to rush into his arms, to tell him she had not cheated on him.

'I think we should both go to bed before we say something we will regret. You can sleep in the spare room,' he said walking away.

'I was raped...'

He stopped and stared hard at her.

'Don't you dare say that,' he growled. 'It's bad enough that you've slept with someone else, please don't lie to me too.'

'I'm not lying,' Catherine said, her voice was low, and she felt her throat tighten.

Without a word, he walked away. She stood still, frozen to the ground. Her body was shaking. Her world had stopped, yet she was still breathing. She held on tightly to the table and collapsed into the chair.

'I need some air, don't wait up,' he said reaching for his car keys.

She watched him go. She refused to cry, to beg.

Half an hour later, she fled David's house in turmoil, only pausing to catch her breath and collect her suitcase. His angry stare flashed before her eyes; his cruel words kept ringing in her ears. She took one last glance towards the house before the taxi disappeared into the dark. The next day, she was back in London in her bed, not knowing exactly how she got there. Wrapping her arms around her, she sobbed until her body was totally exhausted. As hard as she tried to block David's pained face, she couldn't. Damn Brooke, she whispered and pushed herself further into the bed.

Chapter Seven

David paced up and down the living-room floor, his face unshaven, and his eyes red from lack of sleep. This was the lowest he had ever felt in his life, and he didn't know how to handle it. Images of her face came flashing back each time he tried to close his eyes. It was as if she had taken over his body and mind. When he couldn't walk around anymore, he sat by the window. He had come back downstairs expecting to find her sitting on the sofa, but she wasn't there, even though he could still sense her presence and smell the scent of her perfume. Sighing heavily, he got up and poured himself a drink, hoping it would help him blank her out of his mind.

On a nearby low table, was a big picture of Catherine? She looked happy, different from the woman he had faced two nights ago. He threw down the glass of brandy he was holding, smashing it to the floor. He didn't try sweeping up the scattered pieces of glass, but walked away and poured himself another drink, hoping it would make him feel better. It didn't. The more he drank, the worse it got. Memories came flooding back, and he tried to push away the image of another man touching her and kissing her. He held onto a chair for support as a thundering pain ripped through his body.

He could not tell morning from the afternoon, as the pain grew deep inside him. He could not even bring himself to call her, as he didn't know what to say. The house with all its beautiful surroundings wasn't that appealing to him anymore, but it was the only place he could be alone. He couldn't eat, and no matter how hard he tried not to think of her, her face haunted him. She was everywhere: in his dreams and his every waking thought. He did not want to close his eyes in case she came back; he needed answers from her, wanted to feel her body next to his. To hear her say it was just a dream.

Suddenly he remembered the ring he had bought for her. This was supposed to be the weekend when he was going to propose. He had worked on his poem for weeks. That was the big surprise, not the house. He recalled how she had joked about his proposal and shook his head.

It all seemed such a long time ago. He had booked a table for them at a restaurant and, thinking about it; he realised he hadn't called the restaurant to cancel. For almost a month, he had waited for this weekend and now it had turned out to be a nightmare.

He had spent the whole weekend with his younger sister looking for the ring.

'I want something special for her,' he had told Gabrielle.

'You do love her, don't you?' Gabrielle said, wrapping her arm around his.

'Yes,' David said without hesitation, 'I can't wait for her to be my wife.'

'For your sake, I hope she says yes. You cannot spend so much money on a ring and not get married,' Gabrielle teased, staring at the price.

Now he walked up the staircase to his bedroom. The ring was still where he'd left it. The roses and flowers he had bought to give her that evening had all dried up. He took the ring in his fingers and sat heavily on the bed. Nothing made sense to him as he tried to remember her words. He couldn't believe this was happening. He put the ring in his pocket and walked around the room. The phone rang again, and he ignored it. He listened as the caller left a message.

It was his sister. 'Hi, David, it's Gabby. Just wanted to know how things went on Saturday. Call me; I want to come and celebrate with you.'

His voicemail was full of messages, but he didn't want to talk to anyone. He called his secretary and asked her to cancel his appointments for the whole week; his assistant could handle them. She couldn't even wait to go back to her lover, he thought miserably.

The morning turned into evening, and he suddenly found himself in the living-room, unable to remember how he'd got there. He moved his chair away from the window and put on the television. The house felt quiet, and David wished he could just sleep and not think of her, but he was still reminded of her presence. Some of her clothes still hung in the wardrobe. He felt her presence in every room. Why me, he thought reaching for his drink. To think, he had wanted to marry her, to spend the rest of his life with her. He wiped away the tears with the back of his hand. He recalled the first time he had taken her out. She looked so beautiful, he found himself staring at her, and even then, he had wanted to ask her to marry him. Flashes of their last conversation sparked in his mind, and he closed his eyes.

He must have dozed off for a few minutes or even hours, because when he opened his eyes, the table looked clean. The empty bottles of champagne and brandy were gone.

'Catherine,' he whispered without opening his eyes fully. 'Catherine, you came back. Sit next to me, darling. I missed you.'

There was no answer. He heard a cough and saw Gabby standing behind him with a glass of water in one hand. She pulled up a chair and sat next to him.

He did not need to tell her things had not gone according to plan. She saw the ring on the floor as soon as she walked through the door. Catherine was nowhere to be seen and her brother looked a mess.

'I'm sorry,' she said, touching his hand.

David was silent. As much as he wanted to be alone, he was glad his sister was there. He was tired of seeing Catherine's face everywhere he looked.

'When I didn't hear from you, I got worried. I rang Natalie, and she asked me to come and check on you. What happened, if you don't mind me asking?'

David looked at his sister. She is so young and so innocent, I hope she never has to go through something like this, he thought. He held his face in his hands and took a deep breath. There was silence between them as David tried to fight the truth; he couldn't say the words out loud, not yet anyway.

'How did you get in?' he asked her.

'Natalie told me where to find the keys,' said Gabby. 'So are you going to tell me what's going on?'

'Catherine and I have broken up,' David said, his eyes cast to the floor. Saying the words, he wished the ground would open up and swallow him. He didn't want pity from his little sister or anyone else. He walked away, fighting the tears that were threatening; he couldn't cry, not in front of Gabby, and the worst thing was, he still wanted Catherine, despite her deception.

That was not what Gabby had expected to hear. 'What happened?' she asked confused.

'I don't want to talk about it. Please don't bring up her name again?' he added, his voice filled with emotion. 'I'm going to take a walk.' He blamed himself and hated her for what she had done. How could he ever trust anyone ever?

Gabby watched him go, her body paralysed. He was the one who always made her feel strong and now that he needed her, she did not know how to help him.

'There's plenty more fish in the sea,' he'd tell her jokingly.

This was different. Her brother truly loved Catherine, and she could only guess at what he was going through. She couldn't understand why they had broken up. They seemed so happy together, so much in love. She didn't get it at all.

She picked up the phone and rang Natalie; her sister was stunned when she told her.

'Are you certain?' she asked repeatedly.

'She's not here, Natalie, so I suppose it is true. I don't know what to do. David is in a state, and I don't think he's had anything to eat since he came to your house.'

'Just be there for him,' Natalie said. 'I wish I could come, but I doubt he would welcome all of us. Just stay with him and don't let him drink too much,' she added before hanging up. Gabby stared at the phone long after her sister had said goodbye. She was tempted to call Catherine but thought better of it. She doubted her brother would be pleased if she talked to Catherine. She went to the kitchen to find something to cook, but the fridge was empty.

Her brother was still not back an hour later, so she put on her jacket and went to look for him.

He was sitting by the lake, staring at the water. She joined him, and they both stared at the lake in silence.

In the days that followed, Gabrielle thought only of her brother. He spent most of his time in his study; he hardly ate and told her to take messages whenever the phone rang.

'Have patience with him,' Natalie had said when she rang to tell her what was happening.

She was trying her best, but she could not stay with him for too long. She needed to be back in college.

As the days crept forward, her hopes of having a conversation with her brother died and her tension began to mount. She couldn't understand why he shut himself away from everything. He needed to talk to Catherine, to patch things up. It was clear to her that he still loved Catherine. His male ego prevented him from doing what he really wanted to do because he did show interest each time the phone rang and yet he wouldn't pick it up.

On the day she was due to go back to college, he came downstairs quite late, and she had to cancel her flight; she couldn't leave without making sure he would be all right. She decided to visit Natalie and convince her to talk to him. She left later that evening.

The next morning, David woke up early. After having a shower and a shave, he decided to try and get a grip on what had happened between him and Catherine. He wanted to forget about her and move on with his life. He remembered his little sister telling him to talk to Catherine; he wondered what she would say if she knew the whole truth. Even if they got back together, he would always worry about her cheating on him and the child too. Was he strong enough to watch the child grow knowing he wasn't the father? I have to get away from here. He told himself. He dialled her number, but nerves took over, and he switched off the phone.

An hour later, he switched on his mobile phone, rang his brother in Japan and made plans to visit him. As he stood by the window, he remembered her smile, her expression when she first saw the house. He had bought it for them; now he hated the house; he wished he had never bought it in the first place.

He packed a bag and left. The clouds drifted across the sky, and the air was fresh. As much as he was hurting inside, he was glad to be out of the house. There has to be something more to this story he told himself as he drove away. He couldn't bring himself to believe she would ever cheat on him.... but he couldn't believe she had been raped. She would have told him when it happened. They didn't keep secrets from each other. He switched on the CD player and tried to focus his mind on the road ahead.

Chapter Eight

Catherine was dismayed to find the flat in a mess when she got back from the States. Obviously, Sally had had her friends over, probably the moment Catherine had been off. She could smell the cigarette smoke everywhere. She was about to start tidying up when the phone rang.

'Hi, not sure if you remember me, it's Jay, Sally's boyfriend…I can't get hold of Sally, so you're the next best thing…'

'Why are you calling me so late?' Catherine asked shocked that he was calling her at such a late hour unless something was wrong with Sally.

'Is Sally OK? She asked anxiously.

'I'm at the police station. I can't explain on the phone. Please, I really need your help. I'll explain later.'

Sighing deeply, she wrote down the details. She put on her brown tracksuit bottoms and top, tied her hair in a ponytail and left. She didn't bother putting on makeup. She was tired, hungry and angry. The last thing she needed was a visit to the police station in the middle of the night. She tried Sally's number before driving off, and it still went to voicemail.

Half an hour later, she was standing outside Lavender Hill police station.

'How dare you drag me here at this time of the night,' she hissed at him as soon as they were alone. She didn't realise she was shaking with anger until she was out of the police station. The officer on duty had asked her to sign some papers before releasing him on bail.

'I'm sorry I called you,' Jay said again sitting next to her. 'Sally always said you were always there for her during her dark days.'

'Dark days,' she said staring at him.

'Yes, we all have them, don't we? I appreciate what you did for me tonight. I want you to know I don't do drugs; someone must have left them in my car. I know you don't know me very well, but you need to trust me. I would never do anything to hurt Sally. Please don't say anything to her cousin about the charges. She doesn't need to know.'

Catherine wanted to say something but changed her mind. 'Where should I drop you.' she asked him instead.

'He talked all the way to Balham, and she was glad when she dropped him off.

'Thank you for everything,' he said opening the door.

Catherine narrowed her eyes and then sighed. 'Next time you get into trouble with the police please don't call me. If Sally calls, do ask her to call me.' She drove off at top speed through the lighted streets.

Kim watched Catherine as she picked at her meal. She had not said a word about David or the baby, and Kim longed to find out what had happened. Catherine had not even called her to tell her she was back in London.

'She came back two days ago,' Sally had informed her when she called to inquire about Catherine since her mobile phone was switched off.

She let herself in after ringing the bell repeatedly. Good thing I have spare keys, she told herself. Her fears were confirmed when she saw the state Catherine was in.

It was mid-day and yet she was still in her nightgown.

There were empty packs of ice-cream on the table, and she

looked as though she had not slept for days. Fear raced through Kim. She had never known Catherine to be so down before. Catherine didn't speak but fell into Kim's open arms.

'You should've told me you were coming,' she said, pulling back. 'I could have cleaned the place up.'

'What happened over there?' Kim asked her voice soft.

'I told him about the baby; he didn't believe I was raped. End of story.'

'Seriously, that doesn't seem like David.'

'Well, believe what you like. It's over,' she spoke with conviction.

Kim stared at her friend, not believing a word she was saying. She could not imagine David doing that to her. Anyone could tell they loved each other.

'I've called him, at least, three times since I got back, but he won't pick up my calls. Anyway, I've decided not to call him again. If he wants to talk to me, he knows where to find me.'

'Give him time,' Kim said, moving closer. 'He's behaving this way because he doesn't know the full story. David loves you. He will come round; I 'm sure of it.'

'I wish I could be as certain as you.'

Kim put her arms around her. There was no point in telling her everything was going to be fine, so maybe having a good cry would easy some of the pain. Kim brushed her hair until she calmed down.

Catherine was reminded of the time when they didn't know anything about relationships with men. They had brushed each other's hair just for the fun of it. Then the phone rang, and Kim went to pick it up.

She hesitated for a moment, looking at Catherine. 'She can't come to the phone right now,' she said ringing off. 'It was his sister,' she told Catherine. 'I doubt you want to speak to her,' Kim said sitting down. 'Have you had anything to eat?' she asked.

Catherine shook her head.

'Right, take a shower; we're going out to lunch.'

'I don't feel like going anywhere,' said Catherine. 'I have everything I need right here, and besides, I just feel so sick I don't think I would be good company for anyone. Can you believe that before I told David about the baby, I actually thought about having an abortion?'

'Are you still thinking about it?' Kim asked.

'No, strangely enough, I find myself longing to be a mother. I close my eyes at night and pretend it's David's baby. How sad is that? She added her voice low and sad. 'I only wish someone had warned me about the morning sickness, though,' she added, and Kim could almost see a smile on her face.

'You get ready. We're going out,' Kim said.

'I don't feel—' Catherine began before Kim cut her off.

'You've been stuck in this apartment too long. You need some air to clear your head. Besides, we haven't gone shopping together for a while. I'm told there's a good musical from South Africa at the Shaftesbury Theatre. Maybe we can check it out.'

'What about Jason?' Catherine asked, trying to find an excuse.

'He won't be back till the weekend, so you have no excuse,' Kim told her, smiling. Catherine may want to shut herself off from the world, but she wasn't going to let her. She needed to keep busy and take her mind off David and the baby, even if it was just for a few hours.

It was much later in the evening when Kim finally dropped her off, and Catherine admitted herself that she felt much better. For a few hours, her troubles were forgotten as she and Kim moved from one store to another in Knightsbridge, trying on different clothes, shoes, and ended up buying clothes she didn't need. They had afternoon tea at Harrods before heading home.

In the days that followed, Catherine experienced the full impact of David's rejection. Although she was determined not to call him again, she could feel her willpower deserting her, so, in the end, she switched off her mobile phone and unplugged the house phone. She was tired of running each time it rang, thinking it was him.

She thought about calling Melissa to tell her about the baby but decided against it. With everything else going on in her life, she decided to put the adoption process on hold.

She was not the only person who adored the little girl; her parents were so proud of her and her mum sometimes jokingly called Melissa, her first grandchild. She touched her stomach and wondered what life would be like for her and her baby. All the worries she had in the beginning about motherhood didn't seem to matter anymore. She found herself crossing off dates on the calendar and reading books on motherhood and nursery schools.

During the day, she spent most of her time in the study, writing articles and replying to emails, most of them to do with work.

At first, she was angry with herself for not telling David immediately after the rape, but she had been so humiliated and ashamed when it happened. She could also not forget how many times he told her not to trust Brooke. At the time, she had just dismissed his concern, but he had been right, she didn't know Brooke very well.

When her mum asked her about David, she simply said he was too busy to come to London. She also avoided meeting her parents or her friends. She couldn't look them in the eye and lie. She managed to keep her emotions hidden from everybody apart from Kim and Richard. She spent most hours away from her flat; there were just too many memories of him, and she didn't want to risk running into Brooke.

Richard, who didn't like shopping, even escorted her to Harrods and other shops in Knightsbridge. They went to movies and shows together, and he made a point of not mentioning David's name. She had told Richard what had happened in America. He simply told her to give David time. Catherine wished she could be as certain as Kim and Richard, but as time went by, she made herself accept the painful knowledge that she might never see him again.

Chapter Nine

Brooke stood by his car wearing jeans and a black polo-neck top. Anger and contempt burst into her chest seeing him at her office. She quickly turned away, she ran instead of walking in the other direction to get a taxi, but she was not quick enough. He saw her and called out her name. She felt her heart beating with anger. She moved on, without looking back, wanting to put some distance between them, wanting to be as far away from him as possible.

'Catherine,' he said, closing the gap between them. 'Didn't you hear me calling you?'

'What do you want?' she asked, turning to face him, her face was hard and filled with anger. 'Please just leave me alone,' she said frostily moving away. She heard his footsteps behind her, and she quickened her steps.

'Please stop,' he begged. 'I need to speak to you.'

'About what exactly,' she said slowing down.

'We can't talk here; can I give you a lift so we can talk?'

'Have you lost your mind?' She screamed not caring who heard her. 'Just who the hell do you think you're showing up here, and since when did I need a chaperone?' She asked sarcastically. She knew the only person who could have told him where she'd gone to was Sally. 'I've told you; I don't want anything more to do with you. I don't want to talk to you or see you and I can't make it clearer than that.'

She walked away, shaking with anger. She was annoyed that Sally could do that to her when she knew how she felt about Brooke. She didn't understand why her friend even bothered talking to him. She had not been friendly towards him when they were together, and yet she couldn't help feeling Sally was in contact with him. She wondered why he was taking such an interest in Sally, or she in him, when she had her studies and Jay to keep her busy.

'I just want ten minutes of your time,' she heard him say right behind her.

'Listen, and please listen carefully because I don't want ever to say this to you again, you've got to stop harassing me, stop following me. You have hurt me more than anyone has ever done, and I would appreciate it if you kept your distance from now on otherwise I won't be held responsible for my actions. Get a life, and leave me alone.' She got into the taxi, slamming the door. She didn't realise her hands were shaking and sweaty until the car started moving.

She calmed down as the taxi drove through the busy roads, stopping every five minutes to let tourists and shoppers cross. She saw young girls pushing prams, getting onto and off the buses. She knew many of them were probably single parents with no partners or families to help them. She had once done an article on single parenting, and she had been amazed to realise how many girls were having children at a young age; many of them even found the whole idea of having a baby fashionable. It was only afterwards, when the young men ran away, that they realised it wasn't easy to bring up a child when you're young and penniless.

Sally wasn't around when Catherine finally got home.

An hour later, she heard footsteps and the front door opening. Sally walked in carrying shopping bags.

'Can we talk?' she said to Sally, catching her before she went to her bedroom.

'If we must,' Sally said, looking tense. 'I will just get changed.' She went to her room, came back a few minutes later and sat down facing Catherine.

'Well, first of all, I don't want you discussing my business with Brooke. Honestly, Sal, you know what the man put me through. Do you think I want him hanging around me?'

'You've got to be kidding me, why would I be talking to Brooke, especially about you. Do you really think I would sink that low? I haven't seen him in a long time, besides he wouldn't be calling me he hasn't got my number.'

Catherine stared at her, wondering if she was telling the truth. She had lied to her so many times in the past; it was hard to tell when she was being truthful. 'I'm sorry, I had to ask. You're the only person who knew where I was going to be.'

'Well, he didn't hear it from me,' Sally said. 'Perhaps he's stalking you,' she added jokingly.

Catherine didn't find Sally's statement funny. She shook her head and took a deep breath. She was beginning to worry. The thought of Brooke stalking her was very alarming.

'Brooke and I have nothing to resolve, and please do remember that the next time you talk to him. And the other thing is next time one of your friends' needs bailing out, please don't get me involved. Really Sally, why can't you date normal people like everyone else?'

'I'm sorry about what happened; I had no idea that he was selling drugs. He said he worked in the City, and I had no reason to doubt him. I'm so sorry he called you. He had no right to involve you, and I have told him as much.'

'You believe him?' Catherine said. Surely Sally couldn't be that naïve. She'd heard all these stories before. Some men lied to buy time and how was Sally going to know he would do as he said? She only hoped she wouldn't get dragged too much into it; as a friend she didn't want to stand by and just let it happen.

'Do you love this man?' she asked.

'What kind of a question is that?' Sally asked her voice tense. She was shaking inside and hoped Catherine didn't notice.

'Just answer the question, Sal. Do you love him?'

'I don't know,' Sally said after a while, 'but I can't leave him now. He needs me.'

'If the tables were reversed, do you think he would do the same for you?' Catherine said. 'I don't mean to be nasty, but I don't understand why you seem to be attracted to men who are so destructive. You told me yourself he said he had a job in the City. If he can lie about something like that, what else isn't he telling you and what's happened to the new man you were telling me about?'

'I'll get it sorted,' Sally said, her voice tight. 'I know I've let you down.' She did seem to be contrite.

'Don't worry about me. You need to figure out what you want in a man before you go looking for one. There are some good men out there, so why should you settle for the losers? Every woman deserves a man who will treat her well and make her feel good about herself.'

'Once you know where to find such a man, let me know,' Sally said. She did want such a man. A man who would treat her like a queen, who would love her, the way David loved Catherine. She had tried to dress up well, study hard for her exams, but she never seemed to attract the kind of people Catherine was talking about. She made up her mind to talk to Brooke; they needed to sort things out. He was her only hope, and he was the reason she was still smiling after what Jay had put her through.

Not wanting to discuss Brooke and the men in her life anymore, Sally changed the subject. She discussed her lecturers. 'You should see the man, he's so fat and old, and he thinks I would be interested in going to bed with him. He would probably end up with a heart attack.'

'Sal!' Catherine said, surprised.

'Well, you don't think he's interested in me do you? He just wants sex, and he thinks I'm stupid enough to fall for his sweet talk.'

'There are laws about such things? You could report him, you know.'

'I was tempted, but I can't be bothered really. Besides, I will be out of there in less than six months. The sad thing is, I'm not the first person he's tried it on with. He has slept with some girls who thought he could help them pass the exams, anyway enough about me. How are things between you and David?'

Catherine was silence for a few seconds. She realised Sally probably knew things were not as they should be with David, but she wasn't ready to talk to Sally about him. 'Things are OK,' she finally said. Talking about David was too painful, and she wished everyone would stop asking her.

'How does he feel about becoming a dad?' Sally asked hoping Catherine would open up. 'Don't get this the wrong way but you just don't seem yourself since you got back. You would tell me if there was something bothering you, wouldn't you?'

'Everything is fine,' Catherine said trying hard to sound confided.

As Sally watched Catherine staring at her late brother's picture, she realised all was not well. Sally had learned that Catherine always shut down when her eyes pored over her late brother's picture. She didn't get it but never asked. Frankly, she would rather the picture wasn't on the wall. It made her feel eerie. He had those dark deep blue eyes, which always made her feel as though he was watching her even though he was dead.

'I'm sorry about Brooke,' Sally said softly. 'He did come here when you were away; I didn't want to upset you, and that's why I said I haven't seen him. But I never told him where you were today. If I had known things were bad between you, I would

66

never have let him into the house. I never invited him; he just showed up and started asking about you.'

'Was he now!?' Catherine said, getting upset.

Sally saw her expression; it was exactly what she had hoped for. It was obvious to everyone else but Brooke that she didn't want him back.

'Listen, Sal, Brooke and I haven't been together in a long time. I haven't got time for him.' she stated wondering what Sally would say if she knew Brooke had forced himself on her. 'I know you may be trying to help, but you're doing him more harm than good. He needs to realise that I've moved on. I've lost count of the times I've told him to leave me alone, and I can't go on telling him. He says he loves me and yet he can't even respect the fact that I'm with someone else now.' She stopped, realising that she wasn't actually with David anymore. 'If Brooke loved me as much as he claims, then he should let me go. The problem with Brooke is he only wants what he can't have, and I'm tired of it. Anyway, next time he asks you questions about me, tell him to talk to me. I don't want him using you for his own selfish needs. He has a dark side. I would advise you to stay away from him.' she added, stood up and left. She went to her study and tried to do some work, but all the words were blurred. She picked up her phone and called her grandmother.

'Are you okay?' her grandma asked her as soon as she heard her voice. 'I've been calling you the last five days.'

'I'm sorry,' Catherine said. 'I was going to call, but I've been so busy with work, I hardly have enough time in the day.'

'You work too hard, and how is David?' her Grandmother asked.

Catherine hesitated. 'I'm not sure; we had a misunderstanding, and now he's not talking to me. Has Melissa arrived? She asked, changing the subject.

'No, she decided to stay in school and study. They close for holidays next month. I'll see her soon. As for your young man, I wouldn't worry much about him. You'll make up. Anyone can tell he worships the ground you walk on. Your mum told me the good news. I'm so happy and if you need to get away from London, just call me and I'll get your room ready.'

'OK, I'll let you know.'

'If you don't come, I'll understand,' her grandma said. 'I'll let Melissa know you called.'

Sally sat still long after Catherine left. She had called Brooke, telling him where to find Catherine. She had wanted Catherine to have it out with him, so he would realise she was totally over him, and there was no point in delaying telling her about them. She was tired of keeping their relationship a secret; he used Catherine as an excuse all the time even though she was with David. Sometimes in the still dark hours of the day, she did wonder if Brooke still had feelings for Catherine, but brushed them aside. He was her man now, and it was going stay that way. The affair had begun almost three years ago when he was still with Catherine. She had gone on one of her assignments. Brooke came to the house to leave some stuff for Catherine. Sally had been looking after the house. She always looked after the house, when Kim and Catherine went away on long assignments. She couldn't recall which one of them had made the first move, but she woke up in his arms, and they had stayed in bed the whole day making love. He stayed over that whole week until Catherine came back. She hated how he tried to ignore her when Catherine was around. How attentive he was …

Consumed with guilt, she did not sleep with him again until Catherine finally broke up with him. She had been with him the day Jay got arrested. But Catherine must never find out. They would tell her together once David got back. She smiled thinking about her life with him. She realised not everyone would be happy, but they loved each other. He had not told her in so many words, but she knew deep in her heart she loved him more than Catherine ever did.

'I'm going out,' she called out to Catherine half an hour later.

'Where are you off to?' Catherine asked walked into the living room. 'I thought you said you have exams on Monday?'

'I do, but I need to get out, I've studied enough unless there is something you need me to do for you.'

'I'm good and if I don't see you before Monday, good luck with your exams.'

'Thanks,' Sally said anxious to get away. Brooke normally left the office early on Fridays, and she wanted to surprise him. Taking off her underwear, she called a taxi and went to wait outside. When she got to his house, it was quiet, but his car was parked in the driveway. She rang the buzzer several times until she heard soft footsteps moving around the front door. She pressed it again, harder this time, almost getting angry. It was then she remembered that Brooke normally left the spare key for the housekeeper under the flowerpot. Hurriedly she went to get it and let herself in.

She stopped in her tracks, her heart stopped. For a few minutes, she froze. Sitting at the kitchen table, drinking water was a woman half-naked wearing Brooke's shirt.

'Hi,' the woman said softly.

Sally stared at her; she didn't answer. Her body was too shocked to speak.

The woman looked up at her and their eyes locked. She stood up and poured the rest of the water into the sink.

'Who are you?' Sally asked her expression was of pure outrage. The woman just rolled her eyes at her, dismissing her completely and walked towards the stairs. Sally stood still and watched her as she took the steps. A moment later, she heard heavy footsteps, Brooke stopped in his tracks when he saw her. His hair was wet, and his face was as white as a ghost.

'Sally...listen I'm sor...' he began, but she silenced him.

'You bloody bastard,' she hissed at him. I never want to see you again. Stay away from me, and stay away from Catherine. She reached for the vase and threw it at him. Glass shattered all over the floor. She opened the door, walked out without looking back.

Chapter Ten

Catherine Walker sat at the cafe; it was windy. She smoothed her dress over her knees. She watched as Kim walked awkwardly across the street staring at the parking meter. She waved to her, and they shared a smile.

'I'll just go and find parking,' Kim shouted.

'OK,' Catherine said. She ordered another coffee.

The cafe was deserted, normally it was bustling. She watched as shoppers moved along King's Road carrying huge shopping bags. There was a huge sale sign at John Lewis. She made a mental note to pop in and get some shoes. Most people were at the Chelsea flower show. She and Kim had gone once, but she realised long ago, she wasn't a flower person.

She pressed her knees tightly together and tried not to think about the sharp pain that pierced inside her. Across the road, she saw a couple walking a dog holding hands. She thought about David and their last meeting. There was still no communication between them. Her friends had stopped asking, and as much as she tried to forget about him, it was difficult. When her parents asked, she told them he was busy. Her father said David needed to get his priorities right. She couldn't tell them about Brooke; they had been through so much. Even through her mother seemed to be getting better; her father buried himself in work. If he wasn't at work, he was visiting his sister in the states. Her mother was worried about him too. Her mother was a strong person, but Catherine had noticed the cracks when she talked about her father. She said things like going for counselling, which was a word she had never associated with her mother. She was happy they were going away to Spain again. He always seemed happy and relaxed after those visits.

In the weeks that followed, Catherine felt as if she was falling through the air in slow motion, waiting for someone to rescue her, someone to hold her, to tell her she was having a bad dream. She took a sip of water and tried to rid herself of the bad thoughts. A fleeting memory passed through her mind, and it left her feeling empty and sad. She thought about her brother, about their childhood and how happy they had been. She could clearly picture her brother laughing and playing hide and seek. He always played the doctor, while she played the nurse. A passion he had developed from childhood. Tears streamed down her cheeks. She wiped them away, took a magazine and tried to read.

'Would you like to order some lunch? Louisa, her friend and the owner of the cafe asked pulling a chair to sit down.

'I 'm not hungry, I'll wait for Kim,' Catherine said. Over the years, they had built up a relationship. She had even introduced her to both David and Brooke.

'If I was ten years younger, I would fight you for him,' Louisa had said the first time she met David.

'When is lover boy coming?' Louisa asked pushing her bottom comfortably into the chair.

'We broke up,' Catherine said softly. She watched the horror on Louisa's face.

'You've got to be kidding me,' Louisa said staring at her.

She glanced over her shoulder and was relieved to see Kim walking towards her. She was wearing a lovely beige scarf around her neck. Her hair was short, and her face radiant.

'Hi, you OK? That took ages,' she said giving Kim a big hug.

She could almost feel Louisa's eyes staring deeply into her skin. Their eyes met, and they both realised the moment had passed. She didn't want to discuss David.

'Let me know when you're ready to order,' Louisa said walking away. She looked at Catherine again for a few seconds and disappeared into the cafe.

'You look well. Pregnancy suits you,' Kim said, pulling up a chair.

'Flattery won't get you anywhere. I feel so ugly, fat and so useless. I have to go shopping soon; I can't fit into most of my clothes.'

'Let me know, I'll come with you,' Kim said. 'Thanks for sending the scan, by the way. Jason is getting all broody now. He's been giving hints. Men, huh? He's the one who said we should put off having a family for the next three years. One look at your scan and he wants a baby.'

Catherine smiled.

'I told him I was sure you wouldn't mind sharing your baby. I haven't really thought much about having children. I think I'll wait to be a proper godmother before I have my own.'

They ordered some more coffee while Kim filled her friend in with ideas about her new house and some of the projects she was working on. She and Jason had just moved to a house in Richmond. Catherine had not had the chance to see it yet. 'What's the big news you had to drag me out here for?' Catherine asked, resting her chin on her hand. Surely Kim hadn't wanted to meet to talk about work?

Ignoring her, Kim changed the topic and started talking about David. Catherine wondered if the two of them were communicating.

'Are you going to tell me what's going on?' Catherine asked. She didn't want to be reminded of David. It was too hard to think about him; to know he was only a phone call away yet so far away from her.

Kim hesitated.

'Catherine—' Kim began, fiddling with her napkin, 'I'm afraid you're not going to like what I have to say.'

'What is it?' Catherine asked, panicking.

'It's about Brooke and Sally. I found out last week that they've been sleeping together. I don't know how long it's been going on, but I thought you should know. I am sorry. I know you always wanted to see the good in Sally. I still can't believe it, but I just had to tell you.'

Kim saw Catherine's face pale at these words. She wished she could spare her more pain.

'This can't be true,' Catherine said. Her hands began to shake, and she held on tightly to her chair. She closed her eyes and tried to block out Kim's words. Sally would never do that to her; they were friends and friends never crossed that line. 'How certain are you? 'She asked still hopeful that Kim was joking. 'I can't imagine her with Brooke; it's impossible.'

'I'm sorry,' Kim said softly. 'I couldn't believe it either until I saw them together at Ricardos yesterday having dinner. The body language wasn't right. They left together. I don't think they saw me.' She pushed her chair and wrapped her arm around Catherine.

Catherine sat still, trying to register what Kim was saying. It all began to make sense to her – the secret phone calls, Sally's interest in her relationship with David.

'Why did it have to be Brooke?' she murmured. 'She can have any man she wants.'

'I'm sorry,' Kim said again, feeling her friend's despair as if it was her own. She was reminded of some years ago when Sally had wanted the guy; she had been dating. She had laughed about it with Catherine and even teased Sally, who sometimes joined in the joke. 'I think you need to tell her Brooke raped you,' Kim said, her voice faint and soft.

'I need to go home. Do you mind giving me a lift?' Catherine said avoiding Kim's last sentence. She had no feelings whatsoever for Brooke; part of her was beginning to let go of the pain he had caused her ...and now this?

'Are you sure you're up to facing her?' Kim asked. 'I'm off work this afternoon, why don't you come home with me, Jason won't be home till late?'

'No, I'll be fine. Besides, I'm meeting Mum and Dad for dinner.'

They drove in silence. Catherine was too shocked to speak. Nothing Sally did surprise her anymore, but this was too much, even for her. She wondered just how long the affair had been going on. What if they slept in my bed? She wondered. The very thought disturbed her. She stood still; her legs felt heavy, and she could not move.

She couldn't see the attraction between the two of them unless, of course, he wanted to use Sally to get to her.

Kim didn't have any nice thoughts for Sally and Brooke. She hated what this was doing to Catherine. She wondered if she had done the right thing, but there was no other way. Brooke did not deserve to be around her and after what had happened; she couldn't understand how Sally would want anything to do with him, knowing very well he was obsessed with Catherine.

Catherine gently rubbed her hand. 'I'm glad you told me. Can you imagine I would have gone on without knowing she was inviting him to my flat? I'll be fine. I just need to sit here for a minute,' she added when they got to the flat. For a few seconds, she wondered why she had not perceived Sally's attitude towards Brooke then the way she did now. She had not questioned their closeness; instead, she had encouraged her to leave Jay not realising Sally had moved on already.

Kim opened the car window. She watched as Catherine struggled to take all in. Her heart was beating with anger, and she wondered whether she would be able to control her tongue if she came face to face with Sally.

Catherine's heart sank as she tried to digest the news. A part of her could not believe this was happening right under her nose. She was a journalist and a psychologist; she was supposed to know those things. She could see the signs very clearly now, like the secret middle- night phone calls when Sally kept telling her it was Jay.

She could not begin to imagine what had happened to make Sally behave in such a manner. What was she trying to prove?

'How did you find out?' she finally asked.

Kim watched and wished they were not having this discussion. She felt her anger towards Brooke and Sally building up. She reached for her bottled water and took a sip.

'Tapiwe told me,' Kim said softly. 'She's been seeing one of Brooke's friends, and he said Brooke told him he hopes you never find out about him and Sally. He wants you back, but he's worried she might say something to you. Tapiwe was going to tell you herself, but you know what she's like, she can't bear the thought of giving anyone bad news. She rang me last week when I was in Paris and asked me to tell you. I think she dislikes him as much as we all do for what he did to you.'

After Kim left, Catherine sat by the lake and watched the birds as they flew, shrieking, onto and off the water. She resisted the urge to go upstairs and pack Sally's bags for her. She was too angry to face her right now, and she didn't want to get into a confrontation with her. Her parents were coming to London, and she wanted the evening to be perfect. No one would blame her if she asked Sally to leave; most people her age were independent, but not Sally; she was not uncomfortable to keep taking.

'Not anymore, not from me,' Catherine said out loud. Fury burned in her as she walked to the flat. Catherine remembered her grandma's words: 'You watch out for that girl. I don't trust her.'

She had laughed then, thinking her grandma was just paranoid.

Sally was not in the flat, but Catherine could tell someone had just left. The water in the kettle was still hot, and there was a smell of food. She went into her room and began checking her emails. Before long, she heard her opening and closing cupboards. A torrent of anger, pain and confusion swelled inside her, fueling her desire to confront Sally and hurt her as much as she was hurting. She remembered the little girl she had befriended, the one who had been so happy, caring and honest. Whatever had happened to turn Sally into such a conniving, manipulating young woman? She stood up and put on a pair of jeans, keeping her expression unreadable as she walked through to the kitchen.

'Hello, Catherine,' Sally said as soon as she heard her coming. 'I'm just making dinner. Hope you're hungry. I've made too much.'

Catherine stared at her without saying a word.

Sally could tell from the look on Catherine's face that something was up, and she wondered what it was about this time; she had stayed out of her way since her last outburst.

'Are you okay? You don't look too good,' she asked, showing concern.

'What happened to you?' Catherine asked. Her arms folded across her chest. She looked at Sally as if she was seeing her for the first time.

Sally was not used to being caught off guard, and she didn't understand why Catherine was looking at her that way. She thought about Brooke for one second and dismissed it. He wouldn't say anything would he?

'What do you mean?' she asked innocently.

'You've changed so much,' Catherine said, ignoring the confused look on Sally's face. 'I don't know who you are anymore,' She faced her, her fury rising.

'How could you sleep with Brooke, of all people? Have you

lost your mind? What I don't understand is why you made me believe you were so much in love with Jay. Is this how you treat people you love?'

Sally felt her world crashing around her. He wouldn't have, she thought, he promised her. Catherine knew, and she couldn't see a way of getting herself out of this one. Feeling herself on the verge of collapse, she quickly pulled out a chair and sat down. She stared fixedly at the floor, afraid to look at Catherine. Her heartbeat was starting to slow. She held on tightly to the chair, afraid she might stop breathing.

'I'm sorry,' she said softly. 'I'm sorry,' she said repeatedly. 'He told me there was nothing between you anymore, and we only started going out after you broke up.'

Catherine stared at Sally. Her felt her jaws tightening. 'Is that supposed to make me feel better? You were here; you knew how it was. If you wanted him so much, why did you encourage me to give him another chance? Or did he put you up to that?'

'I'm sorry,' Sally repeated. 'We never meant to hurt you, it just happened. I swear I was going to tell you. I was just waiting for the right time. I know it is easy for you to judge me for what I have done, but I'm not like you. You have two parents who love you. You have your wonderful job. I have nothing, I'm broken, beyond fixing and I know it's not an excuse. What pains me most is the fact that you have always been good to me. I hope one day you will find it in your heart to forgive us.' She wanted to say more but stopped. Now wasn't the time. It was too late; everything had changed the minute she opened her legs to Brooke.

Catherine stared at her; shocked at the way she was trying to manipulate the situation. For a few seconds, she wondered if she had ever known her. 'I want you out of here by the weekend. I'm going to stay with Kim. I should find you gone by the time I get back. It's Wednesday, so you have enough time to find somewhere else to live – ask Brooke to take you in, seeing as the two of you want to be together. Just don't come running to me when things blow up in your face. Brooke isn't who you think he is. He cannot be trusted.'

A short, difficult silence followed. They looked at each other. Catherine felt her body stiffen with anger. She didn't know which one of them upset her the most. She fled from the room, closing the door behind her.

Sally sat in the kitchen long after Catherine had left. She could still hear the sounds of the door closing behind Catherine. She didn't know how to get past the door and reach her oldest friend. She hated and blamed Brooke more than she did herself. He still had a home while she was homeless. She couldn't think of anyone who would take her in. Jay wasn't talking to her; they'd had a huge fight over the weekend, and she had told him she didn't want to see him again.

She had hoped he would come chasing after her as he normally did, but there had been no phone calls or text messages. As for Brooke, she had only seen him briefly to collect her book at Ricardo's, since she caught him cheating on her. She felt sick even just thinking about it. He had called her, but she never picked up his calls. Let him sweat for a while. She had told herself. The only person who could help her was her cousin who lived in Brixton, but she didn't want to live there. She had never liked the place and besides, her cousin may not even want her there, after the way she had behaved when she lived with her. Joyce, her cousin, had told her right from the day she moved in that she didn't want any boyfriends sleeping over. Sally had not taken much notice, her ex- boyfriend slept over whenever her cousin was on night shift. She didn't realise the woman next door worked with Joyce. She was a nurse too, and she had taken pleasure in spying on her.

Blocking her mind from the dark thoughts about the past, she cupped her face in her hands, wondering what to do. For the first time in her life, she did not like herself. She hated what she had become and how it was affecting other people. Brooke had become a drug to her. She could not resist him; there were more than a hundred reasons why she should never be with him, but she felt alive when she was with him than anyone else. It struck her then that she had fallen in love with him. Shaking her head, she tried to dismiss the thought from her mind.

If I had been nice to Kim, she would have helped me, she thought. For almost two years she had lived with Catherine, rent free, she had taken it all for granted. She blamed no one but Brooke for the situation she was now in. He won't get away with this, she vowed. He had promised her he would never tell anyone without discussing it with her first, and she had been so careful not to be seen in public with him. Why does this always happen to me, she thought bitterly. She thought back to her childhood, to her mother and her stepfather. Hot tears rolled down her cheeks, and all the bad memories flashed before her eyes. Part of her wanted to rush to Catherine to ask for forgiveness, but the look of anger and hurt on her face had frightened her. She could not remember seeing Catherine so angry before. She stood up and slowly walked across to her room; her face was red with rage.

Chapter Eleven

David Alexander was on the lookout for a purpose, something to help him blank Catherine out of his mind. The seven days he had spent with his brother in Japan hadn't helped at all. In the end, his brother had convinced him he hadn't given Catherine a chance to explain. He got upset that his brother was taking her side; even though he couldn't help feeling, his brother was right. Sometimes he would close his eyes and imagine the child was his. He'd picture Catherine heavily pregnant smiling and telling him to get the bag ready, as the baby was ready to pop. He had even thought about names in his head, names that he may never get the chance to use because he could never see himself falling in love again. She had been his one true love, his inspiration and the best thing to happen to him in years.

Catherine's words flew to his mind: I was raped. He closed his eyes tightly for a moment as if trying to shut his mind to her words. When he opened his eyes, he could still see her face, her lovely lips and breath-taking smile. He imagined holding her close to him, telling her he loved her. But that chance was gone for them. There was no going back, even if he had to talk to her, what would he say? In addition, how could he forget what she had done or forgive her.

'Welcome sir,' the driver said to him, opening the door. He wasn't the usual driver he used when he was in London. They drove all the way from Heathrow in silence, which suited him fine. He wasn't in the mood for chitchat. As they drove passed Hammersmith flyover, he almost asked him to drop him off at Catherine's apartment but changed his mind. He fixed his eyes on the traffic ahead; he half smiled when he saw two sports car drivers at the traffic lights sizing each other up.

His thoughts turned to Catherine again; he wondered what she would do if he showed up on her doorstep. He recalled the first time he had spent the weekend at her apartment. He cooked while she read to him. Sometimes she wrapped her arms around him and told him how much she loved him. That Sunday, she woke up early and made breakfast, toast and boiled eggs. He had laughed at her idea of a full English breakfast. They had read the morning papers in bed and he cooked them lunch. They had not left her apartment the whole weekend. It was then he knew deep in his heart he wanted to wake up next to her for the rest of his life.

'We're here,' the driver said intruding into his thoughts.

Thanking the driver, he got his bag and disappeared into the hotel. From his room, he could clearly see Hyde Park. It was bustling with people. He recalled the times he had spent in the park with Catherine. They always took a picnic basket, he prepared the food sometimes and a few times; Cora packed it. Catherine was never into cooking, and it never bothered him. He recalled her telling him on their third date that she was hopeless in the kitchen, he had laughed thinking she was joking. A knock sounded at his door, and he quickly went to let his PA in.

'How was Japan? Jeff asked sitting down.

'It was OK, so what's been going on here?' He asked.

Jeff went into a description of all the completed projects and the meetings he had lined up in London. As much as he wanted to be enthusiastic about his business, David couldn't help wondering if he might run into Catherine.

'Can we do this after dinner? I need to eat,' he told Jeff.

Half an hour later he walked down to the hotel restaurant. The lobby was a bit crowded; everyone was well dressed. The men in black attire while the ladies walked around in lovely long dresses. Dresses that reminded him of Catherine, he could clearly see her in her long black dress, smiling at him, kissing him. Her warm hands placed firmly on his.

'David....' He heard a voice call his name.

'Is this really you?' Jason said hugging him.

David was motionless for a few seconds. It wasn't unexpected that he was going to run into her or one of her friends, but it was far too soon. He wasn't ready to talk about her or face her.

'It's so good to see you man,' Jason continued. He was looking him up and down, his face clearly happy to see him.

'Lovely to see you too,' David managed to say. He looked over Jason's shoulder expecting Kim to come and jump at him.

'Kim is in the States,' Jason said as if reading his mind. 'She would've loved to see you. Why don't you join us? I'm with those guys.' He added pointing to the group seated at the bar.

'It's OK; my assistant is with me.'

'Does Catherine know you're here?' Jason asked casually.

'No, and it's best she doesn't know.'

'I was sorry to hear about you guys,' Jason said softly. 'I always knew there was something dark about Brooke. Kim said he had been stalking her, and she almost took out a restraining order against him. I know it was hard for you to believe her, but she never cheated on you. Brooke forced himself on her.'

David stood still as if rooted to the floor. He could feel his body drowning. He couldn't breathe. She had been the one who rescued him whenever he felt he was going to drown. She had been his fresh breath of air. She had been the best part of who he was, yet he had let her walk away. He had been blinded by jealousy. Brooke, of all people, he thought shaking his head.

83

'Are you OK?' do you need to sit down?' Jason asked.

Unable to speak, David shook his head.

'We can sit at the bar,' Jason said leading the way.

For a long moment, David did not speak. His eyes wandered around the hotel, the guests in their evening wear, and the staff in their uniforms. 'I thought she lied to me,' he finally said. 'I never believed her,' he added. 'How will she ever forgive me?' he murmured.

'Are you going to be alright?' Jason asked. I'll just show my face and come back.'

'I'll be fine,' David said. 'Thanks for telling me.'

Soon after, Jason left; David leaned on a chair and gazed out of the window, watching cars drive by and people walking in the park. He had hated hearing the truth, but he was grateful to Jason for telling him the truth.

The last weeks had been hell for him; he missed her and hated himself for driving her away. She was a warm, clever and beautiful woman and he couldn't imagine his life without her. He only hoped it wasn't too late; he didn't think he could bear it if she didn't want him after the way he had behaved. Tearing himself from these painful thoughts, he asked his PA to let Jason know he was going out. He decided to take a walk in the park. He wanted to keep busy until he could come up with a plan. He watched as the trees swayed. Families were having picnics. Young children were screaming as they kicked each other playing ball.

Chapter Twelve

Catherine felt a nervous wreck as she drove to meet him. She wore a long black dress and pearl earrings her mother had given her. A part of her wanted to turn the car back, but curiosity got the better of her. She needed to know what he wanted.

He was at the restaurant before her and watched as she hesitated by the door, his heart beating rapidly. She looked beautiful, and all he wanted was to take her into his arms and ask for forgiveness. The waiter led her to the table where he sat waiting.

David's heart melted as he watched her walk towards him. Everything about her was radiant: her long curly hair, which she was wearing up, her hazel green eyes glowing with fulfilment. For a moment, David wondered if she had missed him at all.

The waiter pulled out her chair and went away to get her a menu. She glanced at David while she settled herself. He looked thinner, his face gaunt. The anger she had seen in his eyes before seemed to have disappeared. His features softened and for a second their eyes locked. She knew as she turned away that he had finally accepted the truth.

David spoke first; he couldn't stand being so close to her and not be able to touch her. He had thought about her every minute of the day, and the idea of her carrying another man's child cut into his heart like a knife. He had lied to himself, thinking he would forget about her.

'Can we go somewhere private?' he asked, his voice filled with emotion.

'Aren't we going to eat?'

'Sorry, where are my manners?'

'It's okay; I'm not hungry.'

David left a fifty- pound note on the table and apologised to the waiter on their way out.

The night was still young, and they saw other couples walking by, holding hands. She waited for him to say something, to tell her how he felt. The journey to her apartment took longer than normal. They didn't speak as she drove, and she opened the window and felt the breeze on her hands.

He stood by her dining-room table, waiting for her to tell him what Jason had said.

'Do you mind if I get changed?' she said, moving towards her bedroom. She came back a few minutes later, dressed in a pair of jeans and a white top. He was still standing where she had left him, still looking at her paintings.

'Aren't you going to sit down?' she said, moving closer to him.

He didn't move; it was as if his feet were stuck to the carpet.

Catherine looked into his eyes, waiting. It was as if the clock had stopped ticking as she waited for him to respond. She looked away, and the spell was broken.

'I wanted to tell you,' she began, her voice low. Despite her promise to hold herself together, she could feel her eyes filling with tears. 'I tried to tell you,' she said again, between sobs. 'It was just too painful for me to talk about and a part of me didn't want you to do something stupid. I felt so dirty and so ashamed. I know I should have said something when it happened but I was in such a state, it was like a bad dream that I hoped would go away.'

Though he didn't move, the effect of her words rippled through him.

She carried on talking; now that she had started, she couldn't stop herself.

'Do you remember what we said to each other when we met? We said we must always tell the truth, no matter how bad it was. I just couldn't lie to you, David. I couldn't tell you what you wanted to hear. I can't go back and change what happened. This child,' she said, touching her stomach, 'is a part of me and I have to do what I can to protect her.'

David regarded her in distress.

'You should have told me, Catherine,' he said. 'You shouldn't have made me think you were having an affair. You should have told me what that man had done to you. To think, all this time, I didn't know you were going through this pain on your own. That man should be locked up,' he said. He didn't want to say his name or think of him, and he still couldn't understand why Catherine wanted to keep the baby. As much as it pained him, though, he loved her enough to respect her decision.

Catherine could see the pain in his face; she wanted to hold him, to tell him she still loved him.

As if reading her mind, he pulled her to him, and his lips captured hers in a long hungry kiss that drained her mind of all other thoughts.

She was the first to break away. Desperately though she wanted to feel his body next to hers, she knew they still had a lot to sort out. She wanted to know where she stood with him; she needed to be sure he was fine with everything. She needed him to look into her eyes and tell her he would be there not just for her, but for the baby as well.

'Let's sit down,' he said, moving towards the sofa.

Catherine put her finger on his mouth to stop him from speaking; she wanted to tell him what was on her mind. To let him decide if he wanted to go or stay.

'I think I should start,' Catherine said, turning to face him. 'I never asked for this to happen to me. I went out with the man for years and I never once thought he would be capable of doing what he did. I can't turn back the clock. I blamed myself for a while, but not anymore. It is strange how you think you know someone, and then they do something that seems to be completely out of character.'

'And you still don't want to report him to the police?' David interrupted.

'I wanted to, but in the long run, I would be the one to suffer, and I couldn't put both our families through that. Despite everything else he was my first real boyfriend, we do have a lot of history. It doesn't excuse what he did to me. The only problem is trying to convince him to move on. He has been following me around telling me he wants us to be together, but he's not the one I want. I don't love him anymore, and I haven't done so in a long time. The only mistake I made was taking him back the first time he cheated on me. I know it can't be easy for you to be hearing all this, but there is totally nothing between Brooke and me. But he's still very much around, and if he ever finds out that this child is his, he's going to make my life hell. I want you to take your time and decide if this is what you want. I don't want your pity, I want your love and support, but if you can't handle it, I would rather you walked away now.'

'Are you finished?' David asked.

'I think so,' Catherine said softly.

'I can't believe you have such a low opinion of me. I admit I was upset, well, angry – and with good reason. It's not every day you find out your girlfriend is carrying another man's child. I'm still hurt that you didn't think to tell me what he did, and now you think I'm going to walk away again. You didn't have to go through this on your own. That man should be locked up, and I can't understand why you want to protect him, but I guess it's your choice. I don't want him coming between us because that's what he's doing. He wants you back, and he's going to use this child to break us up.'

'David,' she said, stopping him, 'this isn't about Brooke and me, it's about you and me and the child I'm carrying. He doesn't know it's his baby, and he really doesn't deserve to know, unless I choose to tell him. What I had with him was over long before we met, so he's not in the picture. You have to decide whether you can cope with watching this child grow, knowing it's Brooke's child, for the rest of our lives. I can't be with you if you can't handle it. It will be hard, but I need to be strong for this child.'

Catherine wondered what he was going to say. She didn't regret her outburst. It was not the time for empty promises; he was going to stay or go. She was hurting and deep down she knew she would miss him if he decided not to stay. He was the man she had dreamed of spending the rest of her life with. He was loving, caring and strikingly handsome. She also knew he needed time to make up his mind without anyone pushing him.

'I know what you're trying to do,' he told her, 'and don't think I don't appreciate it, but the truth is, I love you. I have never felt this way for any other woman. I cannot say it's going to be easy, but we will never know unless we give it a try. I have never known you to run away from anything, so why not give us a chance?'

Catherine felt a rush of need engulf her. He was right – she was running away. She was afraid of waking up alone one morning. When it came to some situations, love alone wasn't enough. The words didn't sound right, it was more like Cora speaking than her, but she had thought about them since she found out about the baby.

'I think we are both tired. Why don't I get us some dinner and we can talk again tomorrow? Is Chinese all right with you?'

'Yes, that's fine,' David answered. Thoughts of dinner were far from his mind. He had hoped they would patch things up and yet they seemed to be growing further apart from each other. He didn't blame her for feeling the way she did, but he couldn't say any more than he had already said.

When the food arrived, they sat down on an old Chinese rug Catherine had bought on her travels. It all seemed like the old times when they had laughed together, talked until the sun went down. The apartment held too many memories.

They had made love on the rug so many times. Catherine did not have the courage to voice her thoughts. David only had to look at her to know how she was feeling. She wondered, too, if she had been too harsh with him.

She had practised another speech the whole day, but when she saw him sitting there waiting for her, she knew she had to ask him to make a choice; she couldn't handle it if he left her halfway through the pregnancy.

'This is good,' he said, his eyes looking deep into hers. She could feel herself melting under his gaze. She always felt he could see straight through her soul, so she turned away, not wanting to say too much. As a diversion, she asked him about work and his family. She told him about Michael's memorial service; her aunt and her grandmother were both coming. He told her about Gabrielle's new boyfriend. 'I don't know how to tell her to ditch the guy.'

'Why? Don't you approve?' she teased.

'No, it's not that. I just get the feeling he's a bad influence on her.'

Catherine laughed. 'I wouldn't get involved if I were you. If she even suspects that you don't like him, he'll suddenly become even more appealing to her. Trust me, she's young and intelligent, she'll soon get fed up.'

'I hope it's soon because I don't know how long I can watch her with him. I'm afraid his bad habits may rub off on her.'

'No, she's sensible. I think she's just going through a phase, and she probably has to kiss some frogs before she gets swept away by her prince.'

'How come you always manage to make things seem so easy?' David asked her, amused.

'Well, I've been there, and don't forget, I have had the love of a good man,' she added grinning.

'Really,' David said reaching for her. 'I hope you're talking about me,' he said kissing her.

David studied her. She was so beautiful, and she always looked good, no matter what she wore. She didn't even look as though she was pregnant. The thought cast a cloud over his face and Catherine sensed his change of mood.

'I think I should drop you off before it gets too late.'

'It's okay; I will take a taxi. I don't expect you to be driving me at his time of the night.' He looked at his watch. It was four in the morning. 'Is that the time?' He said, shocked. It was only eight when she met him at the restaurant. The time just seemed to fly whenever they were together. He didn't want to push his luck by asking her if he could stay the night or rather morning.

Catherine escorted him to the door, promising to pick him up in the afternoon.

He wanted to go and see her parents and she didn't have the heart to deny him that chance. Besides, her mum kept asking her when he was coming. All in all, the evening had been better than she had expected.

Two days later, she was woken by the constant ringing of her phone.

'This better be good,' she said sleepily. 'Do you know what time it is?'

'Don't tell me you're still sleeping,' Kim said. 'You were meeting me for lunch, remember?'

'Oh, God, I'm so sorry,' she said, peering at her clock. After visiting her parents with David, they had stayed up talking, and cuddling until it was time for him to leave for the airport.

She could hear Kim laughing.

'Tell you what, I'll just have a quick shower and be with you in twenty minutes.'

'Don't worry. Why don't we make it another day? You sound really tired. I'll call you later to confirm the time and date. You can also tell me what happened with lover boy.'

Chapter Thirteen

Sally paced up and down her cousin's little kitchen, her anger building up as each minute passed. She rushed to the phone each time it rang, thinking it was Brooke. She had left over ten messages for him in three days and yet there was still no phone call from him. She didn't have to be a rocket scientist to know he was avoiding her.

'Are you okay?' Joyce asked her, standing in the doorway.

'Do I look okay to you?' she answered briskly.

'Hey, don't take that tone with me, I'm only asking,' Joyce said, retreating to her room.

'Joyce, wait!' Sally called after her. 'I'm sorry. I didn't mean to bite your head off. I just thought he would call or even text to say he got my messages.'

'By "him" I presume you mean Brooke. You know, for someone who claims to be smart and sophisticated, you really are very naïve. What kind of man jumps from one friend to another? Do you really think that man loves you? Come off it, Sally, he is using you just as Kwesi did and you'd be a fool to sit here thinking otherwise. You had a good friend, someone who appreciated you and you just had to go and spoil it. Now you have no friends and no boyfriend. I really feel sorry for you. You can stay here until you find a place, but don't think I will put up with any foolishness. You have to pull your weight and help pay the bills. I think you have grubbed your way long enough. You're lucky I don't hold grudges otherwise— well, let's not get into that. I just hope you've learned your lesson this time.'

Sally sat still for once, not putting up an argument. She knew Joyce spoke her mind, but she didn't think she had the right to tell her how to live her life. There was some truth in what she was saying, but she needed support and love, not resentment.

'I think I'll take a walk,' she said, standing up.

'I'll be in late so you can take the keys. Tomorrow I'll go and get a spare for you – that is, of course, if you decide to stay.'

When Sally shut the door behind her, Joyce shook her head. It was in this room two years ago that Sally had told her she was seeing a married man and they were going to get married. Joyce had told her she never wanted Kwesi setting foot into her flat. She told her cousin she was wasting her youth on a man old enough to be her father. Sally, as usual, thought she knew best. They had a huge fight and later when she got home, she found a note telling her she was moving in with Catherine. They hadn't talked in a long time, but Catherine rang her once in a while to tell her how Sally was doing. She had hoped her cousin had finally grown up and given up her bad ways. She grabbed the phone and rang her mother. She was the one who had begged her to give her cousin another chance and she was beginning to regret it now.

Sally sat in the park and watched the children playing. Her body ached from sleeping on the sofa. There was someone renting the spare room, and since she had showed up unannounced, she couldn't expect her cousin to throw out her tenant, Joyce had offered to share her room until the tenant left but Sally had declined. Her mind wandered back to events over the last couple of days.

She couldn't go to Jay's flat. He wouldn't give her the time of day after she'd told him that she didn't love him. He was a very proud man. He called her later in the afternoon telling her he would send her things over to Catherine's house. She wasn't given the chance to explain. Whatever they had shared was gone, buried never to resurface. He didn't want to have anything more to do with her, and she didn't blame him.

She took out her mobile phone.

'Sally?' Kim said as soon as she heard her voice. 'What can I do for you?'

'Hello, Kim,' Sally said. Her fingers were shaking like a leaf, but this was her last shot to patch things up with Catherine. 'I'm worried about Catherine. I was just wondering if you have seen her lately.'

'Catherine is fine,' Kim said sharply. 'Why are you calling me?'

She didn't think Sally was interested in Catherine's health. The only time she called Kim was when she wanted a favour.

'I know we haven't always been the best of friends but can we, at least, try, for Catherine's sake? I don't think she should be on her own right now.'

Kim laughed. 'You know something, Sally; you 're just so transparent. Why don't you just say what you want to say? Do you honestly think Catherine would take you back after what you did? You should have thought about that before you jumped into bed with Brooke – in fact, why don't you move in with him? I think the two of you deserve each other.'

It wasn't what Sally wanted to hear. She had rung hoping to get on Kim's good side and maybe get her room back.

'Just tell Catherine I said hello,' she said and disconnected. It's all Brooke's fault, Sally thought bitterly. He had told her she could move in with him if Catherine ever found out about their affair and now he was avoiding her as if she had a contagious disease. She got off the bench and walked to the flat, her mind in turmoil. One thing she knew for sure: she wasn't going to let Brooke get away without paying for what he had done to her. She wasn't prepared to take any responsibility for the predicament she found herself in. Cursing, she dabbed her eyes with a tissue.

When Kim put the phone down, she was even more perplexed and irritated by Sally. She wasn't taken in by her sudden concern for Catherine.

It was about ten in the evening by the time Sally finally managed to get hold of Brooke.

'Hello, Sally,' he said, sounding tired.

'Is that all you're going to say?' she snapped.

'I'm sorry,' Brooke began. 'I was going to call you, just been busy with work.'

'I need to see you tonight,' she said.

He started to speak, but suddenly her rage and frustration burst out of control. 'No, Brooke!' she yelled. 'You're not going to ignore me anymore! If I don't see you tonight, I'm going to tell Catherine everything.' There was silence on the other end. She waited, knowing how much he wanted his precious Catherine back. She was actually enjoying this little game. She had him exactly where she wanted him.

'Give me your address,' he said reluctantly.

She told him where to meet her, and smiled to herself as she put the phone down.

She packed her night bag and wrote a note to her cousin, saying she was staying with a friend for a couple of days. She didn't want to say which friend in case she couldn't persuade him to let her stay. She didn't have to wait long for him. His car pulled up just as she got downstairs.

'I thought we could talk at your house. We don't want anyone taking pictures now, do we?'

He was quiet as he drove through traffic. He felt tired and angry with himself for the situation. He never meant for things to go this far with her, but now it was too late, there was no going back.

Sally was trying very hard to stay calm. She wanted him to ask her to stay: his house was huge and he was hardly ever there.

'Were you ever going to call me?' she asked him suddenly.

'Yes,' he answered his eyes on the road.

She knew he was angry with her for bringing Catherine's name into their conversation, but he had not given her any choice.

'Listen,' he said as they went through the door, 'I'm very tired, so why don't you make yourself something to eat, drink or whatever you want to do. We'll talk tomorrow. By the way, you can sleep in the spare room, he added pointing to a room on the ground floor. He was gone before she could open her mouth to protest.

'Men,' she said, strolling away in the opposite direction. She wasn't interested in his food. She wanted him to give her a hug, to tell her everything was going to be fine. She had spent restless nights thinking of ways to get back at him. Now it didn't seem important.

'Good morning,' he said cheerfully, joining her by the swimming pool the following morning. 'Are you going to get in?'

Sally turned to face him. He was already dressed, and he had a newspaper under his arm. He smiled, and she felt her heart catch at how devastatingly handsome he was.

'I'm fine,' she said eventually. 'I was tempted, but I think I should have stayed in bed.'

'Sorry about yesterday. I hope you slept well,' he said, opening the newspaper.

Chapter Fourteen

The clouds were clear, and the smell of roses rippled through her nostrils. Catherine brushed her fingers through her long curly hair, amazed at how many people had turned up for Michael's memorial service.

She looked across at her aunt, who seemed to be beaming with happiness. They hadn't had a chance to talk but Catherine knew the tall handsome man standing very close to her had everything to do with it. Her grandmother was there, too. She had arrived the previous day from Zambia. She stayed close to her and Catherine held her hand as the preacher said a few words.

They were going to her parents' house for a barbecue. Her dad said that they were celebrating Michael's life, not his death. He was right, of course; her brother had enjoyed life to the full. He wouldn't want them to mourn for him forever.

Richard was talking to some of his old friends from university and Catherine watched him as he walked around, making sure everyone was fine. He was the greatest gift her brother had given her; she wondered at times how she could have managed to get through the last couple of years without him. He had filled in the gaps in Michael's life that she hadn't known about. In a way, she believed they had been each other's support.

'How are you doing?' Kim whispered, standing close to her.

'Okay,' she whispered back. 'I 'm so glad you could come.'

'I couldn't miss this for the world. I didn't realise he had so many friends.'

'He did, my mum used to call him a people collector.'

Kim smiled. Her eyes scanned the area and rested on Joyce, Sally's cousin. She wondered if Sally and Brooke had come too. She quickly blocked out the thoughts.

'I'll see you at the house,' Kim said before moving away to be with her husband.

Catherine's dad said a few words and he invited everyone to come to their house for the barbecue. She felt his presence before she turned, and he smiled as they faced each other. Her eyes told him what she couldn't say, as she slowly slipped her hand through his and he held on tightly to her. He hadn't told her he was coming, but she was glad to see him, to feel his body so close to hers. She looked around and saw her mum look at them and smile. She smiled back and nodded. She guessed her mum had something to do with David being there. Both her parents were wearing black. Her father had his arm around her mother. Catherine wondered if she and David would make it that far.

'Are you going anywhere special?' Sally asked Brooke when he came downstairs dressed in black, looking more dashing than ever.

'I'm going to Michael's memorial service,' he answered casually.

'Are you mad?' she said, astonished. 'When are you going to realise that she doesn't want you? She has David now and besides; I can't imagine anyone welcoming you with open arms, especially her stuck-up friends.'

'What is it with you and Catherine and her friends?' Brooke said. 'You used to like them at one time, or should I say pretend to like them?'

Sally never understood why he always took Catherine's side. She was happy that he was letting her stay at his house until she finished her studies but she wasn't ready to remain in Catherine's shadow forever.

'You need to let her go,' she urged. 'Let her go before it's too late. You can't spend the rest of your life hoping she's going to come back. You haven't seen her with David. She loves him, and I don't think she's ever going to walk away from that kind of love. Can't we just make a go of what we have together and see where we go? I know you like me, we have fun together, don't we?' she added, her voice low. She didn't want to come across like an obsessive girlfriend, but she was tired of his obsession with Catherine.

Brooke was silent for a second, and she wondered if she was getting through to him.

'I wish I could,' he said quietly. 'I really wish I could. I know I've not been fair on you, but I do believe she still loves me.'

'Is that why she's carrying another man's child?' she reminded him bitterly.

She didn't understand why he was lusting after a woman he couldn't have. She loved him, and she could make him happy if he gave her half a chance. What woman in her right mind wouldn't want him? He was rich, young and handsome. She had waited so long for him to dump Catherine. She never considered for one second that he actually loved Catherine.

Brooke's features hardened as he listened to her. He knew she made sense, but he wasn't ready to hear it. He wanted to come to terms with it in his own time and not have someone making that decision for him. He sighed heavily and sank deeper into the chair, all thoughts of going to the memorial services leaving his mind.

'Why are you so consumed with such hate and jealousy of Catherine? She took you into her home, made you feel welcome.

How many people would let you live with them rent-free in London?'

'Don't you dare make me seem like I'm a worse human being,' she said, silencing him before he could say more. 'You have no right to criticise me. You hurt her more than I ever did. If you had been the nice boyfriend she dreamed of, you could be happily married by now.'

'You know what your problem is,' Brooke snapped, glaring at her. 'You want everything she has. Well, I have news for you, it doesn't work like that. You can't be her. You need to get rid of this anger before it eats you up. I can't tell you what you want to hear. You knew even before we started this that I love Catherine, and you said you didn't mind, so why are you giving me such a hard time about it? I don't mind you staying here, but I will not hesitate to throw you out if you carry on this way.'

Despite the pain in her chest, she stepped forward, anger and contempt in her eyes.

'Just what kind of a girl do you take me for, Brooke? I never heard you complain the whole time we were sleeping together, so why are trying to make me sound like some whore? Do you know what would happen if I told Catherine? And I mean everything we did in her house in her bed.'

Brooke stared at her. 'You wouldn't dare; you have as much to lose as I do.'

'I don't actually, she hates me because of you and I doubt she will ever forgive me. I have tried to apologise and I don't care anymore. I'm not going to hang around forever waiting for you to make up your mind. One of these days you will wake up and find me gone.' Wind wafted through the air. She stopped talking and stared at the pool.

Brooke suddenly felt tired and angry. 'I'm going out,' he said, standing up abruptly. 'And don't wait up,' he added.

Sally, upset over Brooke's outburst, sat still, her eyes cast to the ground. It hadn't been her intention to let him see how hurt she was. All she wanted was for him to see sense and to realise that he was never going to get Catherine back; that part of his life he had shared with her was over. He probably thought she hadn't noticed how he sat in his study looking at Catherine's picture; she wished it were her, he was looking at with eyes full of love. She was tired of Catherine having everything. Even when they were kids, she had the best clothes, travelled to places Sally had only seen on television and read about in books, and she had a mother who adored her.

She realised that now the roots of envy of her friend had been there from the start. To her, Catherine was a girl who had everything; she even got the best-looking men who were all educated and rich. Well, I won't let her have Brooke back, she told herself. From now on, I won't mention her name, and I'll make him love me. With that thought in mind, she went to the bedroom she was now sharing with him and changed into a bikini.

There was no one about; the housekeeper didn't work on Sunday. With a bottle of wine in hand and glass, she headed towards the pool. The water was nice and warm, and Sally sang happily, as she swam around, letting her body float wherever she wanted.

Chapter Fifteen

Catherine woke up to the smell of cooked breakfast and smiled as she recalled what had happened the night before. Nothing was mentioned about their last conversation. They had been kissing passionately even before they reached the flat.

'I thought I smelt breakfast,' she said, feeling hungry.

'After last night, I think we both deserve a big breakfast,' he said chuckling.

Catherine pulled him down and kissed him deeply. Emotions overcame her as she held him close to her, her fingers reached for his gown, and it fell to the floor. She pulled his body closer, wanting to feel his soft skin next to hers.

David didn't disappoint her. He squatted on the bed, naked, and all she could do was to stare at him. She pulled him tightly to her and moved on top of him. She knew where to touch him, what he wanted. Back and forth, she rocked and rocked until she felt the spasms of his climax rippling through her.

Later, as they lay in bed, their bodies entwined, he felt her tense, and he pulled her close to him.

'Are you okay, honey?' he asked her drowsily.

'I was just thinking of Grandma. Don't you think she looks different?'

'Well, that's only to be expected. It was Michael's memorial.'

'I don't know,' Catherine said, shaking her head. 'I think I need to spend some time with her.'

'Are you trying to get rid of me?' he asked.

'Don't be silly,' Catherine said, smiling. 'I'm not letting you out of my sight. We've wasted enough time already.' She turned and kissed him passionately.

He pulled her back into bed when she tried to move. 'Stay with me,' he said.

'We can't stay in bed the whole day.'

'Why not, there is no law against it.'

Catherine threw a pillow at him. 'You're a bad influence, David Alexander,' she said laughing.

'I think I have a solution,' David said, throwing the pillow back at her. 'I was thinking perhaps the two of us could go back to Zambia with her. You're off work, and I can get a week or two off. That way you can spend time with both of us.'

'You would do that for me?' Catherine said excitedly. 'Oh, come here,' she said, giving him a hug. 'I love you, David Alexander.'

'I love you, too,' David said, looking deeply into her eyes.

Catherine sighed. 'Jason and Kim have invited us to dinner, remember? Richard'll be there.'

'Do we have to go?' he said, watching her put on her bra.

'Yes, we must,' she answered, her voice filled with laughter. 'Kim has gone to a lot of trouble. I don't think she will forgive us if we don't show up.'

David was returning the following week, and he called her every day just to make sure she was looking after herself. After spending a week together in her flat, he didn't want to go back to New York, but she insisted, and he finally booked his flight.

There was no doubt in her mind about how much he loved her: he had shown her in every possible way how committed he was to her and the baby. The only thing they hadn't discussed was when to tell Brooke. In the last week, they had spent every minute of the day together. They had made love in the bathroom, the kitchen, even her study. He accompanied her to exercise classes, and they went to see her doctor together for her check-up. She laughed at herself when she thought about the past and for doubting him.

The flat felt empty again, but even though she missed David, she was happy to have the time to herself to work on her projects. She was still following up on the slavery in Africa story and she didn't think she would get any work done with him around.

She read parts of the morning newspaper and went to have a shower. Her phone rang just as she walked through to the bedroom.

'Hello, Grandma,' she said when she heard her voice.

'Are we still on for tonight?'

'Yes, that's why I'm calling. Your mum has booked a taxi for me, so you don't have to drive all the way here.'

'I really don't mind. Besides, it will give me a chance to see them as well.'

'Don't worry, darling,' her grandma insisted. 'They're both coming to pick me up tomorrow, so you can see them then.'

'All right then, if you insist,' Catherine said, smiling. 'You can actually come early, and we can have dinner before the theatre.'

She decided to do some work before getting ready. As usual, her in-box was full of new mail. She read a few and decided to make some calls before cooking dinner.

The first person she rang was her informant at a local newspaper in Zambia.

'Oh, hello, Ms Walker,' he said. 'How is the weather there?'

'The weather is fine. How are you?'

'I have been waiting for your call,' she heard him say.

'Is everything okay?' she asked sensing a note of anxiety in his voice.

'I can't talk here' he told her, his voice low. 'Can you please call me on this number?' He gave her his mobile phone number.

She put the phone down, confused. She depended on him to help her talk to the local people. She didn't speak any of the dialects and without him, she didn't know if she could get all the answers she wanted. It had been hard for her to persuade him to help them in the first place, and now that they were, so close...

'I'm sorry about that,' he said as soon as he answered the phone.

'What's going on?' Catherine asked him, not wasting any time.

'The thing is, people are not happy,' he began. 'There were stories going around that you paid those poor people to lie.'

'What?' she exploded.

'I have tried to visit the villagers we saw last time, but no one will talk to me.'

'Who is responsible for those stories?' she asked him more calmly.

He went silent.

'Are you still there?' Catherine asked. She could feel her temperature rising.

'Does it really matter? I think we should give it up and work on something else.'

'I never picked you for a quitter,' she said angrily.

'It's easy for you to say. You don't know what these people are capable of. Besides, it's a local problem. Let them deal with it.'

'Mr Mwanza, you surprise me. You're a journalist. It is your duty to represent those people. If you and I don't address this problem, make everyone aware of what's happening, who else do you think is going to do it?'

'I'm sorry, but I can't help you, and if you want my advice, you should walk away, too. You cannot save those people. No one can save them.'

'Well, thank you, but no one is getting rid of me that easily.

I'm going to talk, write and campaign until no more children are sold into slavery.'

'Don't take this the wrong way, but why do you care so much about those people? They're just doing what they can to survive.'

'These are children we are talking about. You were there; you saw what was happening. If you walk away now, you're never going to forgive yourself. I'm going to be there in two weeks. If you change your mind, give me a call.

You can reach me at my grandmother's house.' She ended the call and rang Kim.

'What?' Kim shouted when Catherine finished telling her. 'What are we going to do? We need to finish the article by next month.'

'Well, I might be able to talk him round. He owes my grandmother a few favours, so I might just ask her to start collecting.'

'You're hardcore, Catherine Walker,' Kim said, smiling.

'I know. I'll call you later. I'm just trying to cook dinner for Grandma.'

'Well, you certainly are keeping busy. Make sure you read the recipes clearly,' Kim joked before hanging up. Kim's last comment made her go and look in the fridge. She and David had prepared hardly any food. They bought takeaways or eat out.

Great, she said as soon as she opened her fridge. There was only water, fruit, yoghurt, cheese and vegetables.

Somehow, I don't think Grandma will be too happy with salad, she thought and laughed as she tried to imagine the look on her grandmother's face.

She changed into a pair of jeans and went to the local supermarket. Her mobile phone went off just as she was getting out of the car.

'About dinner,' her grandma began. 'I would like to cook some Zambian food for the two of us. I haven't cooked for you in ages.

Catherine laughed. 'Have you been talking to mum?' she asked.

107

'No. Should I?'

'Well, she's always telling me I'm a bad cook, so I thought she'd warned you, and that's why you're offering.'

'Don't be silly; I'm offering because I want to treat my grandchild. That's not a crime, is it? Your ma knows nothing about it.'

She told Catherine exactly what to buy, which was one worry off her mind. There was a long queue in Waitrose, she left and headed towards M & S.

By the time, the taxi dropped them off at home from the theatre it was almost midnight.

'Do you want something to drink?' Catherine asked her when they got in.

'Yes, a hot drink will be fine,' her grandma said. 'Your mum told me about the baby. How do you feel – I mean, are you excited?'

Catherine took a sip of her tea and put it down.

'At first, I was scared, I must admit. I never really thought about starting a family at twenty-eight. It took me a while to get used to the idea and now, well, I'm looking forward to it.'

'What about the father?'

'He's fine, and he's been very good and supportive.' She blanked Brooke from her mind and spoke of David. He was going to make a good father to the baby. She had no doubts about that.

'He seems like a nice enough young man. I hope he makes an honest woman of you soon.'

'I hope so, too,' Catherine said.

She felt very secure and confident in her relationship with David. Neither of them had mentioned marriage. She was just happy to have him in her life; anything else would be a bonus.

'He hasn't asked me to marry him yet, so don't go and start planning,' she said jokingly.

'It would have been nice,' her grandma said, 'but I suppose things are different now. In my day, girls had to be married before they had babies. As long as you're happy, that's all that counts.'

Catherine was pleased that her whole family was supportive. 'Thanks, Grandma. By the way, I have a surprise for you,' she went on, pouring more tea into her cup. 'I wasn't going to say anything, but as we are talking about my young man, I might as well tell you now. David and I have decided to come to Zambia with you,' she said. 'Just for two weeks.'

'Really! What about work?'

'He's taking some time off, and I'm off work for three weeks. Besides, it will give me a chance to see Melissa and show David where Mum comes from.'

'Well, this is a surprise. But I'm glad. I haven't seen much of you this year, so it will give us a chance to catch up. I expect a few people will be less than happy to see you, though,' she said, frowning.

'Don't worry about them. I'm a journalist; it's my job. Besides, I can't expect everyone to be happy with what I write. I had a good response from here, and I'm working with a children's charity. We sent clothes and money to the local churches for the community. Kim and I are also working on a project in the east.'

'How is Kim?'

'She is really good,' Catherine answered. 'Jason is one of the good guys, and I think the two of them were meant to be together. It's funny, though, I still can't get used to the idea that she is a married woman. It feels strange and weird but in a nice way.'

Helen suppressed a laugh. 'Do you know I was married to your grandfather when I was only eighteen and a year later your mum was born? Strange how things have changed? In those days, women were more worried about finding a good man, and now your generation thinks more about their careers. But I like the changes. It's good to see women starting to get the respect they deserve. I was lucky I had your grandfather in my life. He made sure I got an education. I was able to support my family when he died.'

'How come you never remarried after granddad died?' Catherine asked.

'I loved your grandfather very much. He was my first love, and when he died, I never felt the need for anybody else in my life. Besides, I had my children and grandchildren to keep me going, and I guess I just wanted to rediscover myself.'

Chapter Sixteen

Sally sat still by the lake, away from the old homeless man, who seemed to find pleasure in showing her his yellow teeth.

'Do you have a pound Love?' he asked grinning at her.

'Here, take this,' she said handing him her untouched coffee and wafers. Her voice was nasal, still clogged with tears.

He looked at her for a second, took the coffee and walked away.

Gazing down at the ducks playing in the lake was like gazing into her heart. Each time she tried to pick up the phone to ring Catherine; her courage was sucked away by an undertow of fear. She wanted to forget, to be free of this pain and hatred, but she didn't know how.

It astonished her to realise she could be so cold and hurtful. She had no reason to hate Catherine, apart from the fact she wanted to live the kind of life Catherine had – money, a good job and a man who worshipped the ground she walked on.

She had been living at Brooke's now for almost two months, yet nothing had changed. He made love to her, shared dinner with her most nights, but he never said the words she wanted to hear, and she had given up nagging him for fear of chasing him away. She tried again to pick up the phone, but quickly put it down.

What would I have said, anyway? she thought, staring at the phone.

When she couldn't think of anything else to do, she rang her cousin. The phone rang for ages.

'How are you?' Joyce said when she finally answered.

'I'm sorry I haven't phoned in a while,' Sally said, her voice sweet and soft. She wanted to stay on Joyce's good side in case Brooke kicked her out.

'How is college?' her cousin asked, ignoring her last remark. 'I hope you're still attending your classes. You've worked too hard to give it all up.'

'Yes, I'm still going. I only have one paper left to write before I throw away the books.'

'I spoke to Mum today. Did you know Catherine is going home with her boyfriend?'

'No,' Sally said, not surprised.

'Well, if you want to send something to your mum, I can take it. I'm going to see her grandma tomorrow.'

'I'll have to call you back tomorrow morning,' Sally said, her mind already working on how she would use this information to her benefit.

She said goodbye to her cousin and headed towards the shopping centre. The day is beginning to look brighter, after all, she thought.

She went to Marks and Spencer and bought wine and food; tonight is going to be my night. She told herself. Forgotten was the remorse she had felt earlier. The news of Catherine and David going to Zambia was too good to be true. Brooke would finally realise he could never have her back. She didn't think Catherine would take David to Zambia unless she was planning on marrying him.

When she finally got home, she told the housekeeper she could have the day off. She wanted to cook a special meal for Brooke and didn't want an audience while having dinner. The house was filled with silence; it filled her with excitement. At that moment, she forgot all about Catherine; she believed Brooke would finally be hers. It began to rain outside. She wished she could run in the rain as she used to when she was a child. It was the only time she was happy.

On an impulse, she opened the window and listened to the rain as it hit the roof. The sky was covered with dark clouds. Her mind turned to Brooke, his beautiful face and the way his eyes lit up when he smiled. If only my mother could see me now, she thought grinning. Brooke's house was very big, with five bedrooms and a swimming pool. She tried to imagine herself as Brooke's wife, showing her friends around. The very thought made her feel excited and anxious to have him home. She danced to the music as she cooked, stretching her neck now and again to check the time on the large clock on the wall. Taking the last look around her, she took a shower, put on her best evening dress and waited for him.

The table was too huge for just the two of them, but that night she was glad. She wanted to sit right opposite him so that he could focus on her. She lit some candles around the whole room, creating a pleasant and romantic atmosphere.

'For a moment there I thought I was in the wrong house,' Brooke said as soon as he went through to the dining-room. 'This is lovely,' he added as he bent down to kiss her.

'Well, I'm glad you like it,' Sally said. There was no denying the fact that he was very pleased.

For a while, they ate and talked just like a normal couple. For the first time since she'd met him, he actually showed an interest in her work; he talked to her about her course and her dreams. Everything seemed so good and right and for a while, she did not think about Catherine.

'I'll just go and catch up on some paperwork, I am due in court tomorrow,' Brooke said sitting up.

'OK, don't be too long,' Sally said reaching for the remote control.

When she couldn't find anything to watch, she fetched a bottle of wine and went to the living room. She wasn't used to being so happy and content, and the very thought of it disturbed her. She watched Brooke as he made himself comfortable in the study; he had his back to her. He was certainly the best lover she'd ever had. He knew exactly how to touch her, where to touch her. An image of Catherine flashed through her mind, and she felt her soul sink with the knowledge that all Catherine had to do was call him, and he would go running to her.

'Why the sad face?' he said, coming to stand beside her.

She shrugged. 'You tell me, you're the one with the answers,' she said bitterly.

Puzzled, he sat down, looking at her. 'We're not going back to the same topic again, are we? Why can't we just enjoy each other's company and see what happens?'

'I think we need to talk,' she said. 'I need to know where we are going with this relationship. I just can't stand all this secrecy. You never take me out or even introduce me to your friends.'

He shook his head in disbelief; he really could not understand why she had to go on about them being a couple.

'I guess you're right,' he said, sounding weary. 'The problem is I don't know what you want from me. I've told you I'm not ready for any long-term commitments, and you said you were fine with it, so what's changed, then? I just can't be the person you want me to be, and I thought you understood that?'

Sally could feel herself getting angry as she listened to him but she tried not to show it. She wanted him to be the one begging her to stay.

'We can't go on like this,' she stated. 'Sometimes I think you use Catherine as an excuse to push me away. Well, I have news for you: Catherine is taking David to Zambia. Do you know what that means? She'll probably marry the guy. You were with her for almost three years and, from what I know, you didn't even get an invitation.'

Brooke felt like someone had just stuck a knife into his heart. He had tried to forget about her despite what Sally said, but how could he when there were so many reminders of her, including Sally?

'Do you know when they're going?' he asked.

'Does it matter?' she hissed back at him.

She had hoped to get through to him, but now all her hopes and dreams crumbled and fell at her feet, along with her faith in men. They had all been a disappointment to her. The only man she thought loved her was no longer in her life because she had wanted Brooke.

'You're such a sad bastard. Frankly, I'm beginning to understand why Catherine left you.'

'Why are getting yourself worked up about this? You've known since day one how I feel. Catherine is my problem, not yours, and if you don't like it, you know where the door is.'

'Are you kicking me out,' she glared at him.

He pulled her closer to him and wrapped his arm around her, 'What are we going to do with you?' he said gently.

For the first time since moving in with him, she sensed gentleness in him towards her that hadn't been there before. He was wiping her tears and telling her everything was going to be okay.

When he thought she had finally calmed down, he turned her to face him.

'You've got to stop this anger you have towards Catherine. You're a beautiful girl, and you can do so much better for yourself. I admit I'm at fault, but would you have been so interested in me if I hadn't been with Catherine? I care about you, but I'm not ready to start another relationship until I sort out my feelings for Catherine, and I suggest you do the same, too. You and I are both broken. We cannot go on like this. It's simply not fair on either of us. I don't mind you staying here until you find a place, but I think it will be best for both of us if you move into one of the spare rooms.'

Chapter Seventeen

As the plane touched down, Catherine turned towards David and their hands clasped together.

'I'm so glad you're here with me; I can't wait to show you around?' she told him softly.

David pulled her to him and placed a kiss on her forehead. 'I love you,' he whispered.

'No regrets,' she asked teasingly.

'Well, it's too late to change my mind now!' David said laughing. 'Unless you're tired of me already.'

'Don't be silly,' Catherine said, her finger poking into his side. 'I just want to make sure you have no regrets.'

'You're joking, aren't you? Any time I spend with you is a precious moment, and it doesn't matter where,' David said, kissing her deeply. 'I hope we have a room far from Grandma,' he whispered into her ear.

Catherine smiled. 'No, actually,' she said softly, 'you have a room close to her, and I'm sleeping in my old room.'

'What! You certainly know how to lower a man's spirit.'

Laughing, Catherine fastened her seat belt. She looked over at her grandma, but she seemed fast asleep.

'Well, this is it,' she said, looking out the window.

'Please fasten your seat belts,' the air hostess said, her body looming over them.

The sky was crystal clear as the three of them stepped off the plane. No one in sight was wearing jumpers or coats. The place was scorching, and the only comfort was that the air wasn't too humid. Catherine slipped off her jacket and breathed a heavy sigh.

'Well, I hope it doesn't get any worse than this,' she said, following her grandmother.

Her grandmother's friend, Grandma Maria, was picking them up. She looked around the lobby searching for her, but there was no sign of her.

'Let's find somewhere to sit,' her grandmother said moving away from the crowd who were waiting anxiously for their families. 'Maria is always late; I should have known better. I always tell her; she's going to be late even for her own funeral.' She added laughing. Not finding a place to sit, they stood inside and held on tightly to their trollies.

Taxi drivers came and waved their car keys in front of them every two minutes. They got tired after a while and ignored them.

Half an hour later, they saw her strolling through the doors. She was a small woman, about five feet three.

'Welcome,' she greeted them brightly. Catherine felt her warm arms circling her in a long embrace. She smelt of fresh lemon and vanilla.

She was wearing a bright orange top and a black skirt. Catherine wondered how she managed to look so cool and be so active at eighty. Catherine loved the way Grandma Maria lived her life. She had lost her husband and two children but not once had she ever heard her complain about the unfairness of it all. A great sense of injustice rose in her heart as she thought about Michael. The driver who hit into his car had never been found. Sometimes she wondered if she would ever have closure.

Blanking thoughts of her brother from her mind, she focused her attention on Grandma Maria. She watched as she put her arms around her grandmother. They were both smiling. Catherine loved how the two woman loved each other and so supportive of each other. Her grandmother said they had known each other since they were babies. Her mother talked about how she had helped look after them when her parents first went abroad. How she had helped her grandmother though the loss. She had been there too when Michael died. She had never regarded her as anything else but her second grandmother.

'Let me look at you,' she said, her eyes focusing on Catherine. She looked her up and down, almost making her feel embarrassed. 'You grow more beautiful and radiant every time I see you. You could do with a bit of meat on your body, though,' she added before she turned her attention to David.

She looked him up and down and smiled. 'Huh, who is this dashing young man with you?' she asked cheerfully.

'Grandma, meet David, my boyfriend. And, David, this is Grandma Maria.'

She ignored David's stretched hand and hugged him.

'You can call me Maria,' she said. Her eyes met Catherine's, and she winked at her.

'Sorry for the delay,' she said when the greetings were over. 'I was waiting for my driver to pick me up. He was running errands in town for me, but you know how slow these people can be when you don't bribe them. I tell you, I feel sorry for the young people in this country. By the time, they get to my age there will be nothing left here for them. Well, I better get you, folks, home. You must be exhausted after such a long journey. I hope you had a pleasant flight,' she added leading the way.

'Yes, we are,' Catherine heard her grandma say. 'And if you don't shut up, we will take a taxi home.'

'Oh, come on, then,' Maria said, laughing.

The two of them chatted happily all the way to the car park. David and Catherine exchanged looks and smiled. It took them almost two hours to get to the farm. Her grandma was staring out of the window telling David about the buildings, about the history of the country.

They passed through Cairo Road, where all the big supermarkets, banks and big office companies were located. There was also a cinema and street vendors who blocked most of the roads. Catherine looked in dismay at what they had done to the city. She never saw people selling things by the roadside when she used to visit as a child.

Catherine and David stepped out of the car when the driver stopped to put petrol in the car.

'They're beautiful aren't they?' David said, looking at the paintings one of the boys was holding.

'Indeed,' Catherine said signing. 'I remember when Michael and I used to come here for holidays, these roads were well maintained, and we didn't see so many people selling food by the roadside. The economy is so bad now; only rich people can afford to take their children to school and enjoy life. Most people just get on with it; not that they have much of a choice. It is sad because they are so many educated people in this country who can make a difference, but they don't care as long as their children are happy and have the latest games and clothes in fashion.'

David took her hand and kissed it.

'I think the driver is back,' he said, giving her hand a squeeze. 'I'm sure one day things will get better,' he said, opening the door for her.

'I hope you're right,' Catherine answered doubtfully. As she settled back into the leather seats of the Land Rover, her mind drifted to her grandma's farm and the memories from the past.

Her grandma lived on the outskirts of the capital city, in a small community where everyone knew everyone else. Most of her neighbours were retired politicians, teachers and doctors. Nothing of interest ever happened in Mpupe, it was miles away from town, buried in farmland and lots of trees. You could walk for miles and not see a soul apart from goats and cows that walked around aimlessly; sometimes you could see young boys in torn clothes chasing after them with sticks. It was a place covered with vast farms full of maize, which was the local food, and orchards that stretched for miles on end.

There was one shop; it reminded Catherine of the old western movies, with groceries squeezed in together. The owner, an old man who had lost most of his teeth, knew everyone. Her grandma used to say; you only need to tell him a name and he would tell you the whole family history of that person.

'Are we almost there?' David asked, his eyes fixed on the road ahead. They seemed to have been driving for hours.

'Yes,' Catherine told him softly. She thought about the old bus stop and smiled. She and Michael used to avoid the place like a plague. Most of the old people loved kissing their hands and most left saliva lingering on. She normally rushed home crying and washed her hands until she was too worn out to carry on. Sally, on the other hand, loved having her hand kissed; she said it was their way of blessing the children. A dark cloud fell over her face, and she quickly blocked away any thoughts of Sally.

'We are almost there,' she whispered to David and immediately realised he had dozed off.

'He must be tired,' Grandma Maria said looking back at Catherine. 'It is such a long journey. That's' why I always have a stopover in South Africa whenever I visit England.'

'I don't blame you,' Helen told her friend. 'So what's been happening in my absence,' she asked.

'I have a lot to tell you, but you must eat and rest first. I will come back first thing tomorrow morning.'

Behind the trees, lay the big houses. It was hard for anyone to see the houses from the main road because of the long driveway and massive avocado trees, that were evident on most farms. As a child, she had loved visiting her grandma during school holidays. Her cousins joined them sometimes. She made a mental note to call them. She had not spoken to them in months. Catherine and her brother always had a ball, climbing the trees and living on fruits for lunch to the annoyance of her grandma and the chef.

She brushed the memory of her brother aside and looked at David as they got closer to the farm. It felt very strange to be there with another man who wasn't related to her. She had never shared that part of her life with anyone. The street was much busier than Catherine remembered. There were other shops on the high street, two to be exact and they both looked as though they could do with a coat of paint. She saw a few people staggering out of what looked like a pub; Catherine had to do a double-take to make sure she wasn't seeing things. She couldn't believe people could get drunk at noon.

'Is the old man still working in the shop?' she asked her grandma, as they drove past the shop.

'God, no, he's too old and can hardly see,' her grandmother exclaimed. 'He gave the shop to his son and the silly boy sold it for quarter its value and spent the money on alcohol. His brothers were so upset with him, but there was nothing anyone could do. The new owner closed his ears to their cries. He had legally signed the papers.'

Her grandma's farm had not changed much.

'I will get them to take your bags,' her grandma announced looking at the young lady who was busy walking up and down the long corridor. 'You relax, and I will get the girl to get your rooms ready,' she added walking towards to the kitchen.

'Just one room will do,' Catherine said when David left. 'You don't expect us to sleep in separate rooms do you?'

'Yes, I do. You're not married yet, and I don't want any funny business under my roof. Your mother will kill me.'

'Ah! Helen, give the girl a break,' Grandma Maria said laughing. Who cares if they're married or not? They're having a baby together aren't they?'

'Maria, don't encourage the girl. I have made up my mind,' her grandma said walking away.

Grandma Maria rose from her seat and winked at Catherine. 'Just move when she goes to bed,' she whispered. Catherine could hear them arguing in the hallway. She smiled.

Hours later, Grandma Maria left. David and Catherine, still feeling tired from the long flight went to bed early. The noise from outside woke up Catherine. The room was bright with sunlight. The leaves rustled outside her window. She lay in bed for a few minutes and watched the man sleeping next to her. Hearing her grandma talking outside, she swung her legs off the bed and looked out the window. It was only eight in the morning, yet the sky was clear and bright. She could hear the workers' children shouting to each other.

She quickly drew back the curtain when she saw who her grandma was talking to. It was Sally's grandma. She had not said anything about Sally, and she didn't think this was the time for her to start narrating any gory details to Sally's grandmother.

She went back to bed and placed a kiss on David's cheek. He looked so handsome and peaceful she didn't have the heart to wake him up.

She sat on the bed for a couple of minutes and then quietly left the room carrying with her a pair of linen trousers and a white cotton top. She was now almost three months pregnant. No one would guess, and yet she felt so fat.

It still felt strange to be back on the farm with David. The only men she had shared this part of her life with were Michael and her dad. Thinking about Michael, she walked towards the living room to look at some old pictures. She stood still when her eyes caught a picture of herself and Sally. Catherine was taken back to eighteen years ago when the picture was taken. They had gone for a picnic with her grandmother and Michael; he was trying to teach Sally how to play cards, but she was more interested in trying on the makeup Catherine had bought for her. He told her she couldn't paint her face until she learned how to play cards. The two of them chased each other around, with Catherine watching how silly they looked and laughing so hard she could barely catch her breath. In the end, they all sat down to play cards and her grandmother took the picture. It seemed like such a long time ago, she thought, putting the picture frame back on the wall.

She still couldn't understand Sally's resentment towards her. She had gone out of her way to try to help her reach her goals and dreams and yet, in the end, she realised, Sally was the only one who could help herself. Her mind drifted to Sally's relationship with Brooke, and she quickly blanked them out.

I can't have any bad thoughts. She said out loudly as she felt the warm water splashing on her silky skin. She didn't want to think or talk about Brooke. She knew she would have to deal with the situation, but not today or tomorrow; she wanted to make sure she and David had a good holiday filled with happy memories.

There was no one in sight when she went outside. She stood in the small patio garden and looked around the long acres of land to see if her grandmother was about.

To one side of the house, there were large trees of avocados, grapes and oranges. There were two cottages for the workers and fields of maize and vegetables. On the other side, there was a guest house and a large swimming pool. Her grandmother had told her the last time she had visited that she was going to fill it up with sand because she didn't want to be responsible for any drowning. She quickly went across to have a look and pool was still there; the only thing different was that there was a fence around it. She smiled, wondering why she had changed her mind.

After sitting around the pool area for almost an hour, she went back to the house to check on David. He was still sleeping so she took a book and walked across to the pool house. She loved how calm and inviting it was. It had always been her favourite place on the farm. It was a place she could relax without the usual human traffic. She held on to her belly as a sharp pain shot through her body.

'Ms Catherine, Are you up there? Sally's grandma is here to see you.' She heard one of the workers call out to her. She closed her eyes and held her breath hoping they would leave her alone. Moments later, she heard footsteps drifting away. She took a deep breath, made herself comfortable and relaxed. She picked up the pencil and started jotting down interesting places she could show David. He had asked about going to see the house where President Kaunda lived before he became president. Catherine hoped someone had taken over care of the house, the last time she had tried to see it; she had been told the person with the keys had travelled. Disappointed she had come back home. She wrote a few more places like Victoria Falls, the David Livingstone Museum. She stared at it for a moment, before putting it away, and reached for her book.

Chapter Eighteen

David reached out for Catherine between consciousness and unconsciousness, yet all his hand could feel was an empty space. His eyes felt so heavy he couldn't open them, and he felt himself falling back into a deep sleep. Children running around woke him up an hour later, and he smiled as he remembered his dream. It was about Catherine and their life together. He stood up and walked to the wardrobe. His briefcase was still where he had left it last night. He opened it, took out the leather tiny jewel box and looked at the ring. His mind drifted to the time he had almost lost her. Out of nowhere he thought about Brooke. He fought hard not to think of the child she was carrying as part of Brooke. Blocking the thoughts, he headed towards the bathroom.

The house was quiet as he took a shower, the smell of cooked breakfast made rumbling sounds in his stomach. He wondered why he was so hungry after the huge feast they had last night. He thought about her response to his proposal as the warm water ran down his body. He found himself whistling a song, which he had not done in ages. He was nervous as well as excited, but he knew deep in his heart this was what he wanted to do. She made him feel that he was the best thing in her life and, despite his reservations about Brooke and the baby, he loved her and wanted to spend the rest of his life with her.

'Have you seen Catherine,' he asked the maid, who was busy placing plates on the table.

'No, I go look for her,' she told him in broken English and left.

Twenty minutes later, she was still not back yet. He remembered Catherine talking about the pool house, and how much she had missed it. He made his way there, avoiding the dogs who were staring hard at him.

She was lying on her back, her knees in front of her and her eyes focused on the book she was holding. His heart melted watching her looking so radiant and relaxed. He loved her so much it went beyond anything he could fathom or maybe, in the end, endure. 'Hi,' he said closing the space between them.

'Hi you, you're awake,' she said sitting up.

'I missed you this morning,' David said kissing her. 'You should have woken me up.'

Catherine grinned at him. He sat down next to her. She put her book down and touched his face. It felt soft, and he smelled good. 'You looked so peaceful; I didn't have the heart to disturb you. Have you had breakfast?'

'No, I wanted to find you first. Has your grandma left? The house seems so quiet.'

'She left early this morning. She said she had some errands to run, and most of the kids are up in the trees eating mangoes.'

'Sounds dangerous and exciting,' David said staring out of the window. The dogs started barking. He heard voices and footsteps running towards the pool house. Then there was silence.

'Are they looking for us,' He asked her.

'I hope not; everyone knows not to disturb me when I am in here. Grandma told them it was my thinking place,' she added laughing.

'Good, I would be happy to stay with you the whole day.'

Catherine beamed with happiness as he wrapped his arms around her. She shivered as their hands touched. He looked so handsome in his shorts; she wanted to hold him to her forever.

He took her in his arms; his mouth found hers and they engaged in a long kiss.

She could feel her body; her soul lifted into another world where nothing mattered but this moment.

'I love you,' he muttered.

She felt him inside her, still hot and large and powerful. They lay down on the mattress, their minds shut to anything else but their breathing.

Later, when she finally opened her eyes, she saw him kneeling beside her, his face calm and collected, like a man on a mission.

'Will you marry me?' He said, his voice deep with emotion.

Catherine looked at him, her heart beating so fast she could hear it herself.

'Oh, David, yes. Yes, I will marry you.'

She collapsed into his open arms and time stood still as they hugged each other. She was crying and laughing at the same time.

'Can we set the wedding date after the baby is born? I want to look beautiful for you on the big day.'

'Your wish is my command,' David said, kissing her.

There were no sounds in the house when Catherine and David entered. She inhaled the smell of freshly baked scones, and she wondered if her grandmother was in the kitchen. Filled with excitement to share her news, she ran ahead, leaving David behind.

'Grandma!' Catherine shouted, looking through the kitchen. When she couldn't see anybody, she moved on to the living room and opened the huge glass doors, leading to the balcony.

'Grandma!' she called again. Still no answer.

She walked back to David, shaking her head. 'I can't find her.'

'Maybe she's not back yet.'

'I thought she would be back by now,' Catherine said glancing at her Cartier wrist watch.

David gave her hand a squeeze and reached for the bottle of water.

'Well, I will just have to wait to tell her. Meanwhile, I will call Mum and Dad,' she said. Breakfast was forgotten for the moment. They were both too excited to eat. Catherine kept looking at her ring, feeling it, making sure she had it on the right hand and finger. It was so beautiful; she felt incredible wearing it.

David was touched to the very core of his heart. This was the moment he had envisaged from the day he met her. He had dreamed about it so many times, and he would wake up in a pool of sweat. Now, almost a year and a half to the day since they met, she was his fiancée. The very sound of the word made him smile. He watched as she picked up the phone to ring her parents and he knew they would have a fantastic life together.

'Oh my God!' her mum said when she told her. 'Wait, let me put your dad on the other line.'

Catherine smiled when she heard her parents' laughter.

'I'm so happy for you,' her mum was saying. 'Both of you,' she heard her dad add.

They were both talking at the same time, and she couldn't make out what they were saying; she could only tell they were as happy as she was.

'How is David?' her dad asked.

'He's right here with me. Do you want to say hello?'

'No, darling, I think we will leave you two to celebrate,' her mum said. 'Call me later when you've rested. We can talk then. And say hi to your grandma.'

She held on to the phone long after she had said goodbye. If someone had told her five years ago that she would be marrying before she was thirty, she would have laughed at them and yet here she was blushing like a schoolgirl. She didn't want to think of the time when she had almost lost him; it all seemed so long ago. They were so much a part of each other's existence now, and their relationship was so strong. She knew no matter what happened they would survive. She believed in him, their love and their brilliant future together.

She rang Kim and Jason answered the phone.

'How are you? We were just going to call but thought we would let you sleep.'

'I am fine. The trip was great, just jet lag at the moment.'

'How is David?'

'He's fine and up as well.'

'I will get Kim,' Jason said.

'What are you doing up this early?' Kim said as soon as she came on the phone.

'It's gone past eleven,' Catherine said. 'Are you sitting down?'

'Why? Has something happened?' Kim asked. 'Just grab a chair then I'll tell you.'

Kim's first thought was the baby; she had been so worried, despite Richard's assurances that she would be fine.

'Jason!' she called out. 'Please sit here with me, I don't like the tone of Catherine's voice.'

'She sounded fine when I spoke to her,' Jason said.

'Just indulge me, darling,' Kim said, pulling his hand.

'Yes, I'm sitting now.'

'David has asked me to marry him,' Catherine said very slowly and calmly. 'And I said yes!' she shouted.

'What!' Kim gasped. 'Jason, did you hear that? They got engaged!' she yelled. 'They got engaged!' she said again.

'Oh my God, Catherine, this is the best news ever. You must be so happy. I mean both of you.'

'Yes, we are,' Catherine answered. She couldn't hide the happiness, which had overcome her.

After Catherine had finished her phone calls, they sat outside and one of her grandmother's girls brought them their breakfast.

'I can't believe we're engaged,' she told him looking at her ring.

It was so beautiful. She couldn't wait to show her grandma.

'Me too,' David said reaching for the bowl of fruits. 'What shall we do today,' he asked.

'Not sure, Catherine said. 'Let's decide when grandma gets back. We can't do much without a car.'

'Oh we could just stay in bed,' he said brightly.

Catherine smiled. Ever since she had met him, she felt as if she were falling through the air in slow motion, waiting for someone or something to shake her and tell her she was dreaming and he wasn't real. She had to pinch herself sometimes to believe this man, living and breathing handsome man loved her. She had watched him cook and iron for her; she had watched him laugh and cry at the simplest things and deep in her heart, she knew she loved him.

'Would you like some more tea?' he asked staring at her.

'Yes, please,' she told him happily. 'We can walk down and check on the new house grandma is building if you like. It's only ten minutes from here. I forgot how hot this place could get. So glad I went swimming this morning.'

'OK,' David said. 'I think I will go swimming this evening.'

Soon after, there was a knock on the door; the workers' children came shyly to greet them when they saw them on the balcony.

David called Natalie and Gabrielle to tell them the news.

They lay together in her late grandfather's rocking chair and before long they fell asleep.

It was in that same position her grandma found them. She smiled and closed the doors, making sure no one disturbed them.

They woke up two hours later to the smell of cooked food. 'I can't believe we fell asleep,' Catherine said, rubbing her eyes. She felt tired, and her body hurt. She touched her stomach as she felt a great wave of nausea.

'Good afternoon,' her grandmother said when she saw them

coming through the door. 'Sorry, I was away for such a long time? I thought you would still be sleeping.'

'Good afternoon,' Catherine said, giving her a kiss. 'It was too hot. I just couldn't sleep.' She thought about the pool house and hoped no one had suspected anything.

'Well, I've cooked some lunch. Hope you're hungry.'

'It does smell good. I will just wash up,' David said, leaving the women staring at him.

'Is that a ring I see on your finger?' her grandmother said as soon as he was out of earshot.

'Yes,' Catherine said, blushing as she showed her grandmother the ring.

'I'm so happy for you. Wow! It's so beautiful,' she said, admiring the ring. 'This calls for a celebration. I will call some friends, and we'll have a party. Have you told your parents?' she asked, already planning the party.

'Yes. Mum is overly excited. He's simply the sweetest man and so much more. I know we will have a wonderful life together,' Catherine said, looking at her ring for the umpteenth time. It was all too much for her, and she could feel the tears starting.

'I'll make the table,' she said, turning away before her grandmother could see.

'Don't worry; the girl has everything in control. You're here to relax.' Her grandmother said.

Her grandmother didn't talk about anything else but wedding plans as they ate. David and Catherine listened, not wanting to interrupt her.

'Did you know your mum had her wedding here?' she asked suddenly.

'Yes, Grandma,' Catherine said. 'I have been told so many times what a grand affair it was; I couldn't forget.'

'Don't spoil my fun. I will soon be a great grandmother. I should be allowed to indulge myself now and again.'

131

'We haven't decided when the wedding will be, so we can't talk about locations yet, but I can promise you, you will be the first to know.'

After lunch, Catherine decided to take David on a tour of the farm. It was quite warm in the house, and her grandmother was having friends over for afternoon tea.

'Wasn't your mum sad to leave all this behind?' David asked.

'She never really grew up here. Her father, my late grandfather, was a diplomat, and he worked all over the world. They lived in America for five years, and when it was time for him to retire, my mother went to Oxford University, and it was while there that she met Dad. My grandfather, of course, didn't approve of Dad, but I guess her being his only daughter, he gave in. I have been told he was a wonderful man, full of life, fun, and very outspoken, too. It's a shame he died before I was born. I never get to see much of mum's brothers. They both work in Foreign Service and always travelling somewhere.'

'Did you know your dad's parents?' He asked, intrigued. She never spoke much about the past, and he didn't push her, but now he wanted to know everything about her, her fears and her dreams.

'Oh yes,' she said. 'They spoiled me rotten,' she added, her voice low.

When my grandfather retired, he decided to settle in America, where my grandmother's family still live. They bought this huge farm, and I remember Michael and I couldn't wait for the summer to visit them. We went swimming, camping and played all sorts of games and they joined in the fun. My grandmother's sister still lives there. I'll take you there one day. It's funny, isn't it, most people grow up knowing exactly where their roots are, but I do wonder sometimes to which part of my heritage I really belong.

'All my life, I mean since I was a little girl, people have told me

I was different – my hair wasn't straight enough to hang out with the white kids, and I wasn't cool enough to be with the black kids. My parents always told me not to worry about what people thought. I guess in a way their love and support made me strong and having Kim as a friend was a blessing. We understood each other's pain to be growing up different and became friend instantly. She has always been my safe place, my person.'

'You're lucky to have her,' David said watching her. 'Is that why you moved to the States?' he asked. 'To escape?'

'Yes, partly but it was mostly because I wanted to prove to everybody that I wasn't just some rich kid, I was a hard-working, intelligent woman who could make it without her parents' help, and it worked. I also wanted to know where my grandmother came from. Sometimes I find myself laughing because, despite what those kids used to say about me, there was some truth in it. I'm different, my father's mother was American, and my mother is African but never grew up in Africa, and I was born in Britain.'

David encircled her in his large arms.

'My poor baby,' he said, kissing her. 'Your mum was right, it doesn't matter what you look like or where you come from, it's who you are that is important. I know I cannot change the past, but I promise to make the future better for you and the baby,' he said, touching her tummy. 'You do know I love you, don't you?' he asked, looking deeply into her eyes.

'Yes,' she answered softly. 'I love you, too. I guess soon I will be Catherine Alexander. Huh, it rather sounds great, doesn't it?'

Chapter Nineteen

Brooke paced up and down the large room in his house, his mind in turmoil. Again he looked at the paper to convince himself the story wasn't a dream. It can't be possible, he told himself, but Sally had confirmed what he already knew and if she was right, then the baby Catherine was carrying was his child.

And there it was in black and white: Catherine Walker Engaged, the headline declared, and the article went on to say that both she and her American boyfriend were thrilled at the prospect of becoming parents.

'Thrilled indeed!' he spat, throwing the paper into the bin. He understood why she probably didn't want to tell him, but he couldn't stand the thought of David bringing up the child as his. A plan began to form in his mind.

He couldn't wait to confront her about it, to make her understand that David would never love their child completely. He sat down on the bed and closed his eyes. He had tried in the last couple of days to make a go of his relationship with Sally, neither of them mentioning Catherine. He took her clubbing and to dinner. A part of him was slowly accepting that he was never going to have Catherine back and then this morning, his housekeeper had given him the paper, telling him to pass on her congratulations.

'Are you okay?' he heard Sally say right behind him.

'Yes, I'm fine,' he said, staring out of the window.

'I have been sitting outside waiting for you. I thought we were going to swim.'

'Sorry, I totally forgot. You go right ahead. There is something I need to do.'

His face was drawn and for a second her heart missed a beat. Whatever was eating at him, she knew it could only be about Catherine.

He paced up and down, wondering whether to tell her. He could picture his life with Catherine and their baby. There was no way his plan wouldn't work, but could he trust Sally? They had become close the last couple of weeks, and the last thing he wanted to do was upset Sally. Thinking of what was at stake, he decided to tell her about his plan to split up Catherine and David.

The minute he finished telling her what he wanted her to do to help him get Catherine back, he knew he should have kept it to himself. There was no need for words; the horrified look on her face said it all. He recalled his conversation with his brother, and he wondered if he was right. He was the one who had done the dirty on Catherine and every relationship he'd had after their break-up had ended because none of them could ever measure up to her. Was he wrong to fight for her?

Seconds ticked by as he waited for her answer. The whole room felt cold and quiet He could almost hear himself breathing.

'You don't have to give me an answer today,' he said. 'Just think it over, but don't take too long. I want to do this before he goes back to the States.'

Sally stared at him, confused. 'You can't be serious. You claim to love her and yet you want to destroy her. She will never believe David would do that to her.'

'I know that,' Brooke said, 'but she will have doubts. And if I know her as well as I do then she'll call off this engagement.'

'I cannot believe you want to do this to someone you claim to love. Do you think she will forgive you if she ever finds out? You need to let her go; she will never love you the way I do.'

Brooke shook his head. 'Me and you don't have a future,' he said and regretted the words as soon as they left his mouth. He needed her on his side until he got Catherine back.

She stood up, confused, and fighting hard not to cry in front of him. It was painful to realise she had just been standing in for Catherine. All those times she had given herself to him. She felt humiliated and hurt. Fury burned in her eyes as she reached for her handbag. 'You're such a bastard Brooke, and frankly, I wish I never let you into my life.' She was gone before he could say anything.

She sank into one of the garden chairs, pulling her feet in under her and closed her eyes, trying not to think of tomorrow. She hated him for what he was doing to her. Her whole life seemed to revolve around him, and she didn't have the strength to fight what she felt for him. All her life, she had wanted a man who could love her and treat her right, but as much as she hated what Brooke was doing to her, she couldn't help the longing and passion she felt for him. No man had ever made her feel as desired as he did. All he had to do was touch her, and she became a slave to him.

Hearing footsteps behind her, she instantly froze. She was not ready to face him. She still had her pride and didn't want him to know just how much he was hurting her.

Her mother's words came back to haunt her: 'What goes around comes around.' Was this her payback for hurting Catherine, she wondered. Her karma? She had tried her hardest to be the best friend, the good daughter, but somehow she always messed up and, this time, she didn't think she could ever make things right between her and Catherine.

He stood still in the doorway and watched her. However much he wanted to go to her to tell her to forget what they had discussed, he knew he would be lying to himself.

He loved Catherine now more than ever. Not a day went by that he didn't think of her. He knew Sally was hurting right now, but he had told her right from the beginning there was no room for anyone else in his life as long as his heart belonged to Catherine. It unsettled him to see her teary face and realise he was the cause of it. He wished things were different for both of them. He never thought for a minute she loved him until she moved into his house and he had made it clear to her where they stood, hoping she would be strong enough to accept the fact that there wasn't going to be a future for them.

'Sally,' he said softly, standing above her. 'I'm sorry about before. I know it was not fair for me to ask that of you and you're right, it was a crazy idea. I also think it will be a good idea if you move out. I can help you put down a deposit. You're a wonderful girl, and I think I have taken too much advantage of you already. You deserve better than I can give you right now and one day you'll meet a man who will love you for who you are. If you don't want to get involved in my plan, you don't have to. I do understand, and I promise I won't mention it again. I think I need a drink. Would you like one?' he asked staring at her.

She pushed her feet back to the ground and faced him as he moved a table closer to her. She glared at him hard enough to stop him from getting any closer.

How could he think she wanted to share a drink with him after the humiliation she had suffered?

'Did I ever mean anything to you?' she asked him.

'After all these months, have I come to mean anything to you at all?' she asked again. 'I've cooked when your housekeeper was ill, cleaned your house, and made love to you every night. What has she got that I can't give you?'

Brooke silenced her before she could go on. 'Listen to me,' he said, looking deeply into her eyes. 'There is nothing wrong with you. This isn't because of you, and what I feel for Catherine is my problem. I suppose in a way I blame myself. I should never have taken advantage of you. We both need to put the past behind us and move on.'

Sally's lips twisted into a sneer. 'So, tell me, what makes you so confident that she'll come back to you?' she challenged him. 'You haven't been together for almost two years, and any fool can tell she's madly in love with David and she's carrying his child. The two of them are so committed to each other; I got sick just watching them. I wouldn't be surprised if she came back a married woman. Not even you with your rotten ideas can put a stop to that.'

'Sally, shut up, you don't know the half of it, and I'm sure as hell not going to bother explaining. But I will tell you this much – that cosy relationship she's having with David won't last another minute if he knew she was carrying my child.'

'What?' Sally said, her face was as white as a ghost. 'What did you just say?'

'Forget it,' he said, putting some distance between them.

'No, I will not, what do you mean she's carrying your child. The two of you are still sleeping together,' she added accusingly.

'That wasn't what I wanted to say – anyway, I thought we weren't going to talk about Catherine again,' he added, turning his back on her.

'Not until you tell me what you meant about the baby being yours.'

Although he stiffened, it was a while before he turned around and sat down.

She waited for him to tell her; it seemed so absurd she didn't want to believe it.

But then she could tell from the way he said it that he did believe the child was his and if it was his child, then how could Catherine lie to everybody? She was supposed to be the clever one, the kind and honest girl next door. She thought of David;

how would he react if he found out? She looked at Brooke, waiting for him to tell her the truth.

'Catherine and I spent a night together almost three months ago, and when I saw the paper, I just wondered if the baby could be mine.'

Sally was silent as his words sank in. This wasn't the news she had hoped to hear, and then again, she wasn't too surprised; nothing he did shocked her anymore. Minutes passed by; she listened silently to the birds singing. Brooke sat looking at her, but she couldn't open her mouth. She was too stunned, not only by what he'd told her but the fact that Catherine would lie to everyone. She was the one who always went on about sincerity and integrity. It was all beyond belief and yet how fortunate this news was. It was beginning to work so hard in her mind she could hardly contain herself. Never in her wildest dreams would she ever have suspected Catherine of cheating on David. As much as she didn't want to hurt Catherine, she realised David deserved to know the truth. Her mind returned to Brooke's idea, and somehow it didn't seem too bad after all. He was never going to love her the way he loved Catherine, so why not get from him whatever she could lay her hands on? And if the plan worked, she would never have to lift a finger for the rest of her life.

'I'll help you get her back,' she heard herself say. 'I think a child needs to be brought up by both its parents,' she added, convincing herself she was doing it for the baby. She thought back to her childhood and quickly blanked out the memories.

'Are you sure?' he asked, surprised.

'I said I would do it, didn't I? Don't patronise me or else I'll change my mind. And I think we should open that bottle of champagne and celebrate parenthood.'

Even though Brooke was amazed by the sudden change in her, he didn't waste time dwelling on it. His plan was working, and he was a happy man. *If I had known she would react this way about the baby, I would have told her sooner*, he thought grinning.

Nothing more was said of Catherine, the baby, or David, as they chased each other around the pool, laughing like two children.

She blocked any thoughts of Catherine from her mind. When he put his arm around her, kissing her passionately, she did not push him away; instead, she pulled him into the pool with her.

Sally woke up an hour later and gently pulled away from Brooke's arms.

She was meeting her cousin for dinner, and she didn't want to be late.

She stared at his relaxed features as she got dressed, and her heart ached when she thought of leaving him. Her body had become a slave to him because she could never resist him.

A part of her wanted to hurt him as much as he was hurting her but she knew it would be a waste of time. She needed to spend her energies on something worthwhile, like earning some money to become financially secure.

She didn't believe for one minute that Catherine would ever go back to him, but since he was too stubborn and so sure of himself, she was happy to go along with the plan, and this was just the beginning. She still believed he would come back to her once he realised he could never have Catherine back. For the first time in her life, she understood why Joyce buried herself in work rather than trying to find a husband.

Her cousin was still a virgin at twenty-seven and Sally wished she could have been like her, but she had no control over her body when it came to men.

'Miss Walker?' Catherine heard someone ask, her voice was charming and courteous.

She turned around and saw a young lady dressed in a long black skirt and white top. She looked quite pleasant and friendly.

'Yes, I'm Catherine Walker,' Catherine said.

'I'm sorry to bother you,' the young lady began. 'My name is Brenda, and I work with Mr Mwanza.'

'I see,' Catherine said, confused.

'Please sit down,' Catherine said, pointing to the chair.

'He asked me to come and meet you as he couldn't come himself. His wife is in the hospital,' Brenda said.

'I'm sorry to hear that,' Catherine said. 'I hope it's nothing serious.'

'She's going to be fine. They are only keeping her in for observation. She had an operation on her leg last week. Mr Mwanza asked me to give you this,' Brenda said, pulling a large brown envelope from her handbag.

'What is London like?' she asked after they had shared a cup of tea. 'I'm told that if you can work in London, you can work anywhere in the world as it is very cosmopolitan. There are so many different cultures and great museums, too. I have lived in Lusaka all my life,' she said. 'I went to a primary school near home and when I left high school; I went to the University, which is just half an hour from where I live. Sometimes I just want to disappear somewhere where no one knows me.' She stopped talking and took a sip of her drink.

'I suppose that's why I went into journalism. I thought it would give me the opportunity to travel the world, meet new and exciting people, but it hasn't worked out like that. My boss keeps telling me I still have a long way to go before he can give me big assignments.'

'Do you enjoy what you do?' Catherine asked her.

'Oh, yes. I have wanted to be a journalist for as long as I can remember. I was one of those girls who was busy reading Things Fall Apart when other students were doing mathematics. I'm sure my parents would have been much happier if I had been good at maths; at least, I could have gone on to study accountancy. I know there is so much I need to learn, and I'm determined to be the best I can be. The children in this town have been let down so many times, and it will be good for them to have a voice. I liked what you wrote in the post about child slavery. I know most people were touched, and I hope you won't give up until both governments can do something about it.'

Catherine's heart went out to her; she was so young, yet so intelligent and mature for someone her age. She reminded her of herself at about the same age, so hungry for big assignments and justice. It only got worse as you grew older, she had realised.

'I'm so sorry,' Brenda said, looking at her watch. 'I didn't mean to carry on and, as my mother would tell you if you ever met her, I talk too much.'

'It's all right,' Catherine said. 'I did enjoy our chat. I'm going to be around for a couple of days, so if you aren't too busy, we can meet again next week.'

They were exchanging phone numbers when a thought occurred to Catherine. She was silent for a moment, wondering whether she was doing the right thing, then she said, 'We're heading off to Victoria Falls tomorrow, and I wondered if you would like to come with us if you don't have any other plans.' She regretted the words as soon as she said them, but she liked the girl and felt Brenda could do with some fun.

'Are you sure?' Brenda asked. 'I mean; you don't know me.'

'Yes, I'm sure,' Catherine said. 'My fiancé and grandma are coming, too. I think we'll all have a good time, and you can tell me all about your work.'

Dawn had barely touched the sky when Catherine heard the car engine. Having spent half the night between the bedroom and toilet, she wondered if she should still go.

After all the planning and excitement, she didn't have the heart to let everyone down. She forced herself to leave the bed to see who was calling so early in the morning.

It wasn't long before she heard the front door open and saw her grandmother talking to the driver. She couldn't make out what they were saying, but the person drove off ten minutes later. Catherine sighed and went back to bed.

Hearing her movements, David sat up. 'Are you okay?' He asked.

Catherine could see that he was as worried as she was; it had been a long night for both of them. He was such a light sleeper, and he had woken every time she went to the bathroom.

'To be honest with you, I don't know,' she said, coming to sit beside him. 'My whole body aches, and I feel so tired and sick.'

He put his arms around her, his eyes filled with concern. 'I don't think we should go to Victoria Falls today,' he said, sitting up. 'You really could do with the rest. We can always see the place another time.'

'Are you sure you don't mind?'

He placed a finger under her chin and looked her in the eye.

'Darling, your health is more important to me, don't you ever forget that. I'll speak to your grandma, and I think she'll agree with me.'

'Since we've already paid for the rooms, maybe Brenda and her boyfriend can still go. She was so looking forward to this break; it'll be sad if she doesn't go because of me. I'll call and let her know,' Catherine said, swinging her feet off the bed.

She met her grandma in the corridor on her way to the living-room.

'Good morning,' she said.

Her grandmother followed her into the kitchen.

'Was that the driver I heard this morning?' Catherine asked.

'Yes. I sent him away. I had the feeling something wasn't quite right with you, as I heard you down the corridor most of the night. Are you okay?'

'I don't know,' Catherine said, shaking her head. 'I just feel so sick, Grandma. I hope nothing is wrong with the baby. I just lay there afraid of waking David up.

Unfortunately, he's such a light sleeper; I don't think he slept much either.'

'I told the driver I would call him back, but I better let him know the trip is cancelled. We can't go with you feeling this way,' her grandmother said. 'And no arguments!'

'Don't worry, none from me,' Catherine said trying hard to smile.

'David was just suggesting the same thing. So how come you left the farm so early yesterday morning?'

'I went to see Sally's mum. Why didn't you tell me she's living with Brooke?'

'It isn't that important, Grandma,' Catherine said and felt happy to hear herself saying it because for a long time she didn't think she could discuss Brooke and Sally with anyone without getting angry.

'You can't mean that,' her grandmother said, looking at her strangely. 'You gave the girl shelter in your home, and she ended up in bed with your partner. What kind of a friend does that?'

'I suppose, in a way, I'm not with Brooke anymore, and he's free to see whoever he wants. I just never imagined it would be one of my friends. I was upset and angry when I first found out, but now it doesn't bother me. I feel quite sorry for her. Brooke isn't capable of loving anyone as much as he loves himself. I only hope she wakes up to the fact before it's too late.'

'Well, next time you see her, tell her she's upset a lot of people here. I spent my entire morning comforting her mother. The poor woman is in such a state, and I don't know if she's going to be all right. She blames herself for the way Sally has turned out, and she's threatening to go to London to sort her out.'

'I wish I could be of help to her, but I haven't seen her since she moved out. I'm sure she'll be all right. She might just be what

Brooke needs,' she said closing her mind to the dark thoughts she felt towards him. She had been tempted to tell Sally the truth about Brooke but realised Sally would never believe her.

'Is everything OK?' her grandma asked staring at her.

'Yes,' she answered as her hands reached out to touch her belly. For a few seconds, she wondered if she should tell her grandma the truth about the baby.

Catherine, exhausted by her bad night, didn't want to discuss Brooke and Sally. She wanted this holiday to be about her and David, without thoughts of Brooke spoiling it. She was glad her grandmother didn't know the true identity of the child she was carrying. There was no telling of what she might do.

Chapter Twenty

Sally's mind was unsettled as she sat down in the taxi on her way to see Joyce. She watched other couples walking about holding hands and wondered if that would ever happen to her, to have a man look at her the way the young couples were doing right now.

She was certain now that she would never mean anything more to Brooke than a sleeping partner. His heart belonged to Catherine and for a second she actually felt sorry for him.

With Catherine on her mind, she couldn't help but travel back to another time, another place, when she had been so proud to tell everyone she had a friend in England.

She was only ten years old, but she knew one day Catherine would help her escape her nightmares at home, and that's exactly what had happened. Catherine had bought the ticket for her and paid her first-year tuition fees.

Thinking back, she realised she had always managed to get any man she wanted until now. She couldn't understand why Brooke couldn't love her.

She tried to establish some sense of what was going on with Catherine. It was still hard to believe the child she was carrying was Brooke's baby. It wasn't the revelation she had expected to hear from Brooke. It pained her to think he had gone back to sleep with Catherine when she had thought he was committed to her. She laughed at herself for even thinking it. Neither of them knew the meaning of the word. She knew he had cheated on Catherine more than once and hadn't she slept with him while he was still with Catherine?

She wondered, too, if Catherine knew who the father was or was she just stringing David along until she was certain.

An hour later she was knocking on her cousin's door, carrying a bag of groceries and presents. She knew Joyce didn't like her showering presents on her, but she didn't have anyone else to give them to. Besides, her cousin just didn't earn enough money to buy herself expensive clothes.

'Hello,' Joyce said, opening the door. 'You just missed your mum.'

'Oh, did you call her again?' Sally asked, confused. She didn't understand why Joyce would call her mum before she got to the flat.

'No,' Joyce said, 'I called mum, and she was at the house. She saw Catherine's grandmother and Mum said she been very upset since then.'

'What's upsetting her? I hope the old witch hasn't been saying things about me,' Sally said, getting angry.

'Well, it wasn't her. I wrote to Grandma telling her that you'd moved in with Brooke. I just didn't want her getting angry with me if something happened to you and since you didn't bother telling her yourself, I thought someone should and, for your information, I don't think Catherine's grandma would be interested in discussing your affairs with your mum.'

'I know,' Sally said, sitting down. 'I'm just a bit touchy when it comes to Brooke, and I didn't tell her because I knew she wouldn't understand. Not that there is much to tell anyway,' she added. 'Brooke and I aren't exactly the couple of the year. I just hope Grandma wasn't told all the gory details; that's all I care about.'

Joyce was silent for a minute, watching her cousin. Sally was three years older than her and yet she acted like such a child. It had always been like that between them;

Sally messed up, and she was left to pick up the pieces. She didn't believe that Sally was there, for once, because she wanted to be; something was up, and it was written all over her face.

'I made us dinner. Hope you are hungry,' she said, standing up.

'Yeah, I guess I could do with some food. What have you cooked?'

'Come and see for yourself,' Joyce said.

'What's getting at you?' she asked as soon as they sat down to eat. 'You have been jumpy ever since you got here, and you keep looking at your watch. Do you have to be somewhere else?'

'It's Brooke,' Sally said, putting her fork and knife down. She looked out the window; it was ten o'clock at night and yet the sky was still crystal clear. 'He's still in love with Catherine,' she said, turning back to look at Joyce. 'I just finally realised he'll never love me the way he loves her. I have done all I can to show him how I feel but this morning he made it very clear we'll never be anything more than lovers.'

Joyce listened quietly as Sally went on talking. 'What are you going to do?' She asked. She didn't want to make any suggestions. Not that her cousin ever listened to her anyway.

Sally shook her head. 'I can hardly force him to love me, can I? The truth is, I have always known the time would come when I had to face up to reality, I just didn't think it would be this soon. I can't let him go on using me. I want to come back and live with you if you'll have me and I promise to get a job and pay my way.'

'That's the most adult decision I have ever heard you make,' Joyce said after a pause. 'You can stay with me as long as you like and no, I'm not going to say I told you so. I just hope that this time you won't let him back into your life. You deserve better. You're young and pretty, why to force yourself on someone who clearly doesn't want or respect you?'

'I know,' Sally said, nodding, 'and thanks for putting up with me. I don't know what I would do without you.'

'You're welcome,' Joyce said. 'You can always repay me when you get your first real job.'

Brooke was just getting ready to go to work when she got back to the house.

She didn't want to see him; she had a note ready in her handbag to leave with the housekeeper.

'Hi,' he said as soon as she walked through the door.

'Hello, I didn't know you would be here,' she said, pushing a hand through her hair.

'You wouldn't be trying to avoid me by any chance, would you?' he asked, smiling.

'No, should I be?'

Brooke was dumbfounded. She looked different from the woman he'd seen yesterday; somehow she seemed a lot calmer and in control. He wondered what had happened to make her seem so indifferent to him.

'I've just come to pick up my clothes. I spoke to Joyce, and she's happy to let me stay with her until I find somewhere else. I want to thank you for having me. I know I'm not the easiest person to live with, but I hope I didn't make life too difficult for you.'

'Are you sure that's what you want? I was upset yesterday and didn't mean it when I said you should move out. Do you really want to stay with Joyce? I thought the two of you couldn't stand each other.'

'I think it's better for us if we don't live under the same roof,' Sally said, looking straight at him. She couldn't believe she was saying the words. 'Besides, I'm family, so she can't kick me out when she gets tired of me,' she added sarcastically.

'Can you, at least, wait till I get back from work? We do have things to discuss, or have you changed your mind again?'

'You call me when you are ready. I've made up my mind, don't try to stop me,' she said, moving past him.

He stood still and watched her go up the staircase. He couldn't understand why he was getting upset. He had been waiting for her to leave ever since she moved in and yet he couldn't help feeling empty inside. He wanted to tell her he was sorry if he had made her believe he could love her. As time stood still, he knew he couldn't turn back the clock. All he could do was to be there for her in future, if she ever needed his help and hopefully become friends. He took out his cheque book and wrote out a cheque in her name for £5,000. He left it on the table where she could see it and then he left the house.

Sally threw herself onto the bed wondering whether to cry or scream. She still loved him, despite his feelings for Catherine. It was the hardest moment for her to be strong in front of him without going to pieces. She could still smell his aroma on the bed where they had shared so many happy moments. She also knew she was doing the right thing by leaving; she could not stay in the same house with him and not want to be close to him, to feel his body next to hers or want to wake up next to him in the morning.

Unable to tear her thoughts away from Brooke and what could have been, she slowly got off the bed and threw her clothes one by one into the suitcase. Most of them were presents from Brooke. The day crawled by slowly as she tried to say goodbye to that Chapter of her life; something inside her wanted her to believe it wasn't over. She was connected to him forever, no matter what he thought, especially if their plan went ahead.

When she couldn't fit all her clothes in the suitcase, she called the housekeeper and told her to give them to the charity shop across the road. She would have loved to send some of the dresses to her mum, but there was no way she was going to fit in them.

She had no relationship with her stepsisters. Royce didn't care much for designer clothes.

Brooke wore a long face throughout the day. He was rude to everybody, including his business partner, whom he normally chatted with happily.

Seeing his mood, she left him to himself and when it was time to go home; she knocked on his door. When he didn't answer, she went in.

He was in a shocking state. His shirt hung out of his trousers; his hair was a mess, and his eyes were red. It was obvious that he had been crying.

'Want to talk about it?' she asked, her voice soft and gentle.

Brooke slumped into the nearest chair and held his face in his hands.

'Not unless you're God,' he said with dry humour. 'It's Catherine. I'm afraid I might have lost her forever. I rang her last night, but she wouldn't talk to me. She's in Zambia with David, did I tell you?'

Louise nodded. 'I thought you said you were moving on. What happened?' she asked.

'I miss her. My life is empty without her. I never once thought I would feel this way about anyone. Have you ever met someone and known deep in your heart that it was the real thing?' he asked.

'I have, but we can't always have everything we want and there comes a time when you just need to pull yourself together and move on.'

'Well, I've tried, but it's not working. Last night, when I rang her, she told her grandmother to tell me not to call again.'

'What did you expect?' Louise asked. She did not have time to sugarcoat him. 'I don't know why you need to punish yourself like this. You've seen how happy she is with David. You surely don't expect him to understand when she receives phone calls from her ex-boyfriend?'

'I don't know what I was expecting. I just thought she would speak to me for old time's sake. I don't know what she sees in that man anyway.'

Louise had to laugh; this had nothing to do with concern over Catherine's feelings. Brooke wanted her back and from the look of things he wasn't having any luck.

'We can't help whom we fall in love with,' she said sympathetically. It was difficult to love a person who didn't love you. She only wished he could get over Catherine before it was too late.

'How is Sally?' she asked, changing the subject.

'She's leaving the house today,' Brooke said softly.

'I hope this time it's for good,' Louise said, fastening her coat. 'There's no point in wasting the poor girl's time when you're not ready for a relationship. If you haven't got anything to do, you can come to my house for dinner. My grandchildren are coming over to spend the weekend.'

'Thanks, Louise, but I can't. I'm spending the weekend with Mum and Dad.'

'That's okay. You have a think about what I said,' she told him.

She was the only person who didn't make him feel bad about himself, he reflected. No one else wanted to hear about his feelings for Catherine. They told him it was his fault. He didn't know who he hated most, himself or David.

He took out his diary and dialled Kim's number.

'What do you want?' Kim asked before he could finish the first sentence.

'Hello to you too,' Brooke answered.

Apologising for disturbing her, he asked if she knew when Catherine was due back.

Kim let out a scream, making him move the phone far from his ear.

'You're a sad man, Brooke. Why would I want to tell you after what you have put her through? I know you called her last night, and if she wanted you to know, she would have told you herself.'

'Can't you just give me an idea? I don't mean to cause any trouble,' Brooke insisted.

'Sorry, you'll have to find someone else to do your dirty work, and if there is nothing else, I have things to do,' she said ringing off.

Kim was shaking even as she put the phone down. He was the most maddening man she had ever met. She had liked him in the beginning. Catherine had fallen deeply in love with him, and almost everyone thought the two of them could end up growing old together. It wasn't until he first cheated on Catherine that she finally saw him for what he was, a manipulating and selfish person who made her friend feel as though it was her fault he was cheating.

She leaned back into her large leather chair, shaking her head as if to clear any thoughts of her conversation with Brooke. She turned her head and looked straight at a picture of her and Catherine taken almost ten years ago.

They had been staying at Catherine's grandparents' ranch in Texas. Most of Catherine's cousins came too, and they all had such a laugh.

She never quite understood why her mother's family had cut them off. She knew nothing about her mother's life before she moved to America. She had tried in her teens to find out more about her Chinese background, but her mother didn't like to talk about it and, in the end, she gave up and never asked the questions again.

Chapter Twenty-One

Sally tossed and turned all night, her eyes wide open, images of Catherine as a little girl haunting her every moment. She wondered if she was doing the right thing. It wasn't something she could share with anyone including her cousin. Her cousin would think she was mad for even considering it and yet something else her darker side people had called it made her think she was doing it for the child. Catherine will thank me one day; she told herself as she tried once more to close her eyes.

She looked at the cheque lying on the table and shook her head. Who the hell did he think he was, trying to buy her silence with money? Nothing of the plan had been finalised, and he was such a fool, he didn't realise that she could do anything for him. He could afford it, and more if he wanted, but why he had done it was a mystery to her. Not that she didn't deserve it, all those times she had slept with him thinking that he was going to marry her. She had never felt so humiliated in her entire life, and she was bleeding inside.

Looking back, she realised she should have known from the way he acted: all the hints and his actions spoke volumes, but she hoped she could do what Catherine had not been able to do. She had never met his family, and the few friends she had met were those who came to play tennis with him. At thirty, he was one of London's most eligible bachelors. He came from a wealthy family.

His father owned a newspaper and property across London and Europe, and his mother was a doctor. Even though his mother was black American, he had been born and raised in England and the family had never spent time in America, apart from holidays and work commitments. She also knew that his whole family adored Catherine and in the beginning, she had convinced herself he was protecting her from being hurt in case they didn't like her, but as time went by she wondered if the opportunity would ever arise. He had his own law firm, and she knew he was doing very well. All those months of plotting how to steal him from Catherine now seemed pointless. He was still in love with her. Catherine had won again, just as she had done when they were kids, always had the nicest clothes, the coolest grandmother.

She sat up and looked at her bedside clock; it was three, and the house was very quiet. Joyce was working the night shift for a month. Sally wondered what to do with herself. She was tired and yet couldn't sleep; she swung off the bed and put on her dressing gown. With Brooke still on her mind, she went to the kitchen and took out a big container of ice cream. She sat down in the front room and switched on the television.

Catherine was due back at the weekend; her mother had told her when she finally worked up the courage to ring her.

'I want you to go to her house and apologise,' her mother had said.

Speaking to me like a child as usual. Sally thought.

Not wanting to argue with her, Sally said yes to everything, though she didn't think Catherine would welcome her apology right now. They both needed time to heal.

She couldn't explain to anyone why she had done what she had. As much as it was her fault, Brooke was to blame, too, but no one pointed a finger at him.

It had been the same with Kim's boyfriend. She liked what she saw, and she went for it; unfortunately, for her, he had told Kim.

It wasn't that she had intentionally gone out of her way to hurt Catherine. Brooke had encouraged her and at the time she did not believe he was in love with Catherine anymore, and he had said so himself. Now she knew he had just wanted to get laid.

She made a note to ring him in the morning and tell him the news: Catherine was coming home over the weekend.

She woke up late and was horrified when she saw what time it was. She hadn't meant to spend half the day in bed, but remembering her troubled night, she was not surprised. She took a shower and went to find something to eat. Joyce's house keys were on the table, so she knew her cousin was in.

She phoned Brooke from the kitchen. A voice answered which she didn't recognise.

'May I speak to Mr Fraser, please,' she said in her most professional voice.

He came on the line even before she could compose herself.

'Sally! How are you?'

'I'm fine,' she responded casually.

'How are things?' Brooke asked, clearly not put off by the tone of her voice.

'I called to tell you Catherine is back on Sunday.'

The line went dead for a moment.

Brooke was so happy; he wanted to shout for joy, but he knew he had to be careful with Sally. She held the keys to everything he was planning, and he was determined to make his plan work.

'Did you speak to her?' he asked.

'No! You're joking, aren't you? She won't talk to me. Mum told me.'

'Can I call you later? I'm just in the middle of something,' he told her.

'Fine,' she said, hanging up the phone.

Brooke rang his brother as soon as he put the phone down

and cancelled their game for Sunday. This was the best news he had heard all week. After calling all her friends, including Richard, he had given up any hope of finding out.

Richard had politely told him to leave Catherine alone.

Brooke couldn't help wondering if Richard knew what had happened, or about the baby. He wished now that he had tried harder to make friends with Richard, but he had been so envious of their closeness that Richard had stayed away, avoiding all the invitations they sent to him. Catherine had told him about Richard and Michael, but he sensed something else from Richard, even though Catherine could not see it. Looking back, he realised just how silly he had been. She looked to him as a brother and, according to his older brother, Richard and Michael had been very close. With nothing else left to do for the day, he told his secretary he was leaving. He found himself driving towards Catherine's flat almost automatically. It was only Tuesday, and yet he could hardly contain his excitement at the prospect of seeing her again.

Next, he drove to his mother's office. He was taking her to dinner. It was something they did once a month and lately he had found himself looking forward to their outings. His brother and two sisters joined them sometimes, and he enjoyed the family get-together. Today, however, he wanted it to be just the two of them. He wanted to talk to her about Catherine and America. When his mother and her family never liked to talk about their life in America.

'Let the sleeping dogs lie,' his aunt said whenever he brought up the subject, but he couldn't let go especially now he knew his child might grow up there.

'Is it okay if we skip the theatre and just go to dinner?' Brooke asked his mother when he arrived at her office.

In the restaurant, she leaned forward and looked straight at him.

'Are you seeing anyone at the moment?' she asked.

He hesitated, wondering just how much she knew about Sally; past episodes made him realise she probably knew more than she was letting on. She had a habit of calling his housekeeper once in a while to check on him and, as nice as the woman was, she never stopped talking. Nothing went by without a member of his family finding out and he only kept her on because he trusted her to be there when needed.

'I'm not seeing anyone,' he told her.

'Well, never mind, I'm sure you will meet someone soon,' she said. The pain he felt was obvious to her.

'I can't stop thinking about her,' he said suddenly.

She did not need to ask him who he was talking about. Everyone knew he was still hung up on Catherine, but the problem was they didn't really know what else to say to him.

'What am I going to do?' he muttered.

'You need to let her go,' she said firmly. 'Much as I'd like to see you two back together, I think it is time to move on. She has a new man in her life now, and if you love her as much as you say you do, then you need to let her be happy. You shared a good part of your life together, and no one can take those memories away from you. It's not healthy for you to go hoping things will change. I know it hurts but whoever said life would be easy?' She took his hand in hers and looked straight into his eyes.

'If you can't do it for yourself, then do it for your dad and me. It pains me to see you so sad. You're still young, and I'm sure there are still a few good unattached young ladies out there who would be happy to have you.'

Later, lying in bed, he tried to remember what his mother had said. It all made sense, but he couldn't help how he felt. Catherine was the only woman who had made him feel he could do anything he set his mind to, and she had touched his heart as no one else had ever done.

He couldn't talk to his mother about the baby. Though he truly believed it was his, he didn't want to raise her hopes. He had to be sure he was the father, even though he wondered what difference it would make to his relationship with Catherine.

'Promise me you'll think about what I said,' his mother had begged him when he dropped her off.

Chapter Twenty-Two

It was mid-day by the time Catherine finally got up. Her grand-mother had taken David into town and the local park to show him some of Lusaka's best sights. She had wanted to go with them but after another sleepless night, she felt too tired.

This time, it wasn't anything do to with feeling ill but with the constant phone calls she had received from London, all to do with Brooke. Richard had phoned her soon after her long conversation with Kim.

'Brooke rang me last night,' he said after chatting for a while about family and friends.

'He rang Kim, too,' she told him, unsurprised that he was calling all her friends.

'You don't suppose he knows, do you?' Richard asked. His voice was full of worry.

'I don't know,' she said. 'I can't help feeling he's up to some-thing. He rang here two days ago, and Grandma just told me yesterday that Sally's mum has been asking when we were leaving. Well, I'm determined not to let him spoil my holiday.'

'What on earth is he up to?' Richard asked.

'I don't know, and I don't think I want to find out.'

She switched on the kettle and tried to blank out any thoughts of Brooke. She didn't share her fears with David. He seemed so happy and relaxed that she didn't want to worry him. In the last week, she had taken him to meet Melissa, and the two had hit it off.

She had grown into a big girl, much taller than the girl in the picture, and the scars of the past seemed to be slowly disappearing. Catherine still couldn't get over the change from the frightened young girl she had rescued to the beautiful, warm child she now was.

As for Mr Mwanza, she never saw him. He seemed to have one excuse after another to avoid a meeting, and Catherine decided not to depend on him for anything.

David sensed great tension around the city as the driver took them through the dirty crowded streets. Children walked around aimlessly, with no direction. The adults held on tightly to their handbags, moving around in dispirited fashion. He was touched, and he felt sad. Catherine had told him about the last time she had visited as a child. Things had been prosperous then; the shops had been full of goods, and the streets were clean.

Thinking about Catherine, he couldn't help wondering about the conversation they'd had the previous night.

She hadn't asked him again what his feelings were about the baby. He had looked her straight in the eye and told her he loved her. It had been hard in the beginning for him to think of the child she was carrying and not feel hurt, but now he wanted to be a part of his or her life. He had made a promise to be a good father and raise the child as his own. Did she still have doubts about their future? he wondered.

'Are you okay?' he heard Catherine's grandmother ask him.

David nodded. 'Sorry, my mind just wandered off.'

'You're thinking about Catherine, aren't you?' She said. She's a strong girl, and she'll be fine. Unfortunately, some women do suffer during pregnancy. Luckily for her, she has you to look after her. I'm really happy the two of you have decided to get married. It's the first time I've seen her happy since Michael's death. It shook all of us, but I think it took her longer to recover. They were very close.' She sighed. 'Anyway, let's not talk about the past. What's important is you have each other, and I do believe the two of you are going to be very happy together.'

'Thank you,' David said. He had come to love this old woman as he loved his grandmother. She made everything seem so simple and easy. He understood why Catherine was such a wonderful person; she had grown up surrounded by good people who loved her.

After the driver had dropped them off at the zoo, they walked together to look at the lion's den. There were a lot of families, children running around laughing and eating ice cream. It was very different from the town centre; the place was calm and peaceful, and he felt himself relax as he tried not to think of Catherine's sad face.

As old as she was, Catherine's grandmother had the energy of a twenty-year-old. They moved from one place to another, enjoying the beauty around them.

Catherine's phone rang just as she put her cup of tea on the table. She sighed heavily before picking it up, wondering if it was Brooke. She was tired of him and his obsession with her. There was no one else in the house, and she had been enjoying the chance to relax on her own.

She cheered up quickly when she heard Richard's voice. 'Hello, Richard. How are you?'

'I'm fine. How is David?' he asked.

'He's well. He has gone out sightseeing with Grandma. The two of them are getting on really well.'

'How come you didn't go with them?'

'I just feel a bit tired, and it's very hot here.'

'Well, I hope you're having enough rest. Just rang to tell you that I'm seeing someone. I know you're coming home this weekend, but I couldn't wait to tell you.'

'Oh, my God!' she screamed down the phone. 'This is the best news ever. When did all this happen and who is the lucky lady?'

'It's Tapiwe,' he said. 'Who can believe that after all these years we finally got together! She's so great, Catherine. I think I have fallen madly in love with her.'

She felt so happy for him and wished she could see his face and tell him so. The news really lifted her spirits. By the time she hung up her tea was cold and she pushed it aside and made herself comfortable on the sofa. David and her grandmother weren't due back for another hour.

Now that she thought about it, it didn't seem strange at all that Tapiwe, and Richard had gotten together. From the moment she introduced them, Tapiwe had told her she fancied him, but because of her job and both their lifestyles, they had never found the time to do anything about it.

She cast her eyes away from the book she was reading when she heard footsteps.

'You're back,' she said putting away the book.

'Yes, did you miss me,' David said lowering his head and kissed her passionately.

She held on tightly to him as he hugged her.

'Did you have fun?' I hope Grandma didn't take you all over town.'

'She was great, at least, I managed to see the lions enjoying their lunch. They must go through a couple of goats a week.

'That's good to know,' Catherine smiled. 'I missed you. I can't tell you how much I've been looking forward to showing you around. Hopefully, I'll feel better tomorrow.'

'You certainly look better than before,' he commented.

'I feel it, too,' she said putting her hand in his. 'Did you have a good time or you're just being polite?'

'Yes, it was good. There is such a contrast between different neighbourhoods. Some of these places make one feel like you've crossed borders. Grandma was great, but I missed you.'

'Sorry, I couldn't make it. I was so tired this morning. I think I would've made all of us miserable.'

'You would tell me if there was something bothering you, wouldn't you?' He squeezed her hand.

She pushed herself up and gave him a huge hug.

'I'm sorry,' she whispered into his ear. 'I think this pregnancy is turning me into a boring middle-aged person.'

David carried her to their room, and before long, they dozed off.

A loud banging on the door woke them. Still half asleep, Catherine went to open the door. Her grandmother was standing in the corridor; her face was as pale.

'What is it?' Catherine said, rushing to her side.

'It's Martha,' her grandmother said. 'Her daughter just called me. She was rushed to the hospital this afternoon, and she was pronounced dead on arrival.'

'What!' Catherine said, not quite believing what she was hearing. She had only seen Grandma Martha two days ago.

'Are you sure?' she asked.

'She had a heart attack.' Her grandmother wiped tears away from her face. 'She had a minor heart attack last year, and the doctor told her to take it easy, but you know what she's like, always wanting to live life to the full. I'm going to her house as soon as the driver comes.'

'Wait, I will come with you,' Catherine said rushing to her room for a pair of jeans.

There was a deadly silence among them as they waited for the driver. Catherine knew life would probably never be the same again for her grandmother. Grandma Martha had been her best friend. She wished her mother was around. She would have known what to do.

Chapter Twenty-Three

She was hugging her parents ten minutes after the plane had landed at Gatwick. It felt so good to be back to the familiar. She had begged her grandmother to come back with them, but she didn't want to come; she said she needed time to mourn and heal.

David was staying with her for another week, and she tried not to think of the time when he was leaving. She had become so used to waking up next to him that the prospect of waking up alone was not appealing at all. She knew he had work to sort out, and she felt guilty for wanting him to stay. Nothing was discussed of their living arrangements once they got married, but she knew she would follow him anywhere. All he had to do was ask her.

'Did you have a great time?' her mother asked as they drove away from the airport.

It was a cold day, and Catherine was missing the African sunshine already.

'It was lovely, too many children on the farm, though. I don't know how those guys cope.'

Her mum laughed. 'I guess some things never change. Your grandma used to get frustrated, but I guess she can't be bothered anymore.'

Traffic was gridlocked; Catherine was so tired that she could hardly keep her eyes open. She snuggled up to David. He cradled her close to him; his palm smoothed her back.

Her parents stayed for dinner. The only people she spoke to that night were Kim and Richard. Her body hurt from sitting on the plane and she and David spent the rest of the day in bed.

Despite her mother's pleas to give them a party that weekend, Catherine said that both she and David needed time to rest, and David wanted to go the States to catch up on work. Also, she wanted time to herself to think about the future, Brooke and the baby. As much as she wanted to know how David felt, she knew that ultimately she was the one to make the final decision. She would have to live with that for the rest of their lives.

She didn't have to wait too long for Brooke to show his face. He was outside the flat the minute she stepped out the next day. She was in a hurry for an appointment, and he was the last person she wanted to see. She had told security so many times not to let him into the building, yet he always found a way to get into the building. She made a mental note to get to the bottom of it.

'What are you doing here?' she asked him before he reached her.

'Good day to you, too,' he said. 'Heard you were back and I thought I should come and see how you are.'

She smiled, not believing a word he said. 'As you can see, I'm fine and happy, engaged as well.'

She saw him try hard not to look too disappointed.

'Brooke,' she said, pulling at his arm. 'Can we do this later? I really have to go.' She looked at her wristwatch.

'Do you want a lift?' He asked. She hesitated.

'I'll take a cab,' she said.

'Please let me give you a lift. I promise to be on my best behavior. Besides, my brother is in the car, and he wants to see you.'

In spite of the heaviness in her heart, she found herself walking with him towards his silver Mercedes. He seemed different, a bit calmer than the last time she had seen him. While she didn't want to be too close to him, she wanted to know exactly what he was up to and why it had been so important for him to go to all this trouble to find out when she was coming back.

'Hi Catherine, it's been a while,' Shannon greeted her cheerfully.

'Hi, sorry been so busy, how are you?' she asked him.

'I'm OK; Brooke tells me you're getting married, congratulations.'

'Thank you.'

There was suddenly a moment of silence in the car.

'How is Sally?' she asked Brooke breaking the silence.

'I don't know,' he answered. 'She moved out a week ago.'

'Sorry,' Catherine said, looking away.

'I'm sorry,' Brooke began. 'I never meant to hurt you. I know we should never have slept together, and I know Sally feels the same way, too.'

'Can we not talk about it?' Catherine said, putting on her seatbelt. 'I think it would be best if we forgot the whole episode. I can't forget what you put me through but I've forgiven you both, and I hope you find fulfilling relationships in the future.'

His brother buried his head in the newspaper and pretended to read.

They waited for her in the car, even though she insisted she would get a taxi back.

Brooke suddenly felt a sense of relief as he watched her walk away. This was the first time he told her how sorry he was about Sally and even though she hadn't said much, he knew she was not dwelling on it as other people would. She seemed very content and happy. There was no bitterness in her voice. He picked up his phone and two minutes later he was talking to Sally.

'Can we meet tonight?' he asked her.

'What time?' Sally asked, not wasting time on small talk.

Seeing Catherine walking towards the car, he quickly told her he would pick her up at eight. He came round and opened the door for Catherine.

'Anywhere else you would like to go?' he asked as if all was back to normal.

'Just home, please,' she answered.

On the way to the flat, Shannon chatted to her about his work and his family. She had a feeling there was something he was holding back, and she wasn't sure she wanted to know. She thought about David and wondered what he would say if he saw her with Brooke.

'Thanks for the lift,' she said and quickly opened the door before he could come round.

'Catherine,' he said, stopping her in her tracks. 'Yes?'

'Congratulations,' he said. 'About the engagement.' And then he was gone before she could respond.

Catherine shook her head. She was surprised how calm she had been to be so near him. All the hurt and pain she had been carrying around seemed to have disappeared.

It was strange how things turned out. Two years ago they could have been laughing and kicking in that car, and now there was a cloud between them. All those old feelings and passion were gone. She suspected he was up to something and only hoped it did not involve either David or herself. The flat smelled of cooked breakfast as she walked through the door. David was nowhere in sight. She rushed through the flat opening all the doors and calling his name. When she had no luck, she sat down heavily by the table. Five minutes later he walked through the door carrying a bunch of roses.

'Oh, David,' she said, rushing into his arms. 'I love you.'

'I love you, too,' he said, kissing her.

'You're spoiling me. Whatever am I going to do when you leave?'

'You can come with me.'

'I'm tempted, but I can't,' she said. 'I have to meet my boss sometime next week, and I think I could also do with some rest. You'll be back Saturday, so I suppose I'll be all right.'

Her mother and Kim had finally convinced them to have an engagement party, and they discussed the arrangements as they ate lunch. His sisters wanted to come, and so did his brother, Kelvin. Catherine's father had kindly offered them their London flat. It was Natalie's first visit to England and Catherine was looking forward to showing her around. The girls were coming, too, and according to their mum, they both had their bags packed, even though there was still a week to go.

David left soon after breakfast. Catherine didn't feel well enough to drive, so he took a taxi to the airport. It was only after he left that she wondered if he had seen her getting out of Brooke's car. She had wanted to tell him, but with all the excitement, she'd become swept up in that. She took a taxi to Richard's house soon after. She had promised to help him choose a birthday present for Tapiwe and didn't want to let him down.

'What do you think she would like?' he asked her as they walked around Knightsbridge. 'I thought about getting her perfume. Do you think she would like that?' he asked again before she'd had a chance to answer.

Catherine laughed, 'You're nervous, aren't you?' she teased.

'It will be her thirtieth birthday. I just don't want to let her down,' he said.

'Well, follow me,' Catherine said, leading the way. 'We'll get her a present she'll never forget.' As they walked towards Harrods, she said, 'I saw Brooke today.'

'Where? Please don't tell me he came to the flat.'

'Yes, he did, he came with Shannon, who is always so sensible and mature. Sometimes I think I chose the wrong brother.' She added laughing. 'Anyway, they waited for me at the clinic and drove me back home. I told him about my engagement; he didn't say anything at first. Then he congratulated me when they dropped me off.'

'What do you think he wants?' Richard seemed to be as puzzled as she was.

'I don't know,' she said, shaking her head. 'Not that he knows what he wants.'

Even though Sally still desperately wanted things to work out between them, to feel Brooke's hands on her body and hold him close to her, she wondered if this was the right way to go about it. She wore a low-cut black dress just up to her knees, with her best shoes making her seem taller than she really was. She was wearing the perfume he had bought for her, which she knew he liked to smell on her, too. Looking at herself in the mirror, she smiled at the transformation. No one would accuse her of not trying.

From their short conversation on the phone, she wasn't quite sure where he was taking her. She was just happy to be with him again.

I have to be strong, she told herself. She had spent many restless nights thinking of him. He was in her dreams every waking moment of the day. There were days when she drank too much alcohol just to keep him out of her thoughts, but it was useless, because as soon as she sobered up, he was in her face as if reminding her what she was missing. She wondered now if she had made the right decision to leave him. Not that he had given her much choice. She had wanted him to beg her to stay, to tell her he could try to love her. But nothing had happened, and only pride prevented her from marching back to his house with her bags. He was too good a man to chase her away or, at least, that's what he wanted everyone to think.

She still could not believe how unfeeling he had been, just to sleep with her and toss her aside when it suited him. She blamed herself for letting him do it to her and for even thinking of him now.

She put on her coat and went to the living room to wait for

him. Seeing her all dressed up, her cousin asked her if she was going out on a date.

'Brooke is picking me up to go for a drink,' Sally answered, trying to sound unaffected.

'Why do you keep doing this to yourself?' Joyce asked.

'I don't know what you mean,' Sally said.

'Don't play coy with me,' Joyce said, glaring at her. 'I wasn't born yesterday. Hasn't he done enough for you to stay away? I thought you were getting yourself sorted and yet here you go getting sucked in by him again.'

'We are only going for a drink, for crying out loud,' she said, getting angry. 'I'm not a child, and I can look after myself.'

'Well, you better stop acting like one, then. You have a job now, and you don't want someone like him messing up your life again. You need to give up this man; nothing good is ever going to come out of it.'

The doorbell rang before she could say anything else. Sally was so relieved that she ran instead of walking to the door. Joyce shook her head and turned back to watch television.

'You look great,' Brooke said when he saw her.

'Thank you and so do you,' she answered, smiling. To her he always looked good, whatever he was wearing.

'I thought we could go to mine for dinner if it's okay with you,' he said as soon as she made herself comfortable in the car.

'That's okay,' she heard herself say, even though she would have preferred a restaurant. A place full of people and destructions from the itching she felt deep in her heart.

There was silence in the car as he drove through the heavy traffic. She was thinking of the conversation she'd just had with her cousin. No one understood why she loved Brooke, and she couldn't explain it to them, no matter how hard she tried.

Sitting next to him now, she wondered whether it was because he had been so committed to Catherine at the time or because he was unavailable that she had gone after him.

The house was the same. It still amazed her how tidy everything was. His housekeeper only worked three days a week, but even when she was off, he didn't dump books and clothes everywhere like most men.

'Do you want some wine before dinner?' he asked her.

'No, thank you,' Sally answered, sitting down.

He came back ten minutes later with plates and Chinese food.

Sally laughed. 'There I was thinking you were going to cook me a meal.'

'Not unless you want to have food poisoning. You know I can't cook.'

'Some things never change, hey. There are always books, and Catherine has stacks of them if you want to borrow one,' she said before she could stop herself. She could almost feel her presence taking over the room, staring at them.

'I'm sorry,' she said quickly. 'I didn't mean to bring her name up. This entire take away just reminds me of her.'

'That's okay,' Brooke said, serving the food on their plates.

He sat down next to her, and they listened to classical music as they ate.

Sally was the first to break the silence.

'Have you spoken to her since she came back?' She asked him.

'I saw her this morning,' he said, wondering which parts of his conversation with Catherine he needed to tell her.

For a moment, Sally felt frozen, a great sadness run through her body. It suddenly occurred to her why he had wanted to see her. This dinner had nothing to do with wanting her company. It was business and everything to do with Catherine.

'She's engaged and looks very happy.' He said the words with difficulty.

'Really?' Sally said, not surprised. Anyone but Brooke could tell that David and Catherine were madly in love with each other.

'Yes, and that's why we need to act fast, because once they marry, there will be no turning back.'

'Did you ask her about the baby?' she asked him.

'No, the time wasn't right, and I only spent about an hour with her. Anyway, I was talking to my brother, and he said Richard has invited him to the engagement party next weekend. He doesn't know exactly when the wedding will be, so I was wondering if there is a chance you might find out.'

'You know she won't invite me and, as for her friends, let's just say we don't get along, so I'll be the last person to know.'

'I think she would talk to you if you rang her,' Brooke began. 'She isn't bitter about what we did anymore and besides, the two of you have been friends for so long it would be a shame not to try and patch things up.'

Sally didn't know what books he was reading. She was a woman, and if anyone had done what she had done to Catherine, she would never speak to them again.

'I can't do it, Brooke. You must find someone else to run this little errand for you.'

'Are you afraid she won't talk to you?' He asked, confused. 'The two of you will have to talk to each other at some point and what better time than now?'

'I'll talk to her when I'm good and ready, so will you please stop going on about it.'

It wasn't until midnight when she realised how much time had passed since they started discussing their plan. The whole thing was putting off any notions of romantic ideas she might have had about the night.

'You can sleep here if you like,' he said, coming to stand next to her.

'No,' Sally said, shaking her head. 'I have a long day tomorrow, and besides, my cousin is expecting me,' she lied. The truth was she didn't trust herself not to give in to him if he touched her in the slightest way.

Her taxi came, and she waved him goodbye, feeling good with herself.

She phoned her friend from her mobile phone, and five minutes later she told the driver to drop her off in the West End.

Before long, she was dancing and laughing on the dance floor, thoughts of Brooke far from her mind. She was glad she had decided to go dancing with her friends. They all left in the early hours of the morning, and she had a few telephone numbers in her bag. She threw them into the bin as soon as she got home. She had made a decision a long time ago not to date anyone she met at a club after one young man had disappeared after sleeping with her.

Catherine sang softly as she showered. She was meeting Kim and Tapiwe for lunch and was quite looking forward to it.

It was the first time in ages that the three of them were meeting. They were all very busy. Even though Kim was married now, she still travelled all over the world on assignments. It was only now that Tapiwe had given up modelling that they were able to go out and relax. Her life had been just as busy as her friends' travelling between Asia, America and Europe.

It had come as a surprise to everyone when Tapiwe had announced six months earlier that she was giving up modelling and opening up her a jewellery shop on King's Road in Chelsea. The last time Catherine had seen her, she seemed quite relaxed and happy.

She looked at herself in the mirror as she dressed. Her pregnancy was now visible, and she was glad she had bought some maternity clothes before going to Zambia.

There were a few articles in the papers about her pregnancy, but she never bothered to read them. The only people who knew the true identity of the baby's father would never betray her. She thought about Sally and, strangely, what she had done didn't seem that important anymore. Life was too precious to stay angry at anyone for too long and now that she was happily engaged to the man she loved, she wished all the best for all her friends, including Sally.

She made a decision to call her and invite her to the engagement party, which she knew would raise a few eyebrows among some of her friends.

Kim was already there when she got to the restaurant. The waiter escorted her to the table and for a moment she stood still, wondering if there was something else going on. The table in the corner far away from everyone else seemed too big for just the three of them.

'What's going on?' Catherine asked, making herself comfortable.

A triumphant gleam appeared in Kim's eyes and her lips parted in a smile. Without looking at Catherine, she turned to the side door and said, 'You can all come out.'

Tapiwe, Richard, her boss and a few close friends all came out from the room smiling. She was too shocked to say anything as they all came round and congratulated her.

'You didn't think we could wait for another week, did you?' Richard said, sitting next to her.

Jason came in just then with two bunches of roses. He gave one to Catherine and the other to his wife. Presents were passed across the table while they waited for their food.

Catherine looked at them in amazement. They were people, friends, who had been there for her in different ways. She felt tears brimming in her eyes as she looked at them and all the presents, piled by her feet. She was deeply touched and wished she could say something, yet could not find the right words.

'Don't you go weepy on us,' Kim said. 'And here is a nice glass of non-alcoholic drink for you.'

'It's all your fault. You should have warned me. I could have come prepared.'

'It was better this way. I wish I had a video camera to capture the look you had on your face,' Tapiwe added.

'Thank you, everyone,' Catherine said, smiling.

'Can we raise our glasses and make a toast?' Richard said, standing up.

'You're not going to make a speech, are you? I can't take any more surprises,' Catherine said.

'Now that you mention it, I think I will,' he said teasingly. 'Don't worry; I won't embarrass you.'

After Richard made his speech, which went along the lines of how much he loved her and what a beautiful mother and wife she was going to be, their food arrived. They talked and laughed, and it was much later in the evening before she finally got back home.

Putting all the presents in the spare bedroom, she changed into her nightgown and rang David.

'Hi, honey,' he said, hearing her voice. 'I thought I had lost you.'

'Don't be silly, you can never lose me,' she said. 'I thought I was just having lunch with Kim and Tapiwe, but everyone was there. Richard, Jason and friends from work.'

'Wow, I guess they couldn't wait for Saturday.'

'You're right, and I got so many presents I don't even know what to do with them. I'll wait for you so we can open them together,' she told him.

'Kelvin arrived this morning. He can't wait to meet you, and I think he's a bit envious of me,' David said, laughing.

'He will meet someone someday,' Catherine told him. 'By the way, I think you should prepare yourself. I have a feeling my mum is inviting everyone in Surrey.'

'Oh, well, it's understandable since you're her only daughter.'

'I hope you will still feel the same way on Saturday. I was thinking of inviting Sally. What do you think?'

David hesitated. He wasn't sure what she wanted him to say.

She was the only one who could make that decision. No one would claim to know how she felt about Sally.

'If you're sure you want her there?' he said.

'I love you, David,' Catherine said softly.

'I love you, too.'

David sat staring at the phone long after their conversation had ended. The house seemed so big and lonely. Memories of their times together made him want her there with him. It was home to him. He loved the peace and calmness he felt whenever he came back. It was the one place he hoped they would live, with their children and grandchildren. They had not discussed it, but he knew she loved the house just as much as he did.

It was only three days since he'd last seen her and yet it felt like forever. He was counting the days to Friday when he would be going back to London. He had not done any work or visited any of his friends; all he could think about was Catherine. It pained him greatly to think she was alone right where Brooke could reach her and put pressure on her about the baby.

Those were fears he wanted to address with her. No matter how much he wanted the child to be his, he knew deep down that he would always be looking over his shoulder to see if Brooke was watching. Maybe Catherine was right after all; they needed to tell him at some point, but when was it a good time, he wondered. Gabrielle had also told Natalie about the baby and he told his elder sister that he didn't want to talk about it, even though she kept nagging him about adopting the baby as soon as he was born. He could tell she was just as worried as he was that Brooke would show up one day and claim the child.

He switched off his mobile phone and shut himself in his office. There was so much work on his desk that he didn't know where to start.

For several hours, he shut himself off from any thoughts of his fiancée and went through everything on his desk. He had dozens of messages. He deleted all the ones he didn't want and worked through the rest.

Chapter Twenty-Four

Sally stood still in the hallway holding on to the phone; she felt her heart beating so fast she was worried it might pop out of her blouse.

'Are you okay?' she heard Joyce ask, her voice sounding faint as if she was far away. 'You look like you've just seen a ghost.'

'I did,' she said, dropping heavily into the nearest chair. 'You won't believe who that was,' she stammered, catching her breath.

Joyce looked at her, her mind already racing to figure out who had died this time. It was not like her cousin to be lost for words.

'What is it?' she asked.

'That was Catherine,' Sally said.

Joyce sighed heavily and sat back on the sofa.

'I see. Is she okay?' she asked.

'I don't know. She just invited us to her engagement party.'

'That's nice of her,' Joyce said, surprised. 'And what did you say?'

'I told her I'd call her back. She sounded normal, even friendly, and I'm just shocked. I really wasn't expecting to be invited.'

'Well, maybe she has forgiven you. I don't think she is the kind of girl to hold grudges. Besides, she's giving you a second chance, and if you want to start afresh, this is your opportunity,' Joyce said, her tone serious.

'Do you want to go?' Sally asked her cousin.

'Of- course. I wouldn't miss it for the world, and you should think hard before declining. I don't think we're going to get any more invitations and besides, I want to meet this American, who's captured her heart.'

Sally stood up and paced around the room. She wondered if she should call Brooke and ask him if he was going. She wanted to go but was afraid of the reception she might get from Catherine's mother and her friends.

Thinking about it, she was still quite bitter. They had portrayed her as a woman who stole her best friend's man, even though Catherine was with someone else. Nothing was said of Brooke's infidelity. Well, I can't change the past, she told herself, walking around the room.

'You're making me tense just watching you,' Joyce said suddenly. 'Why don't you sit down? You don't have to go if it's causing you so much stress.'

'I can't sit down,' Sally said. 'Why is she being so nice to me?'

Joyce shook her head, stood up and pushed her down on the sofa.

'What's wrong with you?' Joyce asked. 'Are you going to eliminate everyone from your life? What Catherine is doing takes a lot of courage, and it's not the time for you to be thinking about yourself. She obviously wants you there; otherwise, she wouldn't have asked you. If you carry on like this, you'll end up a lonely old woman. Since you're the one who did her wrong, anyone else would be grateful to be invited. While we are on the subject of making up, can you tell me what's going on between you and your mum?'

At the mention of her mother, Sally felt herself getting angry. No one in the family knew what had happened between her and her mother, and she didn't like to be reminded. Not wanting to say anything she would regret later, she headed for the door, leaving Joyce looking after her.

It was five o'clock by the time Kim and Catherine got back home. It was Thursday, and they were rushed for time. She rang her mum again to ask her if she needed help.

'You just worry about what you're going to wear,' her mum told her.

Cora was at the flat getting it ready for David's family and Kim had taken the time off from work to be with her.

Looking at her friend now, Catherine wondered which one of them was the more nervous. The last few hours had been surreal for both of them. They had walked into every designer and department shop in Knightsbridge trying any interesting items they found. Catherine wanted to look her best, and she was out to spend.

'What do you think?' she asked Kim, turning round.

'Mmm, not sure, it's not really your color Try this one,' her friend said, giving her a long white dress.

'What do you mean, it's not me?' Catherine asked, ignoring the white dress.

'Because I know you don't like red.'

'Well, you could be right,' she said, laughing.

After trying on, at least, five dresses, they moved on to another shop.

They talked, laughed and tried on so many clothes that by the time they finished shopping, they could hardly walk from exhaustion.

'Did I tell you I asked Sally to come?' Catherine said as soon as they had settled into the taxi.

'Why?' Kim asked. She stopped in her tracks and faced her.

'I don't know. I guess I just feel that it's time to move on.'

'You are too good for that girl. I hope you've told your mum because I know she won't be too pleased to see her there.'

'I'll call her tonight; you will try to get on with her, won't you? I don't think she knows most of the people coming, and I'll be too busy.'

'I can't promise, but I'll try. I just cannot believe you asked her. Whatever possessed you? I hope she realizes just what a friend you've been to her.'

In the flat, Catherine listened to her phone messages. There was a message from Sally telling her she was coming, together with her cousin.

Her mother wanted to know what time David and his family were getting in. Catherine rang her straight back to give her the details.

'How are you feeling?' Kim asked her.

'Tired, hungry and fat. No! I'll rephrase that. I'm perfectly happy. I still can't believe I'm doing this when just two months ago I could have lost him. Sometimes I look at myself in the mirror and think it's a crime to feel this way about another human being. I love him so much and right now I cannot imagine my life without him in it.'

'Wow, you said it, girl. I'm really happy for both of you; you deserve this.'

'Thank you. I got a letter from Melissa,' Catherine said, changing the subject.

'How is she doing?' Kim asked, interested.

'Despite the awfulness of what she's gone through, I think she's learning to put the past behind her. I'm told she's goes to other schools with the sisters to talk to students about child abuse and the importance of education. I'm proud of her,' Catherine said, her face filled with happiness.

'Have you decided where you're going to live once you get married?' Kim asked.

'Well, his house is nice, and I would love to live there. We haven't discussed it in detail, but I know he'll probably want that, too.'

'That's good because there's something I have been dreading telling you. Jason and I will be moving back to the States next year. He's been offered a job, and I was thinking maybe it would be time for me to be close to my parents. Now that I know you'll be in America, I don't feel so bad because I want to be there when the baby is born.'

'Oh, Kim, that's great!' Catherine said, giving her a hug. You must be so happy. I probably won't move till after the baby is born, but hey, you don't have to feel bad about my situation. I will be fine. David will be here, and so will mum and dad.'

'I have a feeling yours won't be the only wedding next year.' Kim laughed. 'I spoke to Tapiwe yesterday, and she's smitten with Richard.'

'I know,' Catherine said. 'Richard is certainly a happy man. Which reminds me, I've ordered some takeaway; it should be here shortly.'

'I guess I can't ask how the cooking lessons are going, then?' Kim said, jokingly.

Catherine grinned. 'Guess not. I'm just lucky David can cook. Otherwise, we would live on takeaways.'

'Well, I don't really think it would get to that, but it would be nice for you to learn a few tricks to pass on to your children,' Kim said.

'Have you been speaking to mum?' Catherine asked. Her cooking was a joke among her family and friends; they found it amusing that she couldn't even cook rice.

She had made an effort to learn when she visited her grandparents in the States, but after a few attempts and with her grandfather's encouragement, she ended up spending more time with him and her brother playing cards.

'So how are things between you and Jason?' she asked, changing the subject.

'Oh, girl, for someone who never wanted to get married, I must say I am enjoying it. He's really good, and we have become great friends. Who can believe that we're both going to be married women?'

183

As if thinking along the same lines about the past, they looked at each other and burst out laughing.

Her doorbell rang just then, and she went to answer it, still laughing and with tears streaming down her cheeks.

She composed herself before opening the door for Richard and Tapiwe. Dressed up in black, they looked the perfect couple.

Chapter Twenty-Five

Catherine impetuously moved into David's arms, throwing her long legs around him and hugging him tightly.

'I've been meaning to do that all day,' she said between kisses.

All the worries about the party and Brooke were far from her mind as she felt his body mould to hers. This is where I belong, she thought.

'I missed you,' he said, returning her kisses.

At last, they were alone. They had spent the afternoon together with both their families. Her mother and Cora had cooked a huge meal for them and after dinner, they all sat together and chatted. Her mother had taken every chance to show them her baby pictures, which left her blushing with embarrassment.

'Why didn't you tell me your brother was so handsome?' she asked David teasingly, sitting down on the bed.

'You don't fancy him, do you?' David said, laughing.

'No, but he's beautiful. So well-mannered too.

'Oh no, you don't! There is no going back. You're stuck with me I'm afraid.'

She threw a pillow at him, and he closed the gap between them and held her.

'How is he?' he asked, touching her belly.

'He could be she, you know,' Catherine said, giving him a

push. 'She's been fine this last week. I think I was just suffering from the heat in Zambia.'

'Still want to wait until she's born?' he asked.

Saying nothing, she turned her face to kiss him.

'You haven't answered my question,' he said, looking deeply into her eyes.

'Yes, I did. I told you with my lips that I love you, married or not. I want to be able to fit into my wedding dress when I walk down the aisle. I want to feel beautiful and look beautiful for you and for me, too,' she said.

'You will always look beautiful to me, pregnant or not,' he told her.

The next morning, Catherine stood still in the doorway looking at Brooke in disbelief. He was the last person she had expected to see.

'What do you want, Brooke?' She asked him, her foot stuck firmly in the door. David was still sleeping, and she didn't want him to know what was happening.

'I thought maybe we could talk.'

'And I'm sure you have never heard of a phone,' she said.

'Well, I did leave a message, but you didn't call me back.'

'Oh, so you thought you could just buzz in here at this time of the morning. You wait here,' she told him, angrily closing the door. She made a mental note to speak to security again for opening the gate for him. She wondered for a moment if he was renting a property in the building and blanked the thought from her mind. She walked through to the bedroom and was just about to pick up a jumper when she felt a hand on her shoulder.

'Good morning,' David said sleepily.

'What are doing up so early?' she asked, turning to face him.

'Are you all right?' he asked, ignoring her question.

'Yes,' Catherine said, kissing him. 'Why do you ask?'

'You just seem so tense. You're not having second thoughts, are you?'

'No, don't be silly. Probably just need to sleep again.' 'Why don't we do that, then?' he said, pulling her towards him.

'I can't,' Catherine said. 'Brooke is here.'

'At this hour?' His face fell.

'Stay here, I will talk to him,' He said firmly.

'I can handle Brooke; I will come and get you if he tries anything.'

'You're joking, aren't you, the man is stalking you, and yet you don't seem bothered, I can't put up with it anymore. I want him out of our lives and if you won't do it. I will.'

'David, I'm only talking to him because of the baby, I don't want him coming between us, I want him gone too, but I can't avoid him forever. Let me talk to him just this once.'

'I've watched you going to pieces over this guy, and I really can't understand why you can't report him to the cops.'

Catherine held on to the dressing table as she felt a sharp pain kick through her body.

David rushed to her side. 'Are you OK?' he asked.

'Yes, I think it was just the baby making her presence known.'

David wasn't convinced she was okay. Her body was too tense.

'I'm not letting you speak to him in this state; he can come back later.'

'David, Please. I need to do this. Her voice wavered, but she recovered and tried again. 'I think it's best he hears it from me. There is no point in dragging it out; he's only going to make it worse for us.'

'Sometimes I wonder just what kind of hold the man has over you,' he said his voice dark.

'Let's not get into a fight, do you think this is easy for me. I'm caught between the two of you, and I never asked for this to happen to me.'

'Do you blame me, he raped you, and he is obsessed with you, and yet you're blind to all his faults.'

For a long time, she just stared at him. She knew he was hurting and struggling to come to terms with her pregnancy, but she couldn't help him, he needed to make that decision himself. 'I have to go; we'll continue with this conversation when I get back.'

She gave his hand a little squeeze as she moved away from the bed. 'I won't be long, I promise.'

'Are you going to tell him?' he asked, his heart beating fast. It wasn't that he hadn't been expecting this to happen, but he wished it was any other day, not after their engagement when all he wanted was to see her happy. Even though he had never sat down to chat with Brooke, he didn't like the man, and this proved all his theories about him.

Catherine paused before answering.

'I can't help feeling he knows, and that's why he is here,' she said. 'Whatever happens, nothing will change between us. You and I are going to raise this child together, and I won't let Brooke or anyone else come between us.'

Anger and pain ran through her as she walked away from the bedroom. This was supposed to be one of the happiest days of her life, and he was spoiling it. She wondered if he knew about the party and Sally came into her mind. 'No!' she cried out. She couldn't have. But then she wouldn't put it past her; anything was possible.

Brooke's heart beat faster as he watched her walk towards his car. He ached to run to her, to hold her in his arms and feel her body close to him but her expression wasn't one to encourage him and for a moment he felt he had made a big mistake.

'I can't stay long.' she said, sitting down on the bench. 'David is upstairs, and we're expected somewhere soon.'

At the mention of David's name, Brooke felt a wave of jealousy run through him.

'This won't take long,' he said, trying to sound casual.

The lakeside was quiet. Even the ducks had disappeared. She was grateful for the peace and quiet and wished he would say whatever he wanted so she could sit there by herself for a moment before going back to the flat.

'I want to know if the baby is mine,' he said abruptly.

'Brooke! Why are you doing this? We have discussed all this before, and I told you I'd tell you once I know.'

'I know what you said,' Brooke answered. 'But you can understand where I'm coming from. The uncertainty is driving me crazy.'

Catherine sighed.

'What difference is it going to make if you know now or later? David and I are very happy now, and I don't want you having any ideas about me and the future. Things are not going to change whether the baby is yours or not. Besides, I don't want to be reminded of the past.'

'Well, if that's how you feel, then why can't you just tell me the truth? You can't honestly tell me you don't know who the father is to this day?' Brooke said, his eyes not leaving her face.

'If you really must know, then yes, the baby is yours. But as I said, I don't want you to cause any problems for David and me. I also want you to promise that you won't tell anyone till the baby is born. I mean it, Brooke. Not a word to anyone, including your family, otherwise I'm going to tell them what really happened.'

'Oh my God,' he murmured, getting off the bench. 'I can't believe this. I am going to be a dad.'

Watching him pacing about, she wished she could take the smug look off his face. She hadn't meant to tell him, not like this anyway. She wondered if anything else she said had registered in his head.

'Brooke,' she said, 'you know that this doesn't change anything between us, don't you? I'm getting married to David, and when the baby is born, we can work something out. I hope from now on you're going to leave me alone.'

She wished David was with her.

He continued to stare at her as if trying to make sense of what she was saying.

'You can't mean that?' she heard him say. 'You're carrying my child, and you want me to pretend nothing has changed? You know as well as I do that a child needs both its parents. David may understand now, but how do you know he's going to stand by you when the baby is born? Can't you, at least, give us a chance to work things out? I love you; I never stopped loving you, if you give me another chance I promise I to spend the rest of my life making up for the past.'

Catherine was getting angry. She wasn't in the least surprised that he could come out with such nonsense. She was used to him by now, always wanting to manipulate things to suit himself. She still couldn't understand what had happened to the kind, sweet loving man she had fallen in love with.

'I'm sorry, Brooke,' she said, 'I don't mean to be rude, but I think you should leave and please don't come back here again.'

'Catherine!' he said, his voice hoarse. 'I didn't mean to upset you, but you know how I feel about you. I know we can be happy together if you gave us a chance and our baby would have parents who will love him.'

'I don't love you, Brooke,' she said, looking straight at him. 'Whatever feelings I had for you ended the minute you forced yourself on me. Any normal person would try and understand and distance themselves. I cannot change who you are, and it's best if you stay away from me from now on. My future doesn't include you, and I wish you could just accept it and move on. I won't have you using this baby for your own selfish needs.'

'Catherine—' he said again, moving closer to her.

'You heard what the lady said,' a voice cut in.

David stood there, glaring at Brooke.

'Your mum is on the phone,' he told Catherine.

'Brooke was just leaving,' she said, moving towards him.

'If you don't mind, I want to speak to him in private,' David said, his eyes still on Brooke.

She hesitated, wondering whether it was a good idea to leave them alone, but from the expression on David's face she knew it wasn't the time to start arguing with him.

'I'll be back shortly,' she said, casting a warning look at both men. She left, her heart beating faster. Even though Brooke looked as if he didn't care, Catherine knew he didn't want to talk to David. It was the first time they had met face to face, and it worried her.

David waited until he couldn't see her anymore and then addressed Brooke.

'What do you think you're doing?' he asked him angrily.

'Haven't, you caused her enough pain already?'

'I don't think this is any of your business,' Brooke began. 'Catherine and I were discussing the future of our child if you must know, and we were getting on just fine until you came along. Are you worried she may decide to come back to me?' He grinned.

David ignored the remark. 'Listen to me, Brooke. I know that she's carrying your child and that you forced yourself on her. You're lucky you're not in prison. That's because she has a good heart and if I were you, I wouldn't push my luck. Leave her alone, or else you'll have me to answer to.'

Brooke decided against chasing after him as he walked away, but he was fuming as he walked to his car. He wasn't used to people getting the better of him. He vowed to get his own back on David.

Catherine stared at the phone. Her mum was not on the phone, of course, he had just made it up to get her away from Brooke, and this is one time she was grateful. She rang her mum, and the two of them chatted while she anxiously looked towards the door. After talking to her mother, Catherine put the phone down and sat heavily on the chair. Apparently, everything was going on perfectly. She wished she could feel that way, too. She hated to think what was happening between David and Brooke. She knew deep in her heart that Brooke would never leave them alone. He had suddenly left a dark cloud on her day, and there was no going back. She had to tell her friends about the baby before he did.

The flat was silent as she walked around the bedroom putting David's clothes into the wardrobe. She had never seen him that angry before, and it frightened her to think that Brooke could have that effect on him. She suddenly felt panic at the thought of him spoiling her relationship with David.

She had wanted so much for this day to be a day filled with happy memories for her and David. A day filled with love and their commitment to each other. She loved him with such a longing that sometimes it scared her to think of life without him.

She didn't have to wait long for David. She went to meet him as soon as she heard the door open.

'Are you okay?' she asked.

He took her in his arms and kissed her softly on the mouth. She held on to him and tried to erase all memories of the last hour.

'I love you, Catherine,' she heard him say softly in her ear.

'I love you, too,' she said, gently pulling his mouth to hers.

'About Brooke—' he began, but she silenced him by placing her finger on his mouth.

'Can we not talk about him today? I'm sorry that I opened the door to him, but I really want us not to discuss him for the rest of the day and concentrate on us.'

'If you're sure,' David said. He knew she must be hurting, even though she was putting on a front for him. He wanted to reassure her if she was having any doubts that he still loved her. Nothing Brooke said could change anything. In fact, he was happy that the truth was out. At least now they could deal with it before things got complicated.

'I'm sorry for lying about the phone call; I just couldn't stand waiting for you anymore.'

'I'm glad you showed up, anyway I rang her to get an update.'

'What did she say?' he asked, sounding brighter.

'She just wanted to let us know that everything is fine.

She sounds very happy. Apparently, everything is going as planned. I think she's enjoying having a full house again. Kim and Tapiwe are there already. I can't believe they went this early. So all we have to do is show up.'

'How did I get so lucky?' David said staring at her adoringly.

'Luck has nothing to do with it,' Catherine answered smiling.

Chapter Twenty-Six

Sally was woken from her dreams by the loud banging on her door. Pushing her bedcovers away, she swung from the bed and opened the door.

'Do you have to bang on that door so loudly?' she complained.

'Hey! Don't take that tone with me. If you told your boyfriend to stop calling here, I would still be in bed. He's on the phone right now, and he says it's urgent.'

'Who are you talking about?' Sally yawned. After all the dancing and drinking last night she wasn't ready for this. She had only managed to drag herself to bed at six and couldn't remember giving her number to anyone.

She tried to push past Joyce. 'Now you've got me, I might as well have some coffee,' she said.

'I don't think that Brooke can be discouraged so easily.

You talk to him and tell him not to call this early again. Some of us work night shift, you know.'

Sally walked to the phone like a zombie. She wasn't in the mood to talk to Brooke after their last conversation.

'Hello,' she said.

'Are you okay?' he asked.

'Yes, I'm fine. Can I call you later? I'm still half asleep.'

Brooke hesitated. 'Just wanted to know if we can meet up later?' he asked her.

Sally looked at her watch. It was just after nine, and she was due to at Catherine's engagement party at five.

'Can't do it today,' she said.

'Call me later, then,' he told her, his tone surly.

Sally went back to bed, but all her problems came piling in on her and she couldn't sleep.

'I wish I'd kept those damn sleeping tablets,' she muttered.

She had been taking them for years until her doctor warned her she was turning into an addict. He'd helped her to stop taking them, and she had been fine for a while until she moved out of Brooke's house. It was as if suddenly she was caught up in the past. She could see her stepfather now walking towards her. His rough hands grabbing her.

Her mother had just kissed her goodbye when the door slowly creaked open again. Huge and tall, he stood there, his frame taking up space in her tiny room. Frightened, she covered her face with her bedcover, her little heart beating as if it was going to pop out.

'No! No!' she screamed, kicking her legs.

'Sally, wake up!' a voice shouted in the distance.

'Sally, wake up!' The voice said again. It wasn't her mother's voice, and she shut her mind to it. She felt someone shaking her and yet she couldn't open her eyes, which felt raw and itchy. Floating away, she felt tears streaming down her cheeks. Then she woke and stared straight into Joyce's big brown eyes.

'Are you all right?' Joyce asked.

'No, not really. What happened and what are you doing here?'

Joyce sat on the bed and put her arms around her.

'I heard you screaming, so I came running, thinking someone was attacking you, but I think you were having another nightmare.'

Sally sat still, numb to any emotion. She remembered now what had made her scream. Terror overwhelmed her, and she wondered if she had said anything in her sleep.

'Want to talk about it?' Joyce said. 'This isn't the first time, you know. I wanted to say something earlier, but I thought you'd tell me when you were ready.'

'It was nothing,' Sally said, lowering her gaze. 'Just a bad dream, that's all.'

Joyce didn't believe her. There had been a terror in her cousin's eyes. The whole episode disturbed her, but she knew there was no point in pursuing the subject.

'I'll wake you up at two, so try and get some sleep.' She moved to leave the room.

'Joyce,' Sally said, stopping her in her tracks.

'Yes?'

'Thank you.' Sally gave a little smile. She was so tired of the nightmares. She wished for once she could avoid thinking of him, but he was always there, laughing at her, cursing her.

The driver of the stretch limousine greeted them and opened the door for them. Her father had insisted they travelled in style, and this was his present.

'Still want to do this?' David asked, sitting very close to her.

'Yes, Mr Alexander! Nothing is going to stop me, and I have a feeling it's going to be a perfect day.'

He smiled and took her hand in his. She was right; it was going to be a perfect day, and his whole family were there to witness it. He wished his parents were there, too, but, wherever they were, he felt their presence there with him.

'I love you, Catherine,' he said, 'and I'm going to make sure you're the happiest woman on earth.'

Catherine shivered, hoping there would be no repeat of the morning's incident.

As they approached the house, she was shocked to see so many cars, and people she hardly spoke to, all of them eager to find out who was invited and what they were wearing.

She had hoped this occasion would be low key, just family and close friends. Now there was no chance of that. As much she wanted them gone, there was nothing she could do about it.

'I'm sorry,' she said to David, who was just as surprised as she was to see so many people.

'It's not your fault. We'll just have to give them what they want.' He kissed her passionately, triggering a storm of flash photography.

Outside the hotel, her friends and work colleagues were walking around all dressed up in their designer clothes and expensive jewel. She told the driver to take them through the back entrance, and they ran for the door, laughing. The rest of the day was a blur to her. All she could remember was her mum and dad making speeches, making everyone laugh, and David holding her hand.

Chapter Twenty-Seven

Sally's heart felt heavy as she waited. The place was getting crowded, and she asked herself again what she was doing there. She had not spoken to Catherine since the party, but after talking to her for a few minutes, she felt as if they could rebuild the bridges between them as Joyce put it. She looked at her watch again and suppressed a heavy sigh as she went to order another drink. It was just like him to keep her waiting. It seemed to her that ever since she had known him, she was always the one who sat around waiting. Sometimes she felt like a fool for letting him have so much power over her. There was nothing she wouldn't do for him; even now that she knew he wanted Catherine, she couldn't help but dream and hope that one day he would realise she loved him much more than Catherine would ever do.

'Sorry, I'm late.' She heard a voice right behind her.

Turning around, she glared up at him, and he sat down before she could say anything.

Not for a moment did she think he meant what he said, at least, not literally. She had heard it all before, and now she wished she was the one who had arrived late and let him sweat for a change.

'Do you want to go somewhere else or stay here?' he asked.

'This is fine,' she said.

'What is so urgent that we had to meet today?' she asked him, once he'd ordered his drink.

'David is in London,' he said, looking around, 'and I thought maybe we could discuss the plan.'

She shivered as if cold water had been thrown over her.

'Are you sure this is the only way?' she asked.

'We've been through this, Sally. Don't tell me you're backing out now?'

'I'm not, just wanted to be sure. Things could go wrong, you know. I want us to think about this before committing ourselves because once it's done, there'll be no going back.'

'Of-course not. I'm not interested in going back. I'll be happily married to Catherine, and you'll have your big house in Surrey, just like you've always wanted.'

'It seems like you have everything planned out, haven't you?' She said, glancing at him. He seemed relaxed and at ease, showing no sign of tension. He was in control, so mysterious and intimidating. She wondered just how many other young women had fallen for his charm.

Catherine was a lucky girl, she thought. To have such a man love her with such passion was like a dream to her. Maybe bringing them together would be a way of paying for the damage I've caused between us, she told herself bitterly, pushing away any thought of David.

'Do you want something to eat?' he said.

She shrugged. 'I don't mind, you decide.'

He looked around, and a waiter came rushing almost immediately. It never failed to amaze her how waiters always leaped instantly to do his bidding.

She couldn't help wondering why a man who could have anyone he wanted was so stuck on a woman who was engaged to another man. Sometimes she wondered if he had ever cared for her at all or just used her to feel close to Catherine. Bitter resentment towards Catherine swelled in her.

'What if the child is David's child?' she asked him, her eyes not leaving his for a moment.

'It's not his child,' he said. 'I saw them on Saturday, and she admitted it.'

'You mean you went there on the day she was getting her engaged?' she asked, surprised.

'It hadn't been my intention, but I guess I couldn't help myself and can you believe, he stood there by the lake telling me what a wonderful life he was going to have with Catherine and my child? I don't know what she sees in the man. He certainly has no morals to think he can just take away another man's child.'

It was almost funny. She didn't know whether to laugh or say something to him. David was getting under his skin and Sally couldn't help but be amused. It made her feel good to see him suffer as she had from the pain he had caused her.

'I've got to give it to you, Brooke. You don't give up easily, do you? You really believe the three of you are going to live happily ever after? I wish I had your faith and determination.'

'This isn't funny, you know,' he hissed at her, draining his glass. 'She's the only girl I've ever loved, and I'm damned if am going to let her go without a fight.'

'So when do you want me?' she asked.

The thought of her part in the plan made her feel bad, as though someone had taken a knife and stabbed her in the stomach. She fought hard to remain calm.

'I'll call you tomorrow once I find out how long he's staying.'

'How come you know so much about his travels?' she asked, troubled.

'I have my sources and the less you know, the better,' he told her.

It was passed midnight by the time they left the west-end.

'Do you want a lift home?' he asked, helping her put on her coat.

'No!' she said firmly. 'I think I'll take a cab.'

He walked with her to get a taxi, and he kissed her goodnight, promising to call her following day.

It was amazing how their relationship had changed. She didn't feel as awkward around him as she had been when they had just split up.

Despite all the heartache Brooke had caused her, in a way it had helped her grow into a woman. She didn't even want to admit it, even to herself, that he had changed her way of thinking. Men and marriage weren't her priority. He had made her want to prove to him that she wasn't just a pretty face, that she could do as well as any other young woman. She wanted to work and make something of herself, like Catherine. Yes, to have it all, like Catherine did.

She wandered around Leicester Square looking at people singing and walking. There was a group of young men all dressed in white dancing vigorously as if they didn't have a care in the world. They reminded her of those birds at home on the farm, flying wherever they wanted to go. She wished she could fly away to a place where no one knew her name or her past.

London had been an escape for her. For a while she had escaped from the past, the ghosts and the painful memories, and yet now she could see his face clearly, laughing, and his massive body crashing into her.

People rushed back and forth, bumping into her. She thought she could have some peace, but this wasn't the place; there was no difference between night and day. People were queuing up to watch movies and get into night clubs. She watched couples holding hands and quickly walked away. When she got fed up, she walked all the way to Trafalgar Square and took a night bus home. The flat was quiet, and she was glad to be alone. Ever since the engagement party, she had been avoiding her cousin. She wished she could tell Joyce about her dreams and fears, but it wasn't something she was comfortable discussing. No one had wanted to listen when she had cried out for help, and she didn't want to wake up any sleeping dogs. No one but her mum knew what her stepfather had done to her, even though she never admitted it ever happened. She had sat her down and told her not to go around telling tales.

'Your father wouldn't do a thing like that,' her mother had said.

But he wasn't her father, and he reminded her of that fact every opportunity he got.

For almost a year, she had suffered. All the children around the farm were older than she was and her grandparents lived far away. It was only when she had her first period and become pregnant that her mother had sent her away to live with some distant cousins. After almost a year, she went to live with her grandparents and had no recollection of the last year, apart from the fact that she had been told she had given birth, and the child had died. She was not given the opportunity even to see the child, and she didn't know if it was a girl or boy. Her mother never talked about it, and she was glad not be reminded.

She pulled her suitcase from the top of the wardrobe. It was full of old clothes and books. There were some photo albums from the time when was she ten and she looked at those first. Both her grandparents stood beside her, smiling. They were the happiest moments of her childhood she could remember. Her grandfather was retired, and he spent time showing her around the farm. It was during one of these occasions that she had met Catherine. She hadn't gone back to live with her mother until she went to boarding school.

To this day, she couldn't help feeling that her grandparents knew what had happened because they never pushed her to develop any relationship with her mother and, as for her real father, no one knew whether he was alive or dead.

She knew little about her stepsisters or brothers; they never showed any interest in her, and she had given up trying long ago. To most people she was her grandparent's child and she never denied it. She was in turmoil over something she could not change or wipe away from her life; the past haunted her wherever she went.

'Oh, Catherine. How could I have done this to us? Why didn't I trust you enough to tell you about the past?' she said, sniffling, her eyes red and her face puffy.

She dragged at the cover and everything went crashing to the floor.

Chapter Twenty-Eight

With Catherine surrounded by David and his family outside Richard's house, Brooke was able to watch her unseen.

Seeing her sitting between David and Richard, Brooke's heart was almost exploding with the need to go to her and beg her to give them another chance, for the baby's sake.

She looked so radiant, beautiful and happy that all he could do was let his eyes follow her wherever she went. He had not been invited to the party, but he had assured his brother he wouldn't cause a scene. Besides, he was Tapiwe's friend as well, even though he couldn't help noticing how she was avoiding him. What about the child, he asked himself? Not finding the answer, he put on his jacket and walked away.

He didn't go far before Kim came running after him.

'Brooke!' she shouted before he could get into his car.

She was the last person he wanted to talk to, but he turned around slowly to face her.

'Hi, Kim.' He smiled at her.

'Can we talk?' she asked.

'Yes, if we must,' Brooke said, locking his car.

She led the way back to the house and went straight to Richard's study, where she knew no one would disturb them.

'Do you want a drink?' she asked him.

'No, thank you,' Brooke said, looking around the room. It was the first time he'd been in it and he was impressed by the paintings on the walls and the books displayed on the bookshelves.

'How have you been?' Kim asked him, sitting down.

'I've been good,' he said, knowing full well she wasn't really interested in his health. 'What do you want to talk about?' He had not forgiven her for interfering in his relationship with Catherine. It was she who had told her about Sally and the other girl he had first cheated with.

He knew deep down she had only done it because she cared for Catherine, but he couldn't help wondering if things could have turned out differently without her.

'I don't mean to tell you how to run your life, but don't you think it's time you stopped harassing Catherine?' she said. 'If you cared for her at all, you would let her be happy. I mean, it's about time you put closure on this, don't you think? She is carrying a child and does not need all this stress.'

Brooke waited calmly before speaking.

'You know something, Kim, you're right. You don't have any business telling me what to do. I've not been harassing her and, for your information, she's carrying my child, and that gives me the right to check up on her. She may be marrying that guy, but she's carrying my child and no one, not even you, can take that away from me. She and I share something precious, a bond that can never be broken and I would appreciate it if you just stay out of it.'

As he finished talking, Kim felt a wave of anger wash over her. She had hoped to talk to him calmly and maybe help him, but now she was totally livid. She wondered what had happened to the kind, funny, charming man she once knew. He looked different, too. She had lost all respect for him the minute she found out he had cheated on Catherine.

She had avoided him even when her friend had given him another chance, but now she couldn't ignore him. He wanted to cause trouble between David and Catherine and someone needed to make him see sense.

'I also know what you did to get her pregnant, and if I were her, you would be in prison. But she has a good heart. It's best not push your luck. She might just change her mind. I really feel sorry for you—' she began to say when she heard Jason's voice in the hallway.

She went to the door and, giving him a meaningful look, slammed the door behind her.

'Where have you been?' Jason asked.

'Just went to look at Richard's new collection,' she said, quickly moving away from the door. She didn't want him to know she had been talking to Brooke. He wasn't one of her husband's favourite people and they were having too much fun to argue.

'It's a great party, isn't it?' she said, putting her hand in his as they walked outside.

They joined as all glasses were raised to toast to the happy couple.

She turned round and kissed her husband. 'I love you,' she told him softly.

'Then you can tell me what you and Brooke were talking about,' he said, poking his finger in her side.

She gasped, taken aback. 'Jason Carrington! Don't tell me you have been following me?'

'Do you blame me? You're a beautiful woman,' he said, smiling.

'Flattery will get you everywhere,' she said, teasing him.

'If you must know, I just wanted to tell him to give those two a break.' She looked towards Catherine and David.

'And there were no kisses?' he said, putting on a mock-severe voice.

'Oh, Jason, shut up,' Kim said, giggling. They went to sit with Gabrielle and Natalie, and they talked about the States. Kelvin had gone back to Japan, and the two women were happy to stay on until the end of the week. From the way they were talking,

Kim knew her friend was going to have a happy life. David's family all adored her.

As for Tapiwe, she was playing the happy lady of the house, going round talking to everyone, meeting Richard's friends. Kim had to laugh at how things were turning out. A year ago, all they had talked about, the three of them, was work and travelling and yet now they were all happily attached to partners. She didn't think it would take long before Richard proposed to Tapiwe.

When David went into the house with Natalie, Richard took Catherine aside, and the two of them took a walk around the garden away from everyone.

'How are things going?' he asked.

Catherine took some time to consider the question. 'I don't know. I feel so happy to be getting married, having this child, and yet I can't help feeling things are going to come crashing down on my head. I saw Brooke last Saturday.

He came to the flat demanding I tell him the truth, and so I did, and now I feel I shouldn't have. I really don't need him stressing me out right now.'

'Have you talked to David about this?' Richard asked. Catherine shook her head.

'Not really. He knows I'm not happy about the situation, but what can he do? We can't change the past. We just have to deal with Brooke and hope for the best.'

'Do you think that's going to work? I mean, waiting for him to make the decision about the baby?' he asked sympathetically. 'The way I look at it; Brooke is still smitten with you. You and David need to sit down with him and tell him exactly how you feel.'

Catherine's heart tightened. 'I know. I had hoped he would go away, fall in love with another girl and we could all live happily ever after. David spoke to him, too, but he's not telling me what they talked about.'

'Talk to him, Catherine,' Richard said. 'You need to sort this out before it's too late. He needs to know you haven't got any feelings for Brooke. He loves you, and I'm sure he's as upset as you are about Brooke's interference in your relationship.'

'Ah, there you are,' they heard David say behind them. 'I was starting to worry when I didn't see you.'

'I'm sorry,' Catherine said, standing up. 'I didn't mean to disappear. Richard and I were just having a chat.'

David smiled. 'Natalie and Gabrielle want to say goodbye to Richard.'

'They're leaving so soon?' Richard asked, surprised. 'Yeah. I guess they want to have an early night, and Miriam is bringing the girls round this evening. It was a great party, though. Thank you for inviting us.'

'You're not leaving, too, are you?'

'I'm afraid so. I need to talk to my assistant, and it won't be much fun for anyone if I call him from here.'

'You don't mind if I go, too, do you?' Catherine asked. It was their last night together and after her talk with Richard, she thought it was a good idea for her and David to spend time on their own.

As the car drew closer to the apartment, she sighed with relief at being back home. Much as she loved her friends, all the dinner parties after the engagement were becoming exhausting. She and David had not had a moment to themselves. She had not even managed to spend time with her aunt or David's family.

Photographers were still hanging around her apartment, trying to get pictures of her and David. They both declined any offers of money for interviews. They were too busy, and Catherine wanted that part of her life to be private. They would print what they wanted without any interviews; gossip was what people craved, and it sold the papers.

She and David sat up that night talking about the baby. When she saw he wasn't going to talk about Brooke, she asked him exactly how he felt.

'He told me he's not going to let you go,' he said eventually.

'What!' She said, shocked. 'He is unbelievable. And you didn't feel the need to share this with me?'

'I just didn't want to upset you,' 'David answered.

'Don't let him destroy us. He can be manipulative, and I really would like you to stay away from him.'

'Anyway, I don't know why we're talking about this. He's the biological father but I will be the real father of the child, and nothing is going to change that.'

David left every early the next day. Catherine didn't know what to do with herself, she was restless and missing having him next to her. She showered, switched off her mobile phone, connected her laptop and got to work.

She went through her emails first. Most of them were reminders of deadlines on projects she was working on, and there were also lots of congratulatory messages. She worked on her project and by the time she switched off her laptop, it was well past midday. She made herself a sandwich and sat down in front of the television with her diary nearby. Tomorrow she was going to the clinic for a check- up, and she was not looking forward to it. At four months pregnant, she wasn't as big as most women would be, even though she felt very fat. She pulled the phone closer to her and rang Kim to confirm if her friend was still coming with her.

'Wouldn't you want to know if it's a girl or boy?' Kim asked.

'No. Please don't put ideas into my head.' She had made up her mind about that.

'I thought not, but couldn't help wondering,' Kim said, laughing. 'I guess I'd better put away all the little pink outfits I've been buying.'

'You're just as bad as David. He has a room full of clothes, both blue and pink. Can you believe that?'

Chapter Twenty-Nine

Catherine woke up in high spirits. David was in town for a meeting and, this time, he had decided to stay at the Lanchester. 'So that I can get some work done,' he told her when she complained. He was right, of course. With everything happening, work took a back seat when they were together. They had other things to talk about, and this was a very important meeting for him. Some of his employees were staying at the hotel, too.

They were meeting for dinner and, strangely, she felt like a school-girl on her first date. Even though they spoke every day on the phone and skyped, it wasn't the same as being close to him, touching him and feeling his lips on hers.

He had sent her flowers and a note that read, 'Would you have dinner with me tonight?'

Smelling her roses again, she smiled. He was the most romantic man, and she just loved him to bits. Everything felt so right and for the first time in her life, she knew what it felt like to have a soul mate.

Stepping out of the shower, she reached for her towel and wandered through to the bedroom. She had a whole new wardrobe filled with maternity dresses and comfortable shoes. Her old clothes were all in black bags in the spare room, waiting to be taken to the charity shop on the high street. She always let Cora pick out whatever she wanted before giving them away. Most of them were clothes bought on impulse that she never wore and with the labels still attached. Cora sent some of them to her nieces in the Philippines. She was visiting her homeland after ten years of absence and Catherine wondered whether she should just leave everything for her to take.

Looking around her bedroom now, she knew things would have to change. She couldn't remember exactly when she had made up her mind to live in the States with David, but it did feel right. She would have to sell the flat, and her cottage in the country. She didn't worry much about her shares in the PR company she and Kim had started; things were going very well, and profits were increasing each year.

Her phone rang, and she rushed to pick it up, still singing happily.

'You sound happy,' her mum said as soon as she heard her voice.

'I was just going to call you,' Catherine said. 'I got a bunch of roses from David this morning, and I'm meeting him for dinner. I'm so used to having him here when he's in town that this feels like a date.'

Her mother laughed. 'I'm glad you have someone to make you feel this special. You deserve it.'

'Have you heard from Dad?' she asked.

'I was just on the phone with him. He's coming back tonight,' her mother answered. 'Anyway, I just wanted to know how you got on at the clinic on Monday.'

'It was good. Great, in fact,' Catherine said. 'For a minute, I thought I saw the baby's little legs kicking. I have the scan, so I'll show it to you next time we meet.'

'And the mother? You are well, I presume?'

'Yes, Mum, I'm fine, and I've been eating well.'

'You know you can always come and stay with us,' her mum said.

'Before I forget, I finally managed to persuade your grandma to come. She'll be here next month.'

'Oh, that's good news. I was beginning to worry about her. Maybe she can stay with me,' Catherine said.

She made a note of her grandma's arrival date in her diary and went through to the kitchen.

Her grandma hated living in London, but if her mum talked her into it, she might come round. She also knew how busy her parents were during September and maybe grandma staying with her would be a good solution.

Sally woke up feeling terrible. Guilt suffused her, and she shrank from what her cousin might say if she knew what she was about to do.

This was far more than anything she'd ever done and, much as she wanted to convince herself that she was doing it for Catherine and the baby, Brooke's offer of money and the house played a big part. She didn't want to be poor all her life, and this was an opportunity for her to move forward and bury the past behind her.

Even though she was trying her best to stay calm, she was scared that something was going to go wrong. She couldn't understand how Brooke managed to stay so calm. She didn't ask him any more questions about how he got his information. She decided he was right; she didn't have to know every little detail.

'Who's died?' Joyce said, coming to sit next to her. 'Are you all right?'

'I'm fine,' Sally said, her head tilted towards Joyce.

'It's sunny and bright outside; you are sat here with a long face, and now you want me to believe you're okay?' Joyce persisted.

'Just let me be,' Sally said, rubbing her face. She wished she could talk to someone other than Brooke about Catherine but she couldn't. It was crazy and too appalling to talk about.

'You know you can talk to me about anything,' Joyce said, seeing the confused look on her face.

'Yeah!' Sally answered. 'And thank you.'

Joyce gave a great sigh of exasperation and settled further into the sofa. Something was bothering Sally; it was written all over her face, and she couldn't do anything about it without knowing the cause.

'Did you call your mum?' She asked.

Sally looked up at her again for the tenth time and then cast her eyes to the floor. She did not reply, but still looked unhappy.

'I'll call her tomorrow,' she said.

'What's going on between you two?' Joyce asked, still trying to find out what the trouble was. 'You cannot avoid her forever, you know. She is your mum after all.'

Sally hastened to get off the subject of her mother.

'Why can't you just let it be?' Sally said. 'I'm a big girl now. I don't need her. She gave up those rights a long time ago. I know you all feel I should be grateful to have lived on the farm with grandma and granddad. Yes, I'm grateful, and I was happy there, but she was still my mother. I needed her then, not now.' She stopped talking and fixed her eyes on her nails.

'You don't mean that,' Joyce said, wondering again, what had happened between Sally and her mum? She couldn't imagine what was so terrible that the two of them barely spoke. She had become the go-between for her, delivering messages from her aunt to Sally. They were always the same. 'Tell her to call me,' her aunt told her every time they spoke.

'Just because you and your mum are the best of friends doesn't mean it would be the same for me,' Sally said.

'I'm sorry.' Joyce felt a great sadness come over her. Even though they had not grown up together, she had always known she had a cousin called Sally.

Everyone in the family knew of her because Sally's mum had been sent away to the village to have her, not being married at the time. No one knew the father and no one talked about him. Her

213

aunt met someone else and married when Sally was only three and seven years later she was sent to live on the farm.

'Can we please talk about something else?' Sally said, stretching her legs.

'That is a good idea,' Joyce said, tired of probing. 'I met someone two months ago.' Her eyes shone.

'Oh, Joyce, you're such a dark horse. Two bloody months and you don't say anything to me. Tell me more,' Sally said, getting all excited. It wasn't every day her cousin spoke to her about her relationships. She must like this one for her to talk about him, she thought.

'He's a doctor at the hospital, tall, handsome and dark. He has incredible brown eyes and a lovely smile.'

'Nice!' Sally laughed. 'I want details, not just nice.'

'Yes, nice is all I can say for now,' Joyce said. 'This time, I'm going to take my time. 'We're going to dinner on Friday and, girl, I can't wait. He makes me feel so good about myself, unlike most doctors who think nurses are just there to make their lives easy.'

'I'm happy for you,' Sally said, and she meant it, too. It was about time her cousin started dating again. 'When do I get to meet him, then?' she asked.

'Not just yet. Just want to make sure he's for real. What about you? Are you over Brooke yet?'

'I don't know,' Sally said. 'Some days I'm fine and some days I'm not. I guess if I met someone else today, I would probably forget about him,' she lied. The thought of their meeting loomed once again.

'What about this man?' she said, moving the subject away from Brooke, and Joyce was more than happy to answer.

That afternoon, she sat in a taxi heading towards the West End. She had tiptoed out of the flat, making sure not to wake her cousin.

Her eyes roved across the streets, looking at other young

214

women walking around with huge designer bags. The area was full of tourists admiring Harrods and the other large shops around Knightsbridge. Sighing heavily, she sat back on the seat and relaxed. She wished now that she'd not taken time off from work, it was the only thing keeping her sane.

Chapter Thirty

Sally didn't have to look too far for Brooke. He was at the bar with his back to the doorway. His broad shoulders made him stand out from the other men.

Sally stood still in the doorway watching him. Her heart missed a bit, and she felt her legs giving way. He had that kind of effect on her, and she couldn't help wondering if she was doing all this so that she could be near him. It pained her deeply to know that no matter what she did or said it was never good enough.

He walked towards her as soon as he saw her and she felt her cheeks warming when he circled her in his strong arms.

She quickly put some distance between them, not wanting him to know that she still wanted him desperately.

Brooke quickly glanced around.

'Do you want to sit over there?' He pointed to a table in the corner away from other tables. She followed him to the table, and he pulled a chair out for her, still the gentleman, just as she remembered him.

'What would you like to drink?' he asked, glancing at the menu she was holding.

She almost said water and quickly changed her mind. She needed something strong if she was going to go through with the plan.

'I think I'll have vodka and coke.'

Although she was trying hard to hide it, he could tell she was nervous and anxious.

He had tried to call her a hundred times since his talk with Kim, to tell her to forget everything, but he couldn't do it. He wanted Catherine back in his life. Nothing anyone said registered.

'So how are you going to try and win her back?' she asked, taking another sip of her drink.

'Do you really want to know?' he asked.

'Yes, I do. I don't want to go away thinking my hard work will be for nothing and you never know, I might offer you some advice, seeing as I've known her longer than you.'

Brooke wished to God he could be the man she wanted him to be, to love her as she deserved to be loved, but it was never going to happen, whether Catherine was in the picture or not. They were better off as friends, and he hoped with time she would come to realise it, too.

Though Sally longed to know more, she didn't want to push him. 'I think maybe we should talk about something else,' she said. 'For a start, do you know exactly which room he's staying in and what time she's coming by?'

'Everything is under control,' Brooke told her. 'We have another two hours before he leaves the conference room, so we can go shopping if you like.'

Sally looked at her watch. She didn't really want to stay there that long, 'That's a great idea. I think shopping will do me good,' she told him.

It was while they walked around the shops that he told her about his plan.

She admitted to herself that he was a very resourceful man and the thought of spending a night at the Lanchester was very appealing to her.

For now, she was glad to have left the hotel. They walked around Oxford Circus like a couple and even though he was not holding her hand, she could still feel the heat from his body next to hers. He took her into Selfridges and waited while she tried on different outfits. There was no question about who was paying. He always had money on him and credit cards.

He bought himself some Calvin Klein t-shirts and by the time they started walking back to the hotel, they were holding, at least, four bags between them. They went straight to his room to avoid running into David before time.

Catherine had just put down the phone down after speaking to her grandma when it rang again.

With a sigh of resignation, she picked it up, looking at her wristwatch.

'Hello,' said a young woman's voice at the other end. 'May I speak to Ms Walker, please?' the person said.

'This is she,' Catherine answered.

'Sorry to bother you,' the girl began. 'I'm calling from the Lanchester. Mr Alexander asked me to call you.'

'Is he okay?' she cut in before the girl could go on. It wasn't like him not to call her himself and he also knew how much she hated giving out her house number.

'He's fine,' the girl told her. 'He's going to be in meetings all day, and he wanted to know if you could meet him here at eight.'

'Oh! I see,' Catherine said relaxing. 'That is fine. Thank you for letting me know.' Her mind was unsettled as she went back to the bedroom. Her long black dress lay on the bed. She had spoken to him almost three hours ago and had confirmed seven o'clock was fine for him to pick her up, and now he wanted her to meet him an hour later at the hotel.

She suddenly felt hungry. She had put off having any food after lunch so that she could eat dinner with him, but eight o'clock was too far off, and her stomach was crying out for food. Since becoming pregnant, her appetite had shot up. She was just about to make a sandwich when her buzzer sounded.

'I was just making a sandwich. Do you want one?'
Catherine asked after Kim had taken her coat off.

'Since when did you start eating sandwiches?' Kim asked her, laughing.

It was true that in the past she had to be really hungry to buy a sandwich. She had preferred hot food, like Chinese and Indian.

'I will have a chicken sandwich if you're still offering,'
Kim told her.

'Sorry, but I haven't got any chicken. Do you want something else? I have gone off chicken, and I haven't bought any since David left.'

'Talking about the man how is he?' Kim asked, following her into the kitchen.

'I don't know,' she answered. 'If I didn't know any better I would think he'd brought someone with him, but no, he's not like Brooke, I do trust him.'

'What happened?' Kim asked, alarm bells ringing in her head.

'Oh, just something he did,' Catherine began. 'We arranged to meet for dinner at seven in Chelsea and just before you came, a girl from his hotel called to let me know David had asked her to call me and tell me to meet him at the hotel at eight. He certainly can't be that busy that he couldn't call me himself and then there is this business of him staying at the hotel. Ever since we met, he has always stayed at his apartment or with me whenever he was in London. He did explain that he was working around the clock, and he didn't want to disturb me, but I can't help feeling there something he's not telling me.'

'Catherine,' Kim cut her short. 'Is this really about David? You know how he feels about you, and I'm sure there's a perfectly good reason why he couldn't call you himself.'

'I know,' Catherine said, more cheerfully. 'I guess being pregnancy just makes me paranoid.'

'You sit down. I will make the sandwiches,' Kim said, opening the fridge. 'Can you believe Jason and I only have ten days before we leave for the States? It feels so strange leaving the house. It was our first home together, and I was just beginning to get attached to it. I actually thought we would have children and grow old together in that place.'

Her eyes brimmed, and she laughed. 'Oh, look at me! I was supposed to be cheering you up, and here I am going all tearful over a house.'

'I know how you feel,' Catherine said. 'I keep changing my mind about selling this place. This is the first place I bought with my own money. You remember the parties and the friends that have passed through here? But hey, life goes on; we will still have our memories.'

'So, you're serious about selling it, then?' Kim asked her, surprised. She knew just how much Catherine loved the place.

'Yeah. I think I have made up my mind. I will probably keep the cottage; Grandma can always live there whenever she's in town.'

'How is she doing?' Kim asked.

'She's getting better; it's going to take a while, but my uncles are there with her. She and Grandma Maria had been friends like forever. I spoke to her this afternoon. She's still not sure about coming, even though she told Mum she would. Apparently the crime rate has been rising so high; she is afraid of leaving the workers on the farm by themselves. She told me that my uncle's car was taken at his daughter's nursery school by a gunman. Can you believe, they followed him in daylight and demanded he hands over the keys in front of children, all under five years old? I don't know if there is going to be a future for children growing up today in that country. The worst thing is, no one cares. People see this happening every day, and it has become a way of life. As for the police, they are even worse. I'm told they give those thieves the guns.'

'Huh, that's bad, hey,' Kim said, saddened by what she was hearing. This wasn't just a problem in Zambia; it was happening all over Africa. Children were being used to carry out all sorts of crimes. Education had become so expensive that their parents couldn't afford to send them to school. She remembered all the orphans she had seen in Rwanda.

She and Catherine had been reporting from Rwanda when the civil war was raging. What had happened to all those children? Were they also going to end up on the street? It had been a distressing sight, and things were certainly going to get worse before they got better. The politicians didn't care; they made promises before the elections and, once voted into government, nothing happened, and things only got worse.

'How is Melissa?' she asked.

'She's really good. She's got exams coming up next month, and the sisters tell me she's been working hard. Come with me; I will show you some pictures. And remind me to give you copies of the work I have done so far on the project.'

'Wow, she looks so different,' Kim said, studying the pictures. 'Do you think she still remembers her parents?'

'I've tried to talk to her about them, but I guess it's hard for her to remember them since she was only three when they gave her away. The poor girl has had so much happen to her in her short life that I'm not surprised she wants to forget most of it.'

'Well, that's what I've been working on.' Catherine handed a big brown file to Kim. 'All we need now are the pictures; Brenda promised to send to me next week.'

'You have been busy, haven't you?' Kim said, taking the sheaf of paper out of the file.

'Oh well, it keeps me occupied. I would go crazy doing nothing.'

'If I were you, I would just sit pretty and wait for the baby to come. You can't save the whole world.'

Chapter Thirty-One

David was feeling disorientated by the time he left the meeting. They had been locked in the conference room for almost three hours, and they were far from reaching an agreement.

He thought he was giving them what they wanted by selling his share in the European offices, but his partners didn't see it that way. He was not giving up, though; he had put in too much hard work over the past year.

Looking at his wristwatch, he shook his head. He had hoped to have at least two hours before going to pick up Catherine, and it was almost six o'clock. He was never going to get there on time. He sighed heavily, heading straight for the hotel phone and tried to ring her but her phone was switched off. He rang his assistant, who had left before him, to cancel their meeting. He wasn't in the mood to look at any more figures tonight.

He decided to ring Catherine again. She didn't answer. He left a message for her to get a taxi. Unsettled, he headed towards the bar and froze when he saw Brooke, the last person he wanted to see.

As Brooke got closer, he saw that David was not pleased to see him; his face was hard with anger. This is not going to be easy, he told himself. He wished he knew the man well enough to make him understand how he felt.

'What do you want, Brooke?' David asked, his eyes blazing with fury.

'Well, I thought maybe we could have a chat,' Brooke said.

'You made your feelings very clear the last time we met. Don't think I don't know what your game is. I can tell you now that you're wasting your time. Catherine and I are very happy, and we're getting married. The sooner you get used to that idea the better, because frankly, I haven't got the energy to be arguing with you. We can sit down and talk when the baby is born, but before then, I would appreciate it if you left us alone.'

Brooke could tell that he meant every word. He looked around him.

'Listen; I'm sorry for what I said to you. I know I was in the wrong, and I had no right to speak to you that way. I guess I was just overwhelmed to find out I was going to be a dad. I was hoping we could clear the air and start again for Catherine's sake. I'm sure life would be much easier if we could all get along. Just give me five minutes, that's all I'm asking,' he begged.

David looked at him and quickly glanced at his Rolex watch for the time.

'Five minutes, that's all,' David said tightly, leading the way.

'I will get the drinks. What would you like?' Brooke asked.

'A brandy will be fine,' David told him. He remembered Kim's words about not trusting Brooke but it was too late, and he really wanted to know what the man was up to so he could put Catherine's mind at rest.

It was just as well Catherine had agreed they could live in America when the baby was born. He couldn't imagine himself having cosy chats with Brooke every week. The man was still in love with Catherine, and he was using the pregnancy to get close to her. Well, he wasn't going to make it easy for him.

'David.' Someone was calling his name. He looked up and stared straight into his assistant's eyes.

223

'Are you OK?' Jeff asked.

'Sorry,' David said, standing up. 'I was miles away. Is everything okay?'

'Yes, we're just going to have a tour of the city and then have dinner. Are you sure you and Catherine won't change your minds and join us?'

'No, you guys go ahead. I think we will just have a quiet night.'

Brooke came back with the drinks.

'What do you want to talk about?' David asked him as soon as he sat down.

'I thought we could come to some kind of agreement about the baby. I know this isn't the time or the place, but I do feel the earlier we know what's expected of all of us, the better. For example, where do you and Catherine plan to live when the baby is born? What names have you chosen, and all that? I want to feel involved in the child's life as much as you and Catherine. I told her I won't be telling anyone else, including my family, about the baby until it's born and I'm keeping that promise. I don't think any of us wants to deal with all the gossip and innuendo if the truth were to come out.'

For a second Brooke thought David was going to hit him. He drew back.

'Just who the hell do you think you are coming here and demanding answers? For a minute there, I thought you were genuinely sorry. I almost fell for your bullshit, but now I realise this isn't about Catherine's happiness or the baby. It's about you and this obsession you have with her. You think you will be hurting Catherine or me if you go to the press. You will be the one to lose because Catherine would never let you near the child and everyone will know you for who you re, a rapist and a stalker.' He took another sip of his drink. Suddenly he felt incredibly weary.

'I'm sorry, I suppose I didn't phrase that well. I don't mean to cause any trouble. Just hear me out.'

'I think you'd better go,' David said.

Brooke almost smiled when he saw David's eyelids drop.

'I'm sorry,' he said. 'Very sorry,' he said again, looking across to the bar for any sign of Sally.

He didn't have to wait long. She moved forward and went towards the lift. She had spent the last hour going through everything Brooke had told her to do.

As the clock ticked, she felt her defences weakening. She drunk more alcohol and tried to convince herself that she was doing it for the baby.

Her mobile was switched off, and she had spent an hour soaking herself in the big bath while Brooke had gone out to make his calls.

It wasn't every day she came to a posh hotel, and she wanted to make sure she made the best of it, despite what she was doing. Whether it was a good idea or not, she didn't think much about it; she blanked Catherine from her mind. All the alcohol she had consumed that evening made her feel she was on top of the world. I wonder if he's going to make love to me tonight for the last time, she asked herself as she pushed the button in the elevator.

A young girl and her mother were chatting away in the lift. They looked so happy together. It made her think of her mother. She realised she knew next to nothing about her or her stepsisters and brothers. They had become strangers to her. Her grandparents had shown her more love and affection than her own mother ever did and to this day, she still regarded them as her parents.

'It wasn't your fault,' she remembered her grandma telling her when she was little. 'It's that man she married. I told her even before he proposed that he came from bad blood. His whole family is full of people who are up to all sorts of things that I can't mention to you, but you know how stubborn she is, just like her father, she wouldn't listen to me. She thought she was doing it for you so that you could have a father, but look what kind of a father he turned out to be. You're better off with us. Someday he's going to realise he did wrong by you.'

Sally wondered if her grandmother knew what her stepdad had done to her. This wasn't something her mother would openly talk about, and anyway, it was only her word against his.

All she had wanted to hear from her mother were words of love, but she got nothing. It struck her that Brooke was the same. He had enslaved her heart with his soft words and expensive gifts and made love to her like she was the most precious thing in his life and yet he never told her what she wanted to hear, words that money couldn't buy.

With tears streaming down her cheeks, she moved away from the elevator and walked down the corridor. Sitting on the bed, she sobbed heavily. She remembered her stepfather's words. He had called her a filthy bastard who would never get anywhere in life.

Maybe he was right. *Why else would I be sitting in a dark room getting ready to destroy the life of someone who had never done me any harm?* She asked herself. This wasn't something she could confess to a priest and be forgiven, cleansed: this would stay with her wherever she went, just as her stepfather had done.

It took another ten minutes before she calmed herself down and when she heard his voice in the corridor, she quickly hid in the wardrobe.

It smelled of rich, expensive suits and shirts. Her fingers itched to touch one of them, to feel the softness and smell his perfume, but he wasn't Brooke. He had never given her any signs of encouragement.

226

Chapter Thirty-Two

Why can't I fit into anything? Catherine said in frustration, trying on the fifth dress. She put it away quickly and rushed to the bathroom when she felt she was going to be sick again. She still didn't get why people called it morning sickness when she was sick most of the day. She had been quite lucky in the days that followed her engagement party; she hadn't felt sick at all, and now she was being reminded that she was pregnant, and she had to look after herself. The only consolation was that she didn't have to go to work because she couldn't imagine herself rushing off to the ladies' every time she felt sick or carrying a bucket like most girls at her workplace did.

Looking in the mirror again, she pushed the hair away from her face and put on her lipstick. She had stopped wearing make-up as soon as she realised she was developing a few spots on her face, something she thought was buried with her teenage years.

She rushed around the room trying to find her shoes that she had taken from the shoe rack less than five minutes before.

'What's wrong with me?' she asked herself, laughing. 'One would think I was going on my first date.'

She had spent the evening trying to find reasons why she couldn't move to the states before the baby was born. She hated been apart from him, waking up to an empty bed. It wasn't as if she couldn't do her work from his house or find a new doctor to help her through the pregnancy. She would miss her parents and friends, but her life belonged with David.

Picking up the phone, she dialled his mobile. When he didn't answer, she rang the hotel. She couldn't wait to share the news with him. He was the one person, who would be as excited as she was, but there was no answer, and the receptionist told her he was not in the lobby.

Disappointed, she sank heavily onto the bed and called for a taxi.

Even though the journey only took fifteen minutes from her flat to the hotel, it felt like the longest she had ever taken. She shut out the noise of the Edgware Road and the tourists, who moved around in huge numbers admiring the casino and carrying huge shopping bags. Young drivers hooting at each other in a hurry to get wherever they were rushing to. She had a meeting scheduled for the following day with her boss, and now that she knew what she wanted, she was looking forward to it. He would be disappointed, of course, but he would also understand. She knew as the car passed through Oxford Circus, that she had made the right decision.

At the Lanchester, she went straight through to the lift and pressed the button to David's floor. Strangely, his door was ajar, and for a moment she hesitated, wondering if she was at the right door. She looked at the door number again.

'David,' she called out, her voice gentle and low. 'David!' she called again, more loudly.

Still no answer. She pushed the door a bit further, her heart missing a beat as she wondered if something had happened to him.

There was stillness in the room, which disturbed her. Unsettled, she reached for the switch on the wall. The light revealed empty champagne bottles and glasses on the floor. Clothes were thrown around the room. She stood still, trying to take it all in.

She was just about to turn around when she heard a moan from the bed.

A loud cry escaped her throat as her eyes took in the occupants of the bed. He lay still, with his arm circling a woman. She wished her eyes were deceiving her, but it was him with his arm around the woman, whose face she couldn't see. His head lay raffishly on the pillow. Her legs froze as she tried to turn around and walk away. She felt sick, and she suddenly felt like throwing up again. Her hands reached for the wall for balance, for a long agonizing moment, she stood still as she felt her world collapse around her.

Anxious to be as far away as possible, she moved forward, and there was a noise as her shoe knocked a bottle.

The woman turned then and their eyes locked. Neither spoke as they stared at each other.

'No!' Catherine cried out and fled the room. She had seen enough. Their images flashed before her eyes. She could barely see where she was going as her legs propelled her forward. Everything was blurred and her heart beat so fast it frightened her. She forgot all about the housekeeping trolley in the corridor, and she cried out as her body crashed to the floor. All thoughts of David went out of her head as a sharp pain cut through her, and everything turned into darkness.

Sally waited until Catherine was out of sight. Quickly, she put on her clothes and picked up the empty bottles and glasses and carried them through to the room next door.

Just as she had thought, Brooke was not in the room. The effects of what she has done were beginning to kick in. She took out a small bottle of Southern Comfort from the fridge and was just about to open it when there was a huge bang, followed by a loud scream.

The bottle fell to the floor, and she ran to see what was happening, already convinced it was Catherine.

Doors slammed as guests came out of their rooms to see what the commotion was all about.

Catherine lay on the floor. There was a man in a suit shouting for someone to call for an ambulance and telling everyone to go back to their rooms.

Sally wanted so much to run out to her, to hold her in her arms and comfort her until the ambulance arrived, but her legs wouldn't move. Like everyone else, she watched from a distance.

'That poor girl,' an elderly woman standing next to her said. 'Does anyone know what happened?' she asked, looking at Sally. Sally shook her head.

'It's the lady from the television,' she heard the maids whisper among each other.

'Yes, the one engaged to that nice-looking American.'

He's staying here, isn't he?' one said as they moved back to their trolleys.

Not wanting to attract attention, Sally went straight to her room. She couldn't sit still, but paced up and down the carpeted floor as she waited for Brooke to show up.

Ten minutes went by. Then she heard someone ask if anyone was with her when she fell and minutes later she heard the wheels in the corridor as a stretcher was rushed to a waiting ambulance. She picked up the phone and rang Brooke.

'Where the hell are you?' she asked him as soon as he answered.

'What's the matter?' he asked, ignoring her question.

'Is that all you're going to say?' she said angrily. 'You were supposed to be here, waiting for me.'

'I'm sorry,' Brooke said, sounding calm. 'Something came up. I should be there in the next ten minutes.'

'Don't bother. I won't be here, and if you know what's good for you, you should stay away, too.'

'What's happened?' he asked.

'Why don't you listen to the ten o'clock news?' She hissed at him.

'Sally, I said I'm sorry. What more do you want me to say? Can't you just tell me what's happened?'

'I'll meet you outside the hotel in ten minutes and don't be late because I won't stay a minute longer.'

She put the phone down before he could say anything. She was tempted to go and see if David was awake but couldn't risk it. She was sure someone was in his room, trying to wake him up. She had not asked Brooke exactly what he had put in his drink, but the man had been fast asleep even before his head hit the pillow.

She quickly put everything in her night bag. The corridor was now deserted, apart from a few maids walking around and she walked down the staircase and through the back door, avoiding the reception area.

Brooke was in the car park waiting, and she told him to drive on before anyone saw them. 'Are you going to tell me what's going on?' he asked, waiting for the lights to change.

Ashamed and afraid, Sally started crying. She could not control herself as tears poured down her cheeks. Brooke pulled the car into a side road and cut the engine.

'Are you going to tell me what's going on?' he asked again.

'It's Catherine,' she said between sobs.

'I know it's about Catherine, what's happened,' he asked anxiously.

Wiping her tears away, she sighed heavily.

'Right now, she's in hospital fighting for her life.'

'What!' Brooke shouted, confusion and shock written all over his face.

'She fell in the corridor,' Sally said. 'I didn't go too close, but there was blood all over the place. What have we done, Brooke? What have we done to Catherine?' She began to weep quietly.

231

Brooke's face collapsed as Sally's words sank in.

'This is your fault,' Sally said, 'you and your obsession with a girl who can't even stand the sight of you. I'll never forgive you if she dies. Do you hear me? I promise I'll never forgive you! I told you, didn't I? I said this was a mistake but you didn't want to listen, and I'm the one she saw!'

'Screaming at each other won't help,' he told her calmly.

'We have to find out which hospital she's in and go to see her. Did you call her parents or Richard?'

Sally looked at him as if he was mad.

'Please don't talk rubbish. I'm the last person they want to talk to. And what exactly should I say? Hello, it's Sally, I'm the one responsible for Catherine's accident?'

'You could, at least, have tried to call Kim. Someone needs to be with Catherine right now,' he told her, his face hard.

'Brooke! You'd better wake up and look around you, if her mother can't stand me, do you think Kim would? That girl is so surly; I can't have anything to do with her. Besides, she doesn't think I'm as swell as her and Catherine. Anyway, I don't know why 're we even discussing this. Just phone your brother as you normally do. He seems to have all the answers.'

Brooke covered his face with his hands and sighed. This wasn't part of the plan. He didn't want to call his brother. What if he asked questions? The fewer people knew of his involvement, the better.

'We need to go back to the hotel and find out what's happening,' he said, turning on the engine.

'I'm not going back there,' Sally said. Shaking, she rummaged through her overnight bag for her mobile phone. 'I'll call Joyce. She'll know where to find Catherine. She's a nurse; she should know.'

He wanted to put his arm around her, and tell her everything was going to be okay, but he couldn't, he was fighting his own demons. His speech was slurred as he tried to speak. He wasn't making any sense and, bizarrely, Sally found herself wanting to comfort him.

Gone was the hard-edged and strong man she had come to love. It was a side of him she had never seen before.

'Brooke,' she said softly, trying to reach out to him.

He didn't reply, thinking he didn't hear her, she said his name again.

'I'll take you home,' he told her, his voice strained.

She didn't have the energy to fight with him. Anywhere away from the West End was good enough for her. She wanted to put some distance between herself and the hotel.

Neither spoke as he drove through Hyde Park Corner and on to the motorway, heading towards his house.

David struggled again to sit up. He was aware of someone knocking on his door. Catherine! This time, he sat up abruptly, startled.

'Mr Alexander?' He heard someone shout his name from the door.

'Yes!' He called back, his voice low and shaky.

Keys turned and, with all the energy he could muster, he managed to sit up straight. He felt as if he had a big hangover and yet all he'd had was one drink with Brooke.

Lights were switched on and a tall white man he recognised as the hotel manager came and stood near the bed.

'Do you mind if I sit down?' he asked.

David nodded, wondering if the man had an answer to his predicament.

'I'm sorry to disturb you,' the manager began, 'but there was no other way of getting hold of you since you were not answering the phone. It's Ms Walker.'

At the mention of Catherine's name, David felt his heart jump.

'What about her?' he asked, fearing the worse.

The manager hesitated. There seemed to be something wrong.

The room smelled of champagne and yet there was no evidence of empty bottles. Should he let him sober up a bit? He pressed on.

'She's had an accident,' he said, 'and an ambulance has taken her to the hospital.'

David's fatigue vanished as horrible images of Catherine flashed through his head.

'Where is she?' he asked, jumping off the bed and almost stumbling in his haste.

'They took her to the Royal Brompton Hospital in South Kensington,' he said.

'If you could please arrange for a taxi for me, I'll be down shortly,' David said. He looked around frantically for his phone.

'I'll take you myself, Mr Alexander,' the manager told him. 'If you just get ready, I will be downstairs.'

In no time he was running downstairs; he didn't bother putting on a jacket and half his shirt buttons were undone.

As promised, the manager was waiting for him. Terror ran through him as he tried to think what could have happened. He could not understand why he had fallen asleep or why his head ached so much.

'Did her parents ask you to get me?' he asked the manager.

'No, sir,' he replied. 'She fell in the hotel corridor. According to the staff, she came running from your room and crashed into a trolley. I don't know if the hospital has contacted her parents yet.'

David didn't know what to say. Nothing was making sense to him. *If Catherine had come to his room, then why didn't she wake him up?* He wondered. A fleeting image of Brooke flashed in his mind, and he quickly dismissed it. No, he couldn't have he told himself.

'Would you like me to come with you?' the manager asked as they drove up in front of the hospital.

'No, thank you. I will be fine,' David said. 'You've been very kind.'

The hospital foyer was empty, apart from a few nurses and doctors rushing around. For a moment, he was taken back to three years ago when his parents died. He felt his steps quicken towards the receptionist.

'Could please tell me where I can find Catherine Walker?' he asked the receptionist.

'Are you family?' she asked him.

He was about to tell her when he felt a tap on his shoulder. Jerking around, he looked straight into Richard's angry eyes.

'Come with me,' Richard said tightly.

Ignoring his unfriendliness, David asked him if he knew where Catherine was.

'Yes!' Richard said as soon as they were out of earshot. 'What I want to know is, where were you when she fell?'

David had never seen Richard so angry before. He didn't understand it.

'Can we talk about that later?' he said. 'I just want to see her. Can you take me to her, please?'

Richard knew that the next twenty-four hours were critical for Catherine, and the doctors were not sure if the baby was still alive. She had lost a lot of blood from the fall.

He wondered if he should tell David the truth or wait for her parents so that he didn't have to go through it twice.

'Can I see her?' David asked again.

Richard looked at David, his mind filled with horrible thoughts. He paced up and down the carpet before sitting down again.

'I need to know,' David insisted.

'She's not doing very well,' he said. 'The injuries she sustained from the fall are quite serious, and she lost a lot of blood. They are not sure if they can save the baby.' He swallowed hard, not sure if he should say anymore.

David felt sick. This couldn't be happening! Oh God, please

don't take her away from me, he prayed silently. Frightening images flashed before his eyes as he thought of Catherine lying on a bed surrounded by surgeons.

His head was full of questions, especially about Catherine coming to see him. What had upset her so much that she had to run from his room? And why did his head feel so heavy, almost like a hangover when he only had one alcoholic drink?

Richard was still pacing up and down, looking up each time the porter came in with his trolley.

He thought of the promise he had made to Michael to look after Catherine if ever there was a need. He felt an urgent wish to be in the operating room, to help save her and the baby, but he knew they wouldn't allow that. 'You're too emotionally involved,' the senior surgeon had said to him.

'What's taking them so long?' David asked his face haggard.

It felt as if they had been waiting forever.

'I'll go and check,' Richard said.

'I'll come with you,' David told him before he could stop him.

They were met by a nurse, whose expression wasn't encouraging.

'I'll just get Dr Adams for you,' she said and quickly walked away before David had a chance to ask her how Catherine was.

At that moment, Catherine's parents walked through the door.

Richard couldn't look at them. He didn't want them to see just how hopeless he felt. He had to be strong for everyone.

Chapter Thirty-Three

It was very early in the morning when Sally left Brooke's house. The house was quiet. She let herself out, carefully closing the door behind her. She took a taxi home, hoping Joyce had left for work already. The area was normally crowded with people, but this time, it was quiet, apart from the bin men and their noisy trucks. She wished she had her own place where she could hide away without anyone asking her questions or wanting to make conversation.

Her head felt heavy from lack of sleep, and she longed to close her eyes and lie still for a long time, yet each time she had tried to sleep, memories of Catherine came flashing back.

Nothing Brooke had said helped in any way. He actually made it worse, because she was reminded of the evil they had done. That was the word for it, she told herself; it was nothing but pure evil. For the first time in years, she found herself kneeling by the bed asking God for forgiveness. It had been a desperate prayer and even now she was still praying in her heart. It was all she could do.

The flat was empty as she went to the kitchen to make herself a cup of tea. As usual, the kitchen was clean and tidy; everything put in its place and tea towels are hanging on the wall. She had never known anyone as tidy as her cousin and sometimes she felt like leaving her clothes all over the place to make it feel lived in.

She took her tea with her to the bedroom and stretched across the bed, trying to clear her head. Sitting up, she took a sip and wondered whether to call Kim or Richard to find out how Catherine was.

Having made up her mind to call one of them, she went back through to the living-room. She sat staring at the phone, her fingers longing to pick it up, and yet her courage failed her.

Joyce came in half an hour later and found her sitting in the same position, cup in hand, her eyes fixed on the phone.

'Are you all right?' she asked, wondering why her cousin was up so early.

'I'm fine, just can't sleep,' Sally said, yawning.

'Well, before you go off,' Joyce began, 'I have some bad news. Catherine was admitted in hospital last night, and she's not doing very well, I'm afraid. I tried to call you, but your phone was switched off.'

Sally cried out before Joyce could finish talking, holding the cup to the floor and her tea splashed onto Joyce's white uniform and the carpet. Her hands shook as she tried to pick it up and she began to shiver.

Thinking the news had hit her badly, Joyce came and put her arms around her.

'I'm sorry; it came as a shock to me, too, but she's in good hands. She's going to be fine. She's very strong, and I'm sure Richard will make sure she's well looked after.'

Sally tried to focus on the television and the pictures on the wall. There was a large one of her grandparents. They were both smiling broadly; her grandfather's hand clung to his walking stick. She looked away quickly, suddenly feeling ashamed and dreadful.

'The doctor said she's going to be fine,' Joyce said. 'I'll be going back to check on her in a couple of hours. You can come with me if you're up to it. You look like you haven't slept a wink. I just feel sorry for her parents; they really could do without this after losing Michael, and there are reporters already hanging around the hospital asking questions about the accident. Anyway, I'll go and get some sleep. You call me if there's any news.'

When Joyce came back into the living-room, yawning from lack of sleep two hours later, Sally was standing by the window gazing at the back yard. Her eyes were red, and she looked flustered.

'Don't tell me you have been standing there all this time? You could've woken me up. Were there any phone calls?'

'I can't come with you,' Sally said turning round to face her cousin.

She had been pacing around the room for the past hour wondering what to do. How can I face everyone and pretend I don't know why she's in the hospital? She had asked herself over and over again.

'May I ask why?' Joyce asked puzzled.

Sally gazed at the family pictures; her mind blank to their smiling faces. Children were playing ball outside, and she wished they would go away. She was back in the hotel corridor watching Catherine lying there so still. She remembered her screams and David, who had been innocent and unaware of what she and Brooke had been up to; their evil plot to split them up.

'Why don't you want to come?' Joyce repeated.

'I'm the reason she's in the hospital. I caused the fall,' she said. She gasped with pain and shame when she saw the effect of her words register on her cousin's face.

'How exactly did you cause her fall?'

Sally closed her eyes, struggling to go on. She couldn't keep it to herself anymore. The guilt was tearing her up inside, and she couldn't breathe.

'I can't tell you; it's too evil! Please don't make me tell,' she heard herself say, her eyes streaming with hot tears. She felt like a child again, begging her stepfather to stop.

239

Joyce leapt to her feet and wrapped her arms around her.

She was reminded of the many nights when Sally had cried in her sleep, and she had been there to comfort her. She could feel her cousin shaking in her arms, and she took her to the leather sofa and sat her down, wiping away the tears.

'What's going on?' she asked. 'You need to let go of all this pain you're carrying inside you. What happened to Catherine was an accident, not even David, I was told, knows what happened, so how can you blame yourself?'

'You don't understand,' Sally said, turning her back on Joyce, her whole body shaking as she held nervously onto the table.

'I don't know if you can take the truth,' she said.

'Sally! There's nothing you can say that will shock me. I have seen too much pain in my short life not to realise that you're in a bad state and if it would help you by talking about it, so why don't you let me be the judge?'

'I was at the hotel when she fell. I was there with Brooke.' She closed her eyes briefly and took a long breath. She could still see Catherine lying on the floor, blood covering the carpet and everyone running around trying to find out what the commotion was all about.

'You don't have to go on,' Joyce began not believing a word, but Sally silenced her.

'No! I need to tell someone; otherwise, I'm going to go crazy. I watched them take her away, and I couldn't do anything,' she said. 'I didn't even ask them if she was going to be all right.'

The words rushed out, she watched in pain as the blood was drained from her cousin's face.

'Brooke promised me she would be fine, that nothing bad would happen to her and I believed him. For the past three months, we have been plotting how to split them up.

Brooke told me she was carrying his child and it all made sense. She was marrying David to punish Brooke and I thought

I'd help heal the wounds by helping him get her back. He drugged David's drink with benzodiazepines and the poor man went out like a light within minutes. Once we were sure he was asleep, we took off his shirt and threw a few champagne bottles and glasses around the room and I lay next to him. We wanted her to believe he was having an affair, but I didn't calculate on her seeing my face. She was out and running in the corridor within minutes.'

She heard Joyce draw in a sharp breath.

'I wanted to follow the ambulance to the hospital but I couldn't, I was just so ashamed.'

Joyce stood up, her legs swaying as she tried to stand still. She couldn't understand how Sally could cross such a line. Hadn't she warned her that Brooke would bring her nothing but pain and despair? Words flew from her mouth. 'How could you?' she hissed. 'After all the discussions we've had, I thought you were finally sorting yourself out. This is more monstrous than anything else you have ever done. *What if Catherine doesn't pull through?* How are you going to live with yourself then?'

Sally raised her head to look at her. She was right, of course. If Catherine died . . . she didn't even want to think about it, but there was no running away from it, she was the reason why Catherine lay in a hospital bed fighting for her life.

Joyce stopped speaking and sat down far from her.

Sally could not look at her; shame and guilt were eating her up. She knew, even without looking into her cousin's eyes, that nothing was ever going to be the same again. The worst part of the whole ugly episode was that she finally realised just how much she had missed Catherine and now it was too late.

'I'm sorry,' said Sally, sobbing. 'I really never meant to hurt anyone, least of all Catherine. I really thought I was doing the right thing. But now that I think about it, I was only thinking about myself, as usual.'

'Did you never sit down and think to ask her if she wanted

Brooke back and what was in it for you? Did he promise you money?' Joyce asked. 'Why, Sally? What was going through your head?'

She stopped before she could say any more. Sally had her faults but this was too much and she couldn't trust herself to be around her, and what about Catherine's family? How could she face them, knowing what she knew? She stood up and walked away without a backward glance.

Moments later, Sally heard doors opening and closing. She sat still for a moment, wondering whether to pack her bags and leave but where would she go? Joyce had not said anything about her moving out, but she had a feeling she would be homeless soon.

Getting up, she slowly walked to the bathroom and locked herself inside.

David sat in the private waiting room, Catherine's parents next to him, waiting and hoping for someone to come and tell them what was happening. Time stood still as they waited. Unable to sit still, he walked to the lobby, the room rustled and swayed as people walked about, enquiring about their own relatives. Reporters stood by, waiting for any news, but David ignored them. He just wanted to be left alone.

Richard was in the waiting room, when he got back. 'Any news yet?' he asked him.

Richard shook his head. Catherine's mother came and put her hands around his shoulders and they nodded at each other. Richard had called them that morning to tell them that she had regained full consciousness, after drifting into and out of sleep for the past two days, coming around just enough to look at their faces.

David had booked himself a room in a hotel in South Kensington, near the hospital. Meetings and offices were forgotten. What mattered now was Catherine. The baby had no heartbeat and the doctors had induced labour while she slipped between darkness and light.

Just then, a tired-looking young doctor came to join them.

'How is she?' David asked, jumping to his feet.

'She's awake at the moment but pretty tired. You can come and see her, but please don't stay too long because she needs all the rest she can get.'

Catherine's eyes were blurred as she tried to look around the room. Her whole body ached and she couldn't feel her legs. Frustrated, she dropped her head back on the pillow. Then her mother walked into the room.

'Oh, Catherine!' her mother said, leaning forward to give her a hug and trying not to cause her any pain. Over her mother's shoulder, she saw her father and David approaching, both un-shaven and looking weary. Her eyes rested on David. Memories came rushing back and she closed her eyes, not wanting to face him or imagine him naked with Sally.

'What's wrong darling?' her mother asked, looking at her. 'John! Get the doctor!' she said as Catherine began to shake, her pulse weakening.

Within minutes, they were all rushed out of the room while doctors surrounded the bedside. A mask was put on her face to help her breathe and David watched from afar, wondering what had gone wrong.

Sally stood quietly between St John's Chapel and the hospital, wondering whether to go in or not. She hadn't seen Joyce since her revelation. Her cousin was avoiding her that much she knew. People passed by looking at her. She didn't care what they thought; she was there on a mission, even though she couldn't move her feet to go forward.

Which was better, the church or the hospital, she asked her-self, looking from one to the other. Joyce's words still hit her like a slug in the stomach every time she thought of them and she suddenly wished she could go far away from there. 'Could you please tell me how Catherine Walker is doing?' she asked the receptionist.

'Are you family?' the woman asked, looking her up and down.

'No, but I am a friend.'

'Sorry, I can't help you. Everyone has been coming here the whole morning asking me the same question, all of them claiming to be friends, but I have been told not to tell anyone anything. You'll just have to wait for her doctor to issue a statement like the rest of them,' she said, glancing towards the visiting room.

Sally walked away quickly. She didn't want to argue with the woman, or worse still, meet Catherine's parents. She took a taxi back to the flat. Joyce was still out and she sighed with relief. Just as she got to her room, the phone rang. She ran to pick it up, thinking it was Brooke.

'Hello, Mother,' she said, recognising the caller. 'Yes, I'm well, so is Joyce.'

'I heard about Catherine,' her mother said.

She couldn't reply.

'Sally! Are you still there?'

'Yes, sorry. I went to see her today but she was sleeping,' she lied.

'Well, her grandmother is not doing too well. The poor woman has been crying all night and I think she's flying out tomorrow.'

'I'll call you if I hear any more news,' Sally told her.

'Your father is here. Do you want to say hi?' her mother asked.

She froze, not knowing what to say. She had not spoken to the man in more than ten years.

'No! I have to go!' she said, and put the phone down before her mother could say any more.

The cheek of that man, she thought, sitting down. She had almost forgotten what he looked like. She still remembered the days when she thought of him every day, touching her and tormenting her until she ran for hours to shake him out of her mind.

She felt as if she was back in Zambia, in her mother's house, with him ever-present, watching her every second and giving her funny looks to remind her not to slip up.

She had not hated him then, she was too young to have such strong feelings, but now she felt differently. It was more than hate; she despised him. Anger washed through her as she tried to squeeze clothes and shoes into her small traveler's bag. She couldn't stay in the flat any more. She had no idea where she could go but she had to get out before Joyce came back.

Looking around to make sure everything was tidy, she took her notebook and wrote a note for Joyce, leaving it in the living-room.

Minutes later she shut the door behind her. 'Heathrow, please,' she told the taxi driver.

She took one last look at the flat and sat back in the seat as the car drove through the heavy traffic.

Kim rushed to Catherine's room instead of walking, less caring of the funny looks the nurses were giving her. Jason followed behind with David and Richard.

'Is she still not talking to you?' Jason asked.

David shook his head. He had tried to think back to the day of the accident, to put the pieces together, but there were no answers. No one in the hotel seemed to know what had made Catherine run from his room. He couldn't help feeling that Richard blamed him, but that was nothing compared to how he felt. Her parents just told him to give her time; no one knew why she didn't want him near her.

Even though her speech was still slurred, she had made it clear to her parents that she didn't want to see him. They were as puzzled as he was, but they had to respect her wishes, so the only time he found himself sitting close to her was when there was no one about and she was asleep. 'I'm sorry,' he heard Jason say, putting his hand on his shoulder and he felt tears prick his eyes. He needed her so much, his heart ached. He hadn't been able to sleep since the accident and the only time he left the hospital was late at night, only to come back early in the morning. Nothing mattered, not his business or the clients waiting. Catherine was all he thought about.

'Doesn't it strike you as very strange that no one knows why she was running?' said Jason. 'Something must have happened to make her run. She was too happy to be having the baby to put it at risk.'

Listening to him, David couldn't take it anymore. He was beginning to remember and, while he hated to admit it himself, he couldn't help feeling that Brooke had something to do with whatever had happened that evening, but he had no proof.

'I think I'll come back later,' he said, looking at both men. 'Will you let me know if there are any changes?' he added before leaving.

The first place he visited was Catherine's apartment.

There was no one about when he got there, which was just as well, because he didn't want to give her any reason to hate him more than she did already.

He searched until he found Brooke's home number, he felt himself shaking as he dialled. He wasn't angry any more, just sad. He had given up calling the mobile. It was on continuous voicemail.

'Mr Fraser is not here,' a female voice said when the phone was finally answered.

'Do you know where I can contact him?' he asked.

'He say he come back Friday,' the woman said. 'I take a message, no?' the woman asked.

Knowing he wasn't going to get much help from her, he said thank you and hung up.

He walked to Catherine's bedroom and opened the window. A picture of the two of them was displayed on a table; they both looked so happy. He took the picture and looked at it more closely.

He could feel the breeze from the lake and the sunlight bright on his face; he couldn't believe how things had changed since the picture had been taken, less than two weeks ago. He had been looking forward to a life full of laughter and joy with the woman he loved.

She was everything a woman should be, his best friend and lover. He was determined to get her back, no matter what. Taking a deep breath, he put the picture back.

That afternoon, while everyone was at the hospital looking after Catherine, David visited the place where Brooke had his office. He knew he couldn't rest until he had spoken to him. He needed answers before he could face Catherine. He had never felt such grief as he did now. It wasn't just for Catherine, but for the baby they had both come to love.

'Brooke is on holiday,' a middle-aged woman told him when he arrived at the office. She offered to take his number and give it to Brooke when he called, but he declined the offer. It became clear to him that Brooke was hiding and he needed to find out why.

Chapter Thirty-Four

'Are you sure this is what you want?' Elizabeth asked Catherine for the tenth time that evening. She had only been out of hospital for four weeks and yet she was determined to go away.

'Yes!' Catherine said, trying to force a smile. 'I can't go on like this, Mum. I need to get away to clear my head and decide what I'm going to do. I know you and Dad are trying your best but I can't expect you to put your life on hold for me.' She moved closer to her mother and took both her hands in hers. 'I'll be fine. The worst is over now, I promise, and I will call you every day.'

'What about David?' her mum asked tentatively. 'I know you said you don't want to see him but, darling, the poor man has been living in London since your accident without a clue as to why you won't speak to him. Don't you think you owe him an explanation? What could he have done that was so terrible that you completely cut him out of your life?'

Catherine looked at the floor. She could not tell her mother of David's betrayal; it was too painful for her to speak about and she was ashamed of the feelings she still felt for him.

I was such a fool to trust him, or any man after what Brooke did, she thought bitterly. As for Sally, she shut her mind to the girl who had let her down so many times. Hatred burned in her heart when she thought of all the chances she had given her.

'Will you at least think about it?' her mother said. 'I know you're hurting, no one should have had go through what you did, but you can't give up on love as well. You need him just as much as he needs you.' She swallowed the words she wanted to say. Everyone wanted to know exactly what had happened on that day, but Catherine had stayed tight-lipped about it. Her only answer was, 'I can't talk about it.'

As for David, he was in the dark, just like everyone else. The hotel manager had confirmed they had to open the door to reach him; he had been fast asleep and disoriented when the accident happened.

It was a relief for Catherine when Cora came to tell her Kim was on the phone.

'If you'll excuse me,' she said to her mother, standing up.

'How are you?' Kim asked her when she answered the phone.

'I'm fine,' said Catherine. 'I still have a lot of packing to do.'

'You're still going, then?'

'Don't you start; too, I need to do this. You do understand, don't you? I'm tired of carrying all this pain inside me. The only way I can get better is if I get away for a while.'

'So why can't you let me come with you?' Kim said. 'You honestly can't tell me you don't want company, and if not me, then why not let David?'

Catherine said nothing.

'Are you still there?' Kim asked.

'Yes! Is David at your place?' she asked, getting suspicious.

'No, don't be silly. I wouldn't be calling you now, would I? I really don't know what happened between the two of you, but don't you think it's time you talked about it?'

'Can we talk about something else?' Catherine said, sighing. 'I really don't feel like discussing David right now. How is work?' she asked.

'Work is fine. Everyone is asking after you. David believes Brooke drugged him,' she added softly and waited.

249

Catherine held on to the phone. She couldn't speak for a while.

'Listen, I have to go,' she finally said. She didn't want to talk about David. 'Please pass my regards to Jason, and tell him I am sorry you had to stay in London.'

'If you say sorry again, I will make you sorrier for learning the word. Jason understands. He knows I couldn't just leave after what happened. Well, darling, have to go. I have a meeting in the West End in an hour's time.'

'See you tomorrow,' Catherine said.

She had just put the phone down when she heard voices in the corridor. There was no mistaking Richard's deep tones; she would recognise them anywhere. Pushing her hair from her face, she went to meet them. Her mother, Richard and Tapiwe were sitting outside, a short distance away in her mother's garden. The weather wasn't too bad for September, she thought, walking towards them. Both her parents loved the outdoors. She understood now why they liked going away during wintertime; it was an escape from the winter blues.

Now it was her turn to escape, even though everyone was telling her to stay. She closed her mind to what Kim had said about Brooke. She was not surprised at all to see Richard. Having failed to convince her on the phone that she should stay, he had come to do it in person. I only hope he doesn't talk about David, Catherine thought. She was tired of putting on a brave face each time his name was mentioned.

'Hello,' Richard said, getting to his feet to give her a hug.

'I take it you're still determined to go, then?' Richard said after Cora had left them with a tray of food.

'Yes, and before you say anything, I need to do this by myself.'

'I know,' Richard said, still unsettled by the whole episode.

Chapter Thirty-Five

'Oh, there you are,' her grandmother said, joining her by the swimming pool. 'I've been looking for you everywhere.'

'Is there a problem?' Catherine answered, toweling her hair.

She was more relaxed than she had been for weeks she couldn't believe she had been in Africa for almost a fortnight.

'There is someone here to see you,' her grandmother told her.

For one agonizing moment, Catherine froze.

'Who is it?' she asked, hoping it wasn't David. Not that she was in a mood to see anyone else.

'It's Sally,' her grandmother said, looking straight at her, her eyes pleading.

There was silence between them as the words sank in.

'I don't want to see her,' she said without emotion.

'I know you don't, darling, but I think you need to talk to her. What she has to say might be healing for both of you. The poor girl looks so thin and miserable; I think she could use a friend right now. Just give her five minutes, that's all I ask. Do it for me, if you can.'

Catherine sighed. She wondered what her grandmother would say if she knew Sally was the reason she had lost the baby and David.

What was she up to? Slightly intrigued, she told her grandmother that she would see Sally in her grandmother's study. She changed into a pair of jeans and a tight-fitting Calvin Klein top.

Her hair was pushed away from her face and tied in a black hair clip.

Sally was standing behind her late grandfather's curved desk, the one that her mother had bought for him on his fiftieth birthday. She looked pale and thin. Catherine could not believe it was the same girl she had seen almost five months ago.

'Hi,' she said, glaring at her.

Sally didn't say a word in response, her eyes fixed to the floor.

'Grandma said you wanted to talk,' said Catherine. She was surprised at herself for staying so calm after all the things she had planned to say, but now they didn't seem important. Nothing could compare with the look on Sally's face. The girl was clearly in torment and Catherine could sense Sally was fighting her own demons.

'Thanks for seeing me,' Sally began. She paused, trembling. It seemed to Catherine she was having trouble just saying the word sorry.

Catherine walked to the window and looked out on the massive acreage.

'What are you doing here Sally?' she asked.

'Can we sit down?' Sally answered. 'I've something to tell you about the night of the accident and I can't do it with your back facing me.'

Catherine turned around. The intense look on Sally's face prevented her from replying.

'This is very hard for me,' Sally began, 'but I have to tell you because it has been eating me up so badly and I can't go on this way. I know that you saw me that day in David's room but it wasn't what you think. Brooke and I planned it. Just before you left for Africa with David, Brooke told me that you were carrying his child. He convinced me you were only marrying David to spite him. I didn't buy it at first but I recalled how cold you were when you first found out about the baby.

The words flowed from her mouth as soon as she began. Catherine could do nothing but stare at her, too shocked and numb to speak.

'I think you can go now,' Catherine said, trying not to believe what Sally was saying. She wanted to say more, to tell Sally what she was feeling right now, but she couldn't. She needed time alone to think. As for Brooke, she wished she had never set eyes on the man.

Sally ignored Catherine's intense look. 'Brooke spiked David's drink. He was out within seconds, and we literary had to drag him to his room.

He was fast asleep before his head hit the pillow. I slept next to him and waited for you to come. Brooke had seen to that too. He was the one who asked the girl to call you.

'Please go,' Catherine screamed. 'Just go and never show your face around here again.'

Her whole body was trembling with anger. She didn't hear Sally leaving or her grandmother come into the room, until she tapped her on the shoulder. She threw herself into her grandmother's open arms and wept. Sally's words haunted her and she was in turmoil. It was like waking up from a nightmare. She couldn't control the tears that streamed down her face.

'I need some air,' she said, wiping her eyes. 'I'm sorry,' she apologised, looking at her grandmother's soaked dress.

Outside, the morning air was fresh. Catherine took a deep breath and walked towards the pool house. She could hear the workers and their families talking and laughing, but nothing mattered to her.

Her mind kept going back to Sally and the past. She couldn't understand how two people she had once trusted could betray her in that way.

And for David, she couldn't think of him. It was too painful to know she would probably never see him again. For weeks he had followed her, from Australia, Hawaii and across America, and each time she had run away before she had to face him.

She shivered, suddenly afraid that he had given up on her. She could still remember grandma Maria's words, 'That girl is going to ruin your life.'

And that's exactly what had happened, because she couldn't imagine having a life without David in it. She was still haunted by the baby she had lost. She had never stopped wondering what life would have been like and Sally had brought the memories back just when she thought she was beginning to recover. Above her, birds in large numbers flew away and for a moment, she forgot her problems and took in their beauty. She walked back to the house. It was only when she smelled food that she realised she had not eaten a proper meal in days, to the disapproval of her grandmother, who kept telling her she looked like a sack of bones.

'How was your walk?' her grandmother asked as soon as she saw her.

'It was refreshing and now I realise I'm hungry.' She tried hard to sound cheerful, but she couldn't fool her grandma. Nothing escaped her wise eyes and Catherine felt that she could see through her soul. After lunch, they sat together on the balcony, sipping tea and enjoying the sunshine.

'I'm sorry about Sally,' said her grandmother.

'It's not your fault.'

'I know, but maybe I should never have encouraged you to be-friend the girl. Maybe one day you'll understand why she is the way she is.'

There was sadness in her voice and Catherine couldn't help but wonder what lies Sally had told her grandmother.

'Did she say something to you?' she asked.

'I wasn't going to tell you,' her grandmother began, 'but that girl is very sad under all that make-up and clothes. For a long time, I wondered why she always seemed so grown up and different, but now it all makes sense. She came back to tell her grandparents what her stepfather did to her years ago. The man was, well, I can't say the word, but you know what I mean.'

'What!' Catherine said, shocked. 'Sally never said anything.'

'I was shocked, too, but they got the truth out of him. Another girl who lives near him accused him of rape but he paid off the family to avoid a prison sentence. Sally told them her mother knew what was happening but turned a blind eye. She got pregnant and, according to her mum, the baby was stillborn. She was only ten years old and it was his child, that's why she never went back. No one knew about it, they were too ashamed and embarrassed to tell anyone. Her grandparents didn't even know about it and her grandfather is threatening to kill the man. It just goes to show how many other girls could be going through the same problem with no one to talk to.'

'So what's going to happen to her stepfather? Has she told the police?' Catherine asked, her voice shaking. She was appalled by the revelation. The day was turning out to be one of horrible revelations and she didn't think she could take any more. She had lived with Sally for almost three years and in all that time, she never knew she had been living with such pain.

'Well, I'm told he's gone back to his farm. The police here don't concern themselves with such matters and I don't think her grandparents want anyone outside the family knowing about this. Her mother, of course, will get a divorce and he'll be free to do whatever he likes. The only person I really feel sorry for is Sally. Can you imagine anyone that young having to go through all that on her own? Maria used to say there was something strange about her, but I never took any notice. She was always so fast on her feet. Thinking back, I know what's why she kept running away from home.'

'No wonder she never spoke of her mum,' Catherine said thinking to all the times she had heard her having nightmares. Her mind turned to Brooke. She wished she had told Sally the truth, maybe things would have turned out differently.

'Yes, it is sad really, isn't it? In this day and age one would think African women had found their voices, but she was too afraid of him. Even after all that's happened, she still wanted to stay with him, but her father told her she would only do it over his dead body. Sally told me she'll be going back to London soon. She doesn't think that farm is big enough for her and her mother. They need time to heal before they can start again.'

They sat on the balcony talking till late evening. Catherine felt herself letting go of most of her anger and pain as her grandmother told her stories about her mother's family, uncles and cousins she had never met. All the time, though, she couldn't stop thinking about David. He was in her thoughts every second of the day. Her only consolation was the fact that Melissa was coming to see her soon. Maybe she can help keep me busy, she thought.

As if reading her mind, her grandmother took both her hands in hers.

'Things will get better,' she told her softly. 'You and David will be fine.'

'I wish I could be as convinced as you. Too much has happened for us to go back.'

'You do still love him, don't you?' her grandmother asked.

'Yes, I'll always love him. I guess somehow I always had my doubts about the whole incident. It was too out of character. I should have listened to him when he complained about Brooke. How could I be so wrong about someone?'

'Hey, don't blame yourself. How could you have known?'

Catherine tossed and turned all through the night as she tried to make sense of everything that had happened during the day. It was like reliving the pain she had felt when she was told her baby was dead. She could not cry anymore; she was tired of crying and of losing people she loved. She remembered Michael and his beautiful smile; he had been so full of life and dreams but he had died too young. He will look after my baby, I know he will, she told herself.

For the first time since she'd arrived, Catherine was up early that morning. She made herself a cup of coffee and decided to take a walk.

Even though it was January, it was still hot. She felt the morning breeze on her body as she took a walk around the farm. The maize stood out tall from the rest of the crops. Someone could hide inside without being noticed and that's exactly what she wanted to do.

Soon she heard voices and car engines driving away from the farm, probably marketers going back, she thought.

The trees swayed and rustled as wind tore through the field. Refreshed, she walked back to the house. She had forgotten how good it was in the morning on the farm. It was so beautiful; nothing stirred but the wind and sunlight. She looked up the sky and watched in awe the bright yellow sunset.

The house was still quiet and she decided to take a swim and it was some while before she saw her grandmother appear outside.

'You're up early,' her grandma said placing a kiss on her forehead.

She was sitting in her grandmother's rocking chair, her hair still damp and her face pale, but she didn't care. All the drama about Sally, David and the baby had left her exhausted.

Rage swept over her. She could not understand how Brooke could have become so conniving and evil. What had happened to the sweet-looking man she had met and fallen in love with? She realised that she'd never known him at all. She felt hot tears start and wished David was there to put his arms around her.

Her grandmother put her cup of tea down and moved her chair close to her.

'You miss him, don't you?'

'Yes,' Catherine said. 'What am I going to do? I should never have chased him away. I should've known he wouldn't do that to me. How can I expect him to forgive me?'

'Well, you weren't to know and who could blame you after what happened with—?'

Her grandmother paused, as if reluctant to say his name. 'Not all men are the same. I know it's easy to get cynical, but sometimes it's best not to dwell too much on the past. David loves you and I'm certain you'll work things out.'

Catherine wished she could be as certain as her grandmother, but the reality didn't look too promising. Their relationship had been based on trust. How could they start again? Maybe it's better this way, she thought miserably.

'I think I'll go and call Kim,' she said, standing up.

'Let's go for a walk when you're done,' her grandmother said.

'You're joking, aren't you?' Kim said when Catherine finished telling her about Sally, her stepfather and Brooke.

'Have you told David?' she asked.

'No, but I spoke to mum and dad. You can imagine their surprise and anger. Not only did they find out the baby wasn't David's but Brooke's, but that he contributed to my accident. I haven't decided what I'm going to do yet. The whole situation is just like a horrible nightmare. I never thought for a second Sally; the girl I welcome into my life would hurt me so much. The worse thing is, she's not even taking responsibility. She still blames Brooke as if he had a gun to her head.'

'I 'm sorry,' Kim said worriedly.

'I will be alright, anyway enough of Sally. What's been happening with you,' Catherine asked changing the subject.

'Oh, I never realised married life could be so blissful. Jason is such a good husband; sometimes I feel like it's a crime to be this happy,' she said, laughing.

'I'm happy for you,' said Catherine. 'You're coming to Richard and Tapiwe's wedding, aren't you?'

'Yes, I wouldn't miss it for the world. Besides, we're brides-maids. I don't know if Jason will be able to take time off, but I'll be there.'

By the time she put the receiver down, she felt a lot happier. Kim always had that effect on her; she made her think of the good things in life.

She rushed off to her room to get changed. With everything happening, she had totally forgotten about Melissa's arrival. Her grandmother's driver was picking her up from the bus station, and she could well be there any moment. She smelled food from the kitchen. Her grandmother's housekeeper had been up all morning cooking. It was enough food to feed an army. Her stomach cried out for food; all the walking and swimming had given her an appetite.

She still couldn't take in what Sally had told her, and as for Brooke, nothing had changed in that regard. He always ran away when things got tough. For his sake, she hoped their paths would never cross again. Moments later, as she made her way to the kitchen, she heard voices coming from the living room. But what was he doing here? And then certain things made sense – her grandmother talking quietly on the phone, the unexpected visit from Melissa. Her heart leapt into her throat.

David had lived this moment a thousand times in his mind. He had seen her, smelt her perfume, felt her soft, silky skin next to his and made love to her a hundred times. She was even more beautiful than he remembered.

Their eyes met and locked in a bond, which only two people who loved each other could share. Time stood still. Neither of them saw her grandmother and Melissa quietly slip away. There was no turning back. Whatever had happened in the past belonged there. He closed the gap between them and took her in his arms.

He held her so close that for a moment she felt he would crush her, but she didn't care. *This is where I belong, with David.* She told herself, wiping away her tears.